HOW TO BE BAD

ALSO BY DAVID BOWKER

I Love My Smith & Wesson
The Death You Deserve

DAVID BOWKER

HOW TO BE BAD

ST. MARTIN'S GRIFFIN ❧ NEW YORK

www.stmartins.com

Library of Congress Cataloging-in-Publication Data

Bowker, David.
    How to be bad : a novel / David Bowker.—1st ed.
      p. cm.
    ISBN 0-312-32826-5
    EAN 978-0312-32826-9
    1. Booksellers and bookselling—Fiction.   2. Women murderers—
Fiction.   3. Serial murders—Fiction.   4. First loves—Fiction.   5. Lists—
Fiction.   I. Title.

PR6052.O879H69 2005
823'.92—dc22

2004065827

First Edition: June 2005

10 9 8 7 6 5 4 3 2 1

To Barbara J. Zitwer, agent and muse

ACKNOWLEDGMENTS

Thanks to my editor, Marc Resnick, for making many vital suggestions. I am extemely grateful to Dr. Alan Wheeler from Oklahoma who really did accidentally kill a pigeon in the manner described in chapter 1. Jane, I love you. Thanks for being a cheerleader when no one was cheering. My sincere admiration goes to my son Gabriel who, at the age of eight and a half, invented the term "butt wax."

A terrible grahzny vonny world, really, O my brothers.
—Anthony Burgess, *A Clockwork Orange*

PART 1

BAD

CHAPTER 1

WHAT LITTLE BOYS ARE MADE OF

AT NINE o'clock that morning, the bell above the front door rang to tell me someone had entered my shop. It was my second customer in two days. Running a rare bookshop can be like that. No customers for an entire year, then two turn up in the same week.

A big man with long auburn hair strode over to me. His neatly trimmed beard was the same color as his hair, and his blue eyes were bright and observant. There was something naggingly familiar about him, but I couldn't think what.

The stranger wore a dark, expensive-looking suit, and rings flashed on his big, brutal hands. He walked up to my desk, smiled, and said, "Aren't you a little young to be running a bookshop?"

"I beg your pardon?"

"How old are you? Twenty-one? Twenty-two? You should be out fucking and getting high. What are you doing in this place, surrounded by other people's dusty old shit?"

I looked at him sternly. "Can I help you at all, sir?"

"Yeah. Yeah. I'd like to see your most horrible book."

"I beg your pardon?"

He spoke really slowly to make sure I understood. "What— is—your—most—horrible—book?"

I looked into his frank blue eyes, still trying to place him. He had massive, square shoulders. Despite his daunting appearance and the strangeness of his request, his voice was light and intelligent-sounding. "C'mon. Books with really nasty pictures. What've you got?"

I thought for a moment. "I've got a copy of *Peter Pan and Wendy*, illustrated by Mabel Lucie Atwell. The pictures in that are truly sickening."

"No, no." He leaned forward and placed his hands on the table, not looking into my face but glancing at the display case to his left. Returning his attention to me, he said, "Perhaps I should explain. My auntie was a midwife, and she had this old textbook full of pictures of malformed babies and vaginal warts. Man, you know the kind of thing."

"Not really," I said, not entirely happy with the direction the conversation was taking.

"I like books like that. Books that make people feel sick," he said. "About Nazi atrocities. Or botched executions. You know. The kind of books that shouldn't be allowed."

I looked up at him. He was beginning to worry me. "Look. What do you want? I'm busy."

He gave a light snort of amusement as he glanced around the empty shop. "Yeah, it looks like it."

"I haven't got any books for sick human beings," I said grandly. "Nor am I interested in selling them."

My customer wasn't listening. He was peering into the cabinet on his right. "What about this?"

"What about what?"

"*Tortures and Torments of the Christian Martyrs*. Any photographs in that?"

"Hardly," I said disparagingly.

"What? Not even engravings by Antonio Tempesta, after the original images by Giovanni de Guerra?" He saw the surprise on my face and laughed. "That's a famous book you've got there."

"Well, obviously not as famous as the original."

He looked at me again, and his eyes darkened. "Obviously. Because the original was printed in 1591. The version you've got was published by the Fortune Press of Paris in 1903."

"You're a serious collector?"

He smiled. "No. I looked it up on your Web site. It caught my attention. Could I have a look at it?"

"Only if you're seriously interested in buying it."

"Man," he said reasonably. "You know I can't answer that. Not without seeing the book."

I was flooded by the familiar misgivings that always plagued me when a sale was imminent, knowing unsold books would always mean more to me than ready cash. And would I charge eighty pounds for it today, only to discover a week later that a similar copy had sold at Sotheby's for thirty thousand?

I took a key from the drawer in front of me and opened the case. I passed the dubious volume to my dubious visitor, and he sat down on my desk, smiling at the nasty pictures. He laughed and pointed at the image of a naked woman hanging by her hair with weights tied around her feet. "Now, that's got to hurt."

"I expect so," I said.

"What does this thing cost? I can't find a price."

"It's a rare book," I said. "Writing in it would lower the value."

"Look. All the fun of the fair," he said, pointing at a picture of a man being broken on a wheel. "What's this book worth?"

"In that condition? Eighty pounds."

He looked at me, smiled, and tore out a page. "How much is it worth now?"

With a yell, I tried to grab back the book. He slapped my hand away. "Right," I said. "Now you're going to pay for it."

"How much?" he said.

"I've already told you. Eighty pounds."

"But it's got a page missing," he said. "You're selling substandard goods."

"Eighty pounds," I said. "Or I'll call the police."

"What will you call them?" he said, laughing at his own pleasantry.

Then he took a lighter from his pocket. Before I could react, he held the book open by the spine and set fire to the pages.

"You mad bastard!" I said, instinctively snatching at the book. He shoved me, not roughly, just hard enough to return me to my seat. When the book was properly ablaze, he let it fall to the floor. I ran round my desk and stamped on the flames until they were extinguished.

"That's not a rare book," said the stranger. "It's a *well-done* book."

"Right!" I said. "Right!"

"Right what?" The arsonist beamed down at me.

I thought for a moment. "Out!" I said. "Now."

"Is that the best you can do?" he said. He turned to leave, his back soaring above me like a sheer cliff face. He must have been about six feet seven inches tall.

At the door, he turned to look at me.

"What was the point of what you just did?" I said.

He winked at me. "Hey. Butt Wax."

Butt Wax?

"You don't like your name?" He smiled and cocked his head to one side, quietly relishing my bewilderment. "Well, why don't you hit me?"

He waited a while, looking down at me. "Are those muscles of yours just for show?" I looked at him, my throat clogged by fear. This was obviously the response he was expecting, because he gave a good-humored laugh and shook his head. "Thought so," he said as he walked into the street.

A pastel blue Porsche was illegally parked on the pavement outside. A young guy with metal studs in his nose and eyebrows was leaning against the car with his hands in his pockets. Nodding to me politely, the young man opened the passenger door, and my visitor got in. As the car moved off, I noticed the registration plate. It read SAVEYA. It was then that I realized who the book-burner looked like. He was the spitting image of the Son of God.

*   *   *

WHILE I was waiting for the police to arrive, I made myself a calming cup of green tea and sat down at my desk. To my right, in a locked display cabinet, stood fine copies of some of the best books ever written by and for men. There was a signed first edition of *The Little White Bird* by James Matthew Barrie, about a lonely and selfish bachelor who pretends he has a son to impress a woman, and Nick Hornby's *About a Boy*, which, purely by coincidence, tells the story of a lonely and selfish bachelor who pretends he has a son to impress a woman. A signed first edition of *Fight Club* stood beside *Iron John*, both books highlighting the spiritual crisis of the contemporary Western male.

There was the seminal *And When Did You Last See Your Father* by Blake Morrison, signed by the author in his nervous, spidery scrawl, and *From Stockport With Love*, David Bowker's haunting journey through spying and fatherhood. Also for sale were the complete works of Tony Parsons, not yet collectible or ever likely to be, yet fairly representative of what men who didn't like reading were reading. Apart from the Barrie, none of these books could command a high price—at least, not yet. Like any collector, I hoped I was ahead of my time. In fact, I was banking on it.

In a case to my left were the first editions that people actually wanted to buy, by people like Patrick O'Brian, Tolkien, and that bloody Rowling woman.

The bell above the door clanged again, and a uniformed constable came in, carrying his helmet underneath his arm. He had rosy cheeks and a frank, unassuming stare. He looked about twelve years old. I mean, I was only twenty-three myself, but at least I possessed pubic hair. Worryingly, the constable didn't seem aware of the seriousness of what had just occurred. "And you say this book is valuable, sir?"

"Yes. Or rather, it was."

"Is your stock insured?"

"Yes. But . . ."

"Well, that's good. The fact you've reported the incident to us will satisfy the insurers. If you want to pursue it in court, we'll support you. But I can tell you now, it'll be difficult to prove. There were no witnesses. It'll just be your word against his."

I stared at him in silence for a few moments while his words sank in. "So that's it?"

"That's up to you. Do you want to make a complaint or not?"

"Yes, I bloody well do. People can't be allowed to just wander about setting fire to private property."

The constable sighed as he took out his notebook.

"What are you sighing for?" I said. (Forgetting that one should never end a sentence with a preposition.)

He seemed reluctant to explain. I insisted.

"Well," he said, smiling. "Don't you think you're getting things a bit out of proportion? It's only a book. You'll get reimbursed.

Try counting your blessings. What's the matter with you? You've got all your arms and legs, haven't you?"

* * *

AT MIDDAY, I closed for lunch, got onto my bike, and pedaled into Barnes. The sun was shining on all the nice clean middle-class people. Say what you like about the middle classes, but they'll never take a dump on your front lawn. At Barnes Pond, I leaned my bike against a bench and sat down. I found a pack of chewing gum in my pocket and rammed three pieces into my mouth, try-ing to calm my nerves. I tried to tell myself that the police officer was right, that I shouldn't let a lunatic book-burner ruin my day. As I was sitting, chewing, and sulking, I noticed the boys.

There were five of them, four of them about fourteen and one at least a year younger. The older four were all ganging up on the younger kid, who looked like Elvis in a shabby school uniform. Little Elvis was blushing in embarrassment, while the leader of his attackers, a fat kid with the thin mouth, tiny eyes, high cheekbones, and jutting jaw of an SS torturer, gripped him by the throat and uttered threats.

Hitler Youth gave Elvis a shove, causing a pile of coins to tumble out of his victim's pockets. The other kids stooped to re-trieve the money, and in the confusion Elvis broke free and started to run. But physical fitness wasn't exactly Elvis's thing—if it had been, perhaps no one would have bullied him in the first place. Elvis had barely reached the curb before Hitler Youth headed him off. Then all four boys escorted Elvis back toward the trees. They passed right by me. There was a resigned look on Elvis's face. The poor little fucker knew he was in for a kicking. I guessed it wasn't the first time. But it was the first time it had happened while I was around.

I can't abide bullies. I left my bike where it was and ran over to them. Little Elvis was lying on the ground with Hitler Youth squatting on his chest, slapping his victim's face with horrible relish. The other kids were just standing around, enjoying the spectacle.

"Get off him," I commanded.

Hitler Youth looked up, his left hand gripping his victim's collar, right hand hovering above his tear-stained face. It was a blank look, devoid of thought or curiosity.

"I said get off him."

Dismissing me as a hallucination, Hitler Youth turned back to Elvis and gave him another slap. I grabbed hold of his arm and hauled him off so violently that he rolled backward and hit his head on the concrete path. "Now go," I demanded. "And if you ever lay one finger on him again, you'll answer to me."

Hitler Youth and his friends slouched off, waiting until they were a hundred yards away before shouting, "Fuck off, Lulu." (I have no idea why they were calling me Lulu.)

I helped Elvis to his feet and dusted him down. There was a red mark under his right eye where Hitler Youth had slapped him. Elvis seemed pathetically grateful for my intervention, acting as if tackling a bunch of fourteen-year-olds required exceptional courage. I was so touched that I gave him a fiver and wheeled my bike alongside him for a few minutes until I was satisfied he was safe.

*   *   *

FEELING VIRTUOUS, I cycled back beside the pond. There were about a dozen pigeons on the path ahead. I was pedaling along at a fine rate and didn't bother to slow down when I saw them, certain that even birds as stupid as pigeons would fly away on my approach. But one bird, evidently a pigeon with severe learning difficulties, stayed right where it was. I felt a nauseating bump as both the wheels of my bike plowed over it.

I didn't want to stop, but nor did I want to leave the stupid bird in pain. So I braked, laid down my bike, and walked back to the scene of the accident. The pigeon was lying flat on its belly, right in the center of the path. Its wings were outstretched, its head to one side. I could see immediately that it was dead. My eyes were drawn to a flash of color about eight inches to the right of the body. It was a blob of bright, fresh blood. Eight inches farther on lay another vivid little spatter. And to the right of that, still beating, lay the pigeon's heart.

I jumped back in revulsion. My amazing powers of deduction told me that the weight of my bike had burst open the bird's breast, sending its heart skimming over the concrete path like a bluey-pink stone.

A couple of middle-aged women came up behind me. Seeing that I was shocked, they commiserated with me. "Pigeons are vermin, dear," one informed me helpfully. "Dirty, dirty things. I wouldn't worry about it."

I was unconsoled. A pleasant cycle ride had turned into a real-life urban myth. "The Legend of the Heartless Pigeon."

The two ladies headed for the snotty shops, and I was about to remount my bike when I heard the pounding of feet. A small, wide guy of about forty with tattoos all over his face and neck ran up to me. He gripped the handlebars of my bike with both hands. His head looked like a potato with jutting ears. His teeth were little more than knarled green stumps, making it look as if he had a mouth full of pistachio nuts. His wrists were as thick as thighs. "Ya fingy faggin har, yeh?" he said. I could smell beer on his breath.

"I beg your pardon?"

"Yoo erd ya cant. I sez yer fingy faggin har? Yer bigugly cant, wod ar ya?"

"Sorry?"

I had no idea why he was addressing me or what he was saying, but I was pretty sure he wasn't inquiring after my health. Then I glanced to my left and saw Hitler Youth standing there, grinning. I felt my guts churn. "Dis der twad, our Darren?" said the guy with the tattoos to Hitler Youth. "Dis da cant wod ad ya? Yeah?"

Darren nodded grimly.

The man with the tattoos hurled my bike to the ground. He didn't need to do that. Breathing on it would have been enough.

"If that bike's damaged, you'll have to pay for the repairs," I warned him sternly.

"Repair mah cantin ring. Yer lige hiddin liddle cants, wod yer lige with someone a bit fackin denner, yer gaylor?"

"Excuse me?"

"Scuse yer twat, ya VD scab."

"I really don't understand what you're saying to me."

"Oh. Yewa fig baster? Iddaddit?"

"I think you should hear what happened," I began. "Your son was picking on another kid. All I did was drag him off."

"No one cobs mah sunny bud me. Laid nuvver fing on im I'll splay ya awl ova da fackin grarn."

"I can't make out what you're saying," I said.

"Der grarn!" he yelled.

"I'm sorry. I'm afraid I don't speak working class."

I don't know why I was surprised when the man with the tattoos punched me in the forehead and I fell over. It had never occurred to me that the forehead was a sensitive area, but the blow hurt like hell, so I decided to remain horizontal for a few moments until I felt better. Someone touched my face and, thinking it was the illustrated scumbag, I told him to fuck off and die.

"Now, there's no need for that. I'm only trying to help."

I opened my eyes. A female paramedic was leaning over me.

"Oh. Sorry."

"What's your name, love?"

I told her.

"My name's Sue," she said, "and this is Geoff."

I was vaguely aware of a male colleague standing behind her, looking bored.

"Mark, I'm not being funny," said Sue, "but you can't stay here."

"I only just this minute lay down."

"No," she said. "You've been here for at least half an hour. That's why we're going to take you for a nice little ride in an ambulance."

"No need to be patronizing," I said. "And I don't need an ambulance. There's nothing wrong with me."

"Mark," explained Sue patiently, "you're lying flat on your back in a public place with a lump the size of a grapefruit on your head."

* * *

THERE WAS an enormous queue at the hospital. Everywhere you looked there were ill bastards. After showing such initial concern, the paramedics just dumped me on a chair in a corridor and left. While I was waiting, a police officer turned up to question me. One of the paramedics had phoned in to say I'd been assaulted. To our mutual dismay, I was attended by the same twelve-year-old constable who'd visited my shop that morning. Obviously thinking he had wasted enough time on me for one day, the rude bastard sighed again as he took out his notebook. "So this man who attacked you. Did he look like Jesus as well?"

"No. This one looked like a tattooed Martian."

The police officer gave me a long, quizzical stare. "Mark, I'm going to ask you a question. I don't mean anything by this, but I've got to be sure."

"Fire away."

"You wouldn't be inventing these attackers of yours, by any chance?"

"No."

"Only I wouldn't be cross with you if you were. In fact, I could put you in touch with some trained counselors who might be able to help you."

"I am not a fucking nutcase!"

"On the other hand, I must warn you that wasting police time is a very serious matter."

"What about the police wasting my time? I haven't invented anything. I've had a terrible day. The Son of Man came down from heaven to insult me. A nasty tattooed cunt hit me in the face and stole my fucking bike. I suppose that's not a crime, either?"

The constable nodded and stared at the wall for a while. I assumed he was just humoring me, but when he looked at me again there was a thoughtful gleam in his eyes. "This man with the tattoos? When he spoke, did it sound as if he was talking a foreign language?"

"Yes."

"And he didn't happen to have his son with him, did he, sir?"

"Yeah! That's it. A horrible fat little Nazi."

"Ah." With an air of hopelessness, the constable closed his notebook. "OK. The man who hit you is called Nigel Barker. Known locally as Wuffer. He's already well known to us, unfortunately."

"Well known as what? Someone else you do fuck-all about?"

"Mr. Madden, if you want to make a complaint about Mr. Wuffer—I mean, Mr. Barker—that's fine with me. But the fact is, people like that aren't like you and me, are they? They can't be reasoned with. It's not just the father. The whole family is competely out of control. You could make a complaint, but what good would it do? These people are the lowest of the low."

"So do you ever do anything about anything?" I said.

He blinked. "What do you mean?"

"I mean is this how you spend your days? Every time someone makes a complaint, you try to persuade them there's not really any point?"

The young police officer looked affronted. "I never said anything of the kind, sir. All I was trying to suggest was that there's no real harm done. And the fact is, a person like Mr. Barker simply will not learn, no matter how many times we fine him or send him to prison."

"So you wouldn't advise me to press charges."

He cleared his throat. "That's up to you."

"I suppose no real harm's done," I said wearily. "I've still got my arms and legs."

Then he smiled. "Exactly. That's exactly the way I look at it."

When the police officer had gone, I went to the coffee machine and bought myself a cup of steaming brown water. When I got back, a young woman with her wrist in plaster walked up the corridor looking for an empty seat. I watched her approach from a distance, saw the heads turning to stare after her. As she passed by, her loveliness hit me full in the face like the heat from an oven.

The only empty chair was next to mine. She sat down without so much as a glance at me, took a book out of her bag, and began to read. She had pale skin and razored pale hair and an aura of casual insolence. Her name was Caro Sewell, and when I was eighteen years old she broke my heart.

Caro was frowning at the paperback in her lap as if it had just said something stupid. It was some kind of self-help book, so it probably had. She must have known she was being stared at, but she didn't look up. I cleared my throat and spoke to her. "Caro?"

She turned to glance at me, then did a double take and almost smiled. "Oh, it's you," she said. The way she said it, you'd have thought she hardly knew me. You'd have thought we had never cried together at parties or taken drugs or lain in a field next to a railway embankment, fucking joyfully as the trains went by. Caro raised the level of her gaze, and I realized she had noticed the bump on my forehead.

"It's just a bruise," I explained quickly.

Caro nodded tersely, and I guessed she didn't want to ask how I'd got it in case I questioned her about her injury. I wasn't that interested, really. It sounds shit when you say it, but I'll say it anyway. At that moment, I was only interested in her face. She was twenty-three, the same age as me. Still young but old enough to start counting the fucking birthdays.

I hate those supermarket philosophers who tell you what a great healer time is. Time is a mere anesthetist. The years numb the pain, but the wound remains. I may no longer have ached for Caro, but nor had I forgotten everything she meant and took away. She had been an exceptionally pretty schoolgirl. She had turned into a startlingly beautiful woman. Just looking at her turned my mouth dry.

"I thought you were at uni," she said. "Weren't you doing English or something?"

"English lit. I left after the second year. I had to. They were putting me off reading."

"What do you do now?"

"I own a top retail outlet in Sheen."

"You mean you work in a shop?"

Ouch.

"It's a bookshop. Mark Madden Books. You can't miss it. My name's above the door in bloody big letters!"

She half-nodded. "I think I've passed it. I didn't think it could be the same Mark Madden. I pictured some fat middle-aged man in a cardigan. Your very own shop. How did you get the money together for that?"

"Um, my dad helped me out. I'm going to pay him back, though."

A nurse appeared and called out my name.

I got up and started to mumble a miserable farewell.

"No, wait," she said. She took a ballpoint pen out of her bag, grabbed my hand, and coolly scrawled a number on it. "If you feel like going out sometime, give me a call."

* * *

AT THE pub that night, Wallace asked why I had a grapefruit on my head. I told him about the book-burning maniac and the incomprehensible tattooed maniac, and he quickly lost interest. But when I told Wallace I'd bumped into Caro, he got all excited. "She asked you to call her? Really?"

"Yeah."

"You didn't say yes?" said Wallace.

"I didn't say anything."

"Thank Christ for that." He set his beer glass down on the bar and looked at me. "Because I hope you haven't forgotten what happened last time."

"Er, no."

Wallace proceeded to tell me anyway. "You went out together for two months."

"Five and a half," I said.

"Then on your eighteenth birthday, she goes and dumps you for Danny Curran."

I nodded grimly.

Wallace laughed. "I hope for her sake he was better as a lover than he was a teacher. God, your face when you caught her sucking his cock at your own birthday party!"

"Get stuffed," I said, blushing at the memory.

"What are you so sensitive about? It was years ago." He smiled and shook his head. "Poor old Danny, eh? I wonder what became of the dirty one-legged bastard?"

"He had two legs," I said. "One was shorter than the other."

"Oh, that's right. I forgot. You saw him with his trousers down, didn't you?" Wallace took a mouthful of his drink and tried not to laugh. He tried so hard that beer came out of his nostrils.

"I'm glad you find it amusing."

When Wallace had stopped laughing, he leaned back on his stool and shrugged. "She didn't do him much good, anyway. Lost his job for fucking a pupil. He and his wife split up, and Caro dumped him. Serves him fucking right."

"If it hadn't been Danny," I said, "it would have been someone else."

"Exactly," said Wallace, spinning on his stool until he was facing me. "That's exactly my point. What do you want her phone number for? You know what you're like. You'll see her once, then you'll start following her about on all fours with your little tail wagging and your tongue hanging out."

"I'm nothing like that."

"Yes, you are. You're doing it now. Why you ever wasted your time on a lying tart like that, I will never know."

This was the trouble with Wallace. He dreamed of being hip, but he used words like "tart," words that even your parents would consider old-fashioned.

"She was a teenager," I reminded him. "Of course she was going to be flattered when her favorite teacher took a shine to her. She's twenty-three now. People do grow up, Andy—present company fucking well excepted."

He sulked for a while, then tried to get his own back. "I'll tell you something about Caro, shall I? Something you didn't know. She used to take the piss out of you behind your back."

"No, she didn't. Other kids might have done. Bastards like you. Not Caro."

"Madden, I'm telling you. Even when you were seeing her, she found you rather amusing. And I don't mean in a nice way. She used to call you Madeline."

"Bullshit."

For a few seconds, Wallace looked at me the way comrades-in-arms look at each other in old war movies, just before they go over the top and get shot to fuck. "Mark?" he said.

"What?"

"Promise me you won't call her."

"Why? What's it to you?"

"Just promise."

"All right, all right. I promise."

As soon as I got home, I called her.

CHAPTER 2

ABOUT A GIRL

THE VERY next night, just before eight, I drove to Caro's address on Kew Road. She lived in a first-floor flat overlooking Kew Gardens. A black BMW Sportster was parked in the drive, next to which my Fiat Uno looked like a car for cautious old ladies. Feeling scared and excited, I rang the bell. Caro, now minus her plaster cast, came down to open the door. She placed her hands lightly on my shoulders and greeted me with those fake kisses so beloved of middle-class women.

We walked to the restaurant on foot, close but not touching. It was a mild but windy night in early February. Litter and dead leaves spun around our feet as we walked. I complimented her on the BMW. "You must be doing all right for yourself, to drive a car like that."

Caro laughed rudely.

The restaurant was that French one at the shitty end of Kew Road. Our table was in the window, giving passersby an excellent view of my appalling table manners. The people around us were all rich and well groomed. In my slightly idiotic best clothes, I blended in rather well. "Have you been here before?" I asked her.

"No. Have you?"

"A few times. It's the second-best restaurant in Richmond. The first is an Indian place called the New Manzil. You know it?"

"Is that the place where they give you free wine?"

"Yeah. And those cute little matchboxes with elephants on them."

I suddenly became aware of the Muzak softly playing in the background. "Listen," I said. "They're playing our song."

To our amusement and distaste, it was a Mantovani arrangement of "Fuck Me but Don't Fuck With Me" by Sol Horror. The song that had been playing at that first party when Caro had puked all over me. The song that brought us together.

"It's an omen," I joked.

"I doubt it," said Caro.

The neighboring table was occupied by a leering white-haired man and a woman who was young enough to be his daughter but nowhere near ugly enough.

"Look at that," said Caro in a loud voice. "Beauty and the beast. She's got her whole life ahead of her, but so what? She's broke. He's promised to leave his wife for her, and with her body, it might just be worth it. At the moment, his money is the only aphrodisiac she needs. But I wonder how sexy he'll seem when she's forty and he's seventy-five and peeing his pajamas."

Caro may have looked like a more beautiful version of her former self, but the feeling she gave off was very different. At seventeen, despite her pretensions to cool, she had been as appalled and bewildered by the world as me. Now, unless it was an act, she gave the impression of being frighteningly self-possessed.

"Wow," I said. "Are you always this cynical?"

"I'm no cynic," she said. "A cynic doesn't believe in the basic goodness of people."

"And how many good people do you know?"

"Donny Osmond."

"Is that it? Donny Osmond?"

"Isn't that enough? I have faith in Donny. If Donny was found to be a junkie, a wife beater, or a pedophile, I wouldn't believe in anything anymore."

We'd ordered a bottle of chardonnay. The waiter who opened

the bottle, a puny French guy in his thirties, fawned over Caro as if she were royalty. He wasn't exactly subtle about it, letting her sample the wine instead of me, despite the fact that I was paying. When Caro said the wine was lovely, the waiter said, "A beautiful wine for a beautiful lady."

"Well, thank you," I said, fluttering my eyelids at him.

Even when he was serving other people, the waiter couldn't help staring at her. Humbert Humbert at the next table was also mesmerized by her. I don't know why I'm acting so superior about it. I couldn't take my eyes off her, either.

I drank the first glass too quickly because I was so nervous. When I was on the second, she patted my hand. "Take it easy, I'm not going anywhere."

"So what do you do?" I said.

She smirked. "Are we making polite conversation?"

"Yeah," I said.

"I do fuck-all," she said. "And what do *you* do? Oh yeah, I remember. You sell rare books. Like Hugh Grant in *Notting Hill*."

"No. He didn't sell novels. He sold travel books."

"How on earth would you remember that?"

"I've got a very retentive memory."

"Retentive anus, you mean."

I decided to let this go. "If you've got any Nick Hornby first editions you want to sell, I'd definitely be interested. That's my specialist area. Books by and about men."

"Ugh, no." She shook her head vehemently. "All that men-with-feelings shit makes me throw up."

I smiled tolerantly to demonstrate that her contempt for my vocation would not affect my desire to sleep with her.

"What's the point?" she said. "Are Nick Hornby books worth anything?"

"*Fever Pitch* would go for about twenty pounds. A signed one could fetch as much as forty."

"As much as that?"

Now I was starting to feel uncomfortable. "Yeah, but you wait. In a few years, the value of those books will skyrocket."

"What if it doesn't?" said Caro. "What if dear old Nick becomes one of those writers nobody bothers with anymore? Like Matthew, Mark, Luke, and John."

"Well, I'll have been wasting my time."

She nodded in satisfaction. I felt we weren't getting on well at all.

"You used to like Sylvia Plath, didn't you?" I said. "I've got a copy of *The Colossus* you might be interested in."

"I've already got it."

"Yeah, you've got an old paperback. I'm offering you a hardback first edition. The first UK edition, published by Heinemann in 1960. You can have it for nothing."

"Why?"

"To say thank you. For coming here tonight."

She frowned. "But has it got the same poems in it as the paperback?"

"Of course."

"Thanks. But no thanks."

"Why not?"

"I'm not interested in first editions. I'm not a collector. I think that collecting things is sick. It's like hamsters filling their pouches with nuts. It's just another way of trying to ward off death. Plus you could offer me as many books as you liked, it wouldn't turn back the clock. I'm not going to suddenly fall back in love with you. I'm not going to want to sleep with you."

This crushed me so comprehensively that for a while I could think of nothing to say.

It was Caro who broke the silence. "To answer the question you asked ten centuries ago, I tried working. Two and a half years on a magazine in Fleet Street."

"You were a journalist?"

"Yeah. I was a staff writer on a women's glossy. I used to make up all those exclusive stories about how to keep your man from straying."

"And what's the answer?"

"The real answer or the one I wrote for the readers?"

"The real answer."

"You mutate into a completely different person every two years. Only way to keep your man. Relationships only last two years. After that, the sex has lost its edge, and all the flowers in the world can't make up for the arguments, the resentments, and the secret loathing."

"You don't really believe that," I said. "Anyway, we were only together for six months."

"That's right." She smiled brightly, and my heart fluttered. "That's why I never got tired of you."

"Oh. So how come you walked out on me?"

"I was seventeen. My lovely teacher made a pass at me. I was a little kid, I was flattered. What was I supposed to do?"

"Report him to the authorities?"

"If I'd thought you'd have been able to handle me seeing someone else, I would never have ended it. Well, not for about another eighteen months, anyway."

The first course arrived. It looked like a giant maggot sitting on a lettuce leaf. Caro ate hers without hesitation, then started on mine. She was welcome to it.

"So in theory," I said, "you and I have got another year and a half?"

"Stop it."

"Then why did you ask me to call you?"

"I thought it'd be nice just to meet as friends and catch up."

"You don't fancy me anymore?"

I saw her hesitate. "It isn't that. You're very nice. That's part of the problem. You're a little *too* nice."

"I'm not that nice."

"You are, Mark. I bet you even wash the dishes."

"I prefer to wipe."

The main course was some kind of fish. I thought I'd ordered a salad, which just went to show how bad my French was.

"How's your love life?" I asked, trying to sound casual.

"I haven't been out with anyone for eight months."

"How many relationships have you had since I knew you?"

"Lost count," she said. "You?"

"Four," I said. "An actress, a kindergarten teacher, a flight attendant, and a girl I met at college."

"Which one lasted the longest?"

"Four and a half years. The girl I met at college. She was my second-favorite girlfriend. You're the first. The kindergarten teacher comes third. The flight attendant and the actress share equal fourth place."

Caro laughed. "Is there something wrong with you?"

"No." I felt myself blushing. "What do you mean?"

"Well, you keep making lists."

"Do I?"

"Yeah. First you did it about the restaurant. Now you're doing it about your girlfriends."

"Ah."

She wasn't just being hostile. The subject interested her. "Listmaking. Making endless lists about stupid fucking things. It's an epidemic, and it's wiping out the modern Western male."

"I haven't really given it much thought."

"I can tell," she said. "Does your dad make lists?"

"No."

"Nor does mine. But he's a complete nutter, so he doesn't really count. My mum's dad got shot in the war—can't remember if I ever told you that. A Japanese bullet went right through him, took out his spleen. Do you think he made lists? His ten best comrades to die in action, in order of likability?"

"I doubt it."

"So do I. He was too busy fighting to survive. No wonder the male sperm count is plummeting throughout America and Europe. Why would men need testosterone when all they do is sit at home being neurotic?"

"I'm not being neurotic. I run a business, I live my life."

To illustrate my point, I accidentally knocked over my wineglass, spilling chardonnay over the tablecloth and the floor.

"But your business is neurotic. Collecting things is neurotic."

I could see what she was saying, just couldn't bring myself to accept it.

"Guys like you are just not equipped," stated Caro.

"Equipped for what?"

"I don't know . . . life and death."

"And what makes you such an authority on men?"

"I've screwed enough of them. And I've perceived a definite trend. Men who lived through the Second World War came out solid. Like Humphrey Bogart. You could see it in their faces. They'd passed through the fire. They weren't just a bunch of compulsive-obsessive faggots."

"Is that what you think I am?"

"Well, you could use a bit of toughening up. You can't argue with that, surely?"

"You sound like my dad."

"He must be partly to blame, even though he doesn't know it. Did he ever take you out into the woods, teach you how to hunt?"

"I worked in his bacon shop every Saturday."

"It's not quite the same thing."

"So what are you suggesting?" I said. "A return to men who never cry, can't cook, or change a nappy?"

Caro lit a cigarette. I have to admit I was shocked. The dangers of smoking are so widely publicized that I'd forgotten that some people are still rash enough to disregard them. "As you know, I used to be into all that feminist shit," she said, blowing smoke across the table. "But I now think women have thrown the baby out with the bathwater. Sure, it's useful to have a man who can wash and iron clothes. It's also useful to have a man who keeps calm in a crisis. A man who would kill to protect his family."

"So marry a soldier."

"I'm getting on your nerves, aren't I? That's good."

"Why?"

"If I irritate you enough, maybe you'll get over all this shit about loving me."

The smoke was making me cough. "Who said anything about loving you?"

She went on as if I hadn't spoken. "You're nice, Mark. You always were. But that's the trouble, Mark. I'm only attracted to bastards."

"I can be a bastard."

She smirked. "Since when?"

"This morning. I walked right past a homeless person without giving him any money."

Caro said, "Yeah, but I bet you smiled at him as you walked past."

I shrugged. "Good manners don't cost anything."

Caro wasn't listening. I followed the direction of her gaze and saw an angry red face leering at us through the window. For a second, I thought the homeless person I hadn't given money to had returned to taunt me. Then Caro said, "Shit!" and I realized she knew the man at the window and he knew her.

A few seconds later, the stranger had gone.

"Who was that?"

"Warren," she said wearily.

"Who's Warren?"

"An ex-boyfriend who can't accept that it's over."

"A pattern seems to be emerging here." I put down my fork and looked at her. "Warren looked a little psychotic to me."

"He's a maniac. That's what I've been trying to tell you. When we met he told me he was a record producer. He turned out to be a small-time dealer. He sells dope and speed to the sweat-stained losers of Richmond."

"You know some very strange people."

"I seem to collect them," she said, looking me directly in the eye.

*   *   *

I PAID the bill and walked her home. On the way, Caro suddenly linked arms with me and said, "That was a great meal. I've had a really nice time."

"Thanks."

She added, "But there's no way I'm going to sleep with you."

"I never imagined you were," I said.

"Yeah. I bet it didn't even cross your mind."

"No," I said. "I never make advances unless I'm invited."

"That's right, I forgot," she said, laughing. "Men like you don't even get a hard-on until a woman gives you permission."

I found this a bit insulting but couldn't think of a comeback. We entered Caro's leafy driveway to be confronted by a bizarre sight. There was a man squatting on the hood of her BMW. As we approached, he leapt into our path and screamed. It was Warren.

"Careful," I warned. "I am armed with a large vocabulary."

"Warren," said Caro, "when are you going to grow up?"

Warren's hair came down to his big, solid shoulders. "Is this him?" he said angrily. "The bastard you're fucking instead of me?"

"Let's be reasonable here," I said. Warren didn't appear to hear me.

"No, no. You've got it all wrong. I'm not fucking him," said Caro. When Warren had calmed down, she said, *I'm sucking his cock.*"

Warren gave us a strange lopsided stare, and for a second I thought he was going to kill us both. Then he grunted and half-swaggered, half-staggered away. I stood at the gate, watching him turn right into Pagoda Avenue. "I think he's gone," I said reassuringly. "What's wrong with his eyes?"

"One of them's false. He had an accident."

"You went out with a guy with a glass eye?"

"Yeah. So what?"

"Nothing. I just think it's laudable that you treat people with disabilities the same as everyone else."

"Don't," she said. "You'll make me throw up."

"Sorry."

"Would you like some coffee before you go?"

I rarely drank tea or coffee, because I liked to keep my body caffeine free, but I was afraid that admitting this would merely confirm Caro's suspicions that I was not a real man. So I nodded confidently and said, "Coffee would be great."

She lived on the first floor of a three-story house. Her front room faced Kew Road, with its roaring traffic. In the distance, the pagoda in Kew Gardens reared above the trees. The walls were lined with shelves, containing, as one would expect, worn paperback copies of all the books that had ever been considered cool. *On the Road, Trainspotting, A Clockwork Orange, The Doors of Perception.* There was even a copy of *Billy Bunter Goes to Blackpool.*

On the coffee table lay a neat pack of tarot cards, which in turn rested on a worn and threadbare copy of Wilhelm's translation of the *I Ching.* Beside them was a dainty ashtray that contained a half-smoked spliff.

We sat in the high-ceilinged living room, listening to the traffic rumble down below. Every so often a plane passed over on its way to Heathrow, flying so low that the roar of its engines drowned out the traffic. "So did your life work out the way you wanted?" asked Caro.

"I think you know the answer to that."

She nodded. "Things are shit for me, too. I'm in debt up to my eyeballs."

"How much?"

"Last time I dared to look, I owed about fifty grand."

I whistled in admiration.

"My mum died," she said. "Did I tell you that?"

"No. I'm sorry."

"Yeah. She built her whole life round Dad, gave him his pills on time, did everything for him. She was meant to survive him so we could have a nice easy life, spending his millions, but she dropped dead from a heart attack last February. Soon as she's out of the way, my dad hires a live-in housekeeper and guess what? He hasn't had a hard-on since 1961, but he gets the hots for her. Last week he told me they were getting married. Pretty soon he's going to change his will, if he hasn't done it already. Where does that leave me? Hopelessly in debt, without a chance in hell of ever climbing out of the hole I've dug for myself."

"The BMW in the drive. Is that yours?"

"Yes."

"Why don't you sell it?"

"I haven't paid for it yet."

"If I had any money, I'd give it to you. In the meantime, if there's anything practical I can do to help, just ask."

"I know," she said sarcastically. "Why don't you give me a job in your bookshop? If I don't eat, buy clothes, or use any electricity, I should have paid off all my debts by the year 3000."

I went into her kitchen to get a drink of water. When I first turned on the light, I thought someone had been sick all over the floor. Then I realized I was looking at hideous orange and brown linoleum. A naked lightbulb hung from the ceiling. There was no curtain or blind at the window. It was a typically delapidated Greater London shithole.

In the fridge, I found a half-empty bottle of flat Perrier. I poured some into a glass, swallowed it, and poured some more. Using the kitchen window as a mirror, I checked that my shirt looked okay and my hair wasn't sticking up. Then there was a violent crash. Something hard and cold burst through the window and hit me on the head. I staggered and had to grip the kitchen table to prevent myself from falling over.

* * *

"WHAT HAPPENED?" I was lying on the sofa. Caro had laid a cold, damp cloth over my brow.

"It was Warren again," she said. "I saw him running away."

"What hit me?"

"It was a brickbat. You're lucky. You must have a very hard head. Now you've got a lump on your lump."

"Have you called the police?"

"No. I just taped cardboard over the window."

"Hadn't you better call them?"

"Why? The police know all about my ex, I've called them a hundred times. He'd have to murder me before they took him seriously."

"But this is Richmond-Upon-Thames. It's meant to be a nice area."

"It is. Warren's the son of a doctor. He just happens to have an addictive personality, and at the moment he's addicted to me."

"How often does he come round?"

"There's no particular pattern. Sometimes weeks can go by. Just when I think I've got rid of him, the doorbell starts ringing at one in the morning, and there's Warren on the doorstep, howling like a stray dog."

I tried to sit up but felt so dizzy that I lay straight back down again.

Caro looked at me and sighed. "Why don't you stay here tonight?"

My dick began to twitch hopefully. It needn't have bothered.

"You can sleep on the sofa," she said. "Why don't you? You don't look well. Go home in the morning."

I wanted to see my head, so she brought over a mirror. On my forehead there was a swelling the size of a poached egg, the most recent lump representing the yolk.

She hauled in some pillows and covered me with a flowery quilt. And when she said good night, she kissed me, once, on the brow, like Florence Nightingale kissing a dying soldier.

CHAPTER 3

FEVER BITCH

IN THE morning, Caro cooked me a full English breakfast: bacon, tomatoes, fried eggs, sausages, beans, and fried bread. I usually avoid fatty foods, but I was so touched by her consideration that I devoured it all, right down to the last heart-stopping morsel. Caro, nibbling daintily at dry toast, sat opposite me, her eyes piercingly blue in the morning sunshine. I felt an overwhelming, hopeless implosion of longing.

"Stop going on about it."

"About what?"

"About how gorgeous I am."

I was astonished. "I didn't say a word."

"You didn't have to," she said, with a sly smile. "It's written all over your egg-stained fucking face."

"Well, of course, I've still got feelings for you."

"Dirty or clean?"

"Pretty filthy, actually."

She nodded. "Just can't let anything go, can you? The way you are about books and songs is the way you are about people. You try to keep everything."

"I try to keep promises," I said, in a tone of hurt dignity. "You once told me you'd never love anyone as much as you loved me. You *did* say that."

"Maybe I did. We say a lot of things when we're seventeen."

"You love someone else?"

"Mark, I don't feel anything. Not just for you, but for anyone. I haven't felt a real emotion since I left school."

* * *

THE TWIN bruises on my head had turned purple and green. I looked like the man from the future in an old *Outer Limits* show. Caro must have felt sorry for me, because as I was leaving she asked me if I fancied a walk. We ambled over to Kew Green and bought some water, hazelnuts, and chocolate. Then we circled the high walls of Kew Gardens until we came to the footpath by the Thames that links Kew with Richmond.

The dark green river slid by on our right. To our left lay the boundary fence of Kew Gardens. Between us and the fence there was a wide ditch. A stout drainpipe emerged from the gardens and passed underneath the path, pumping shit into the river. Caro suddenly mounted the drainpipe and started walking. When she was halfway across the ditch, she turned to look at me. "Come on," she hissed.

"What're you doing?"

"You tell me."

"You're sneaking into Kew Gardens without paying."

"You astound me, Holmes."

"I think I'd rather pay."

"Don't be silly. It costs a bomb to get into this place."

Feeling shoddy and cheap, I followed her, and we passed into the gardens via a gap in the fence. I realized this was how Caro lived her entire life, never answering the door or the phone, sneaking and hiding to avoid admission fees and creditors.

We sat on a bench, eating nuts and chocolate and looking out at the river. Caro pointed out the stone lions on the roof of Syon House. As we passed all the benches, most of them dedicated to dead people who had loved Kew, I found myself thinking of "Everything Is Cool," my favorite song by the Serenes.

And everywhere I turn
I see the ones I knew
For they found heaven here
The dreaming ghosts of Kew . . .

Men of all ages and quite a few women stopped talking as we passed, often smiling as they followed Caro with their eyes. It had been the same when we were seventeen. Some men might have felt proud to be in the presence of such a dazzling creature, yet the attention Caro attracted had always unnerved me. It would have suited me better if everyone else thought she resembled Lon Chaney as the Phantom of the Opera and I was the only man alive to perceive her true beauty.

At the pine trees near Queen Charlotte's Cottage, Caro insisted on stopping to feed the squirrels. The fluffy-tailed rodents were so accustomed to Caro that they ate nuts out of her hands. I copied her, and soon they were accepting nuts from me. One squirrel seemed a little slow and was always looking the wrong way when the nuts were being handed out. Determined to feed the poor little bastard, I waited on one knee with my hand out until he finally got the idea and came up to me.

"Mark, careful," said Caro. "He looks a bit mentally handicapped."

I ignored her. The squirrel sniffed my left hand, then took hold of my thumb and sank his teeth into it. The pain was instantaneous and appalling. I felt the yellow rodent teeth grinding against my thumb joint. I leaped up, roaring with furious pain, a cute furry retard dangling from my hand like some kind of sick fashion accessory. It was only a few seconds before the squirrel released me, but it felt as long as a seventies guitar solo.

My thumb was spurting blood, and a great flap of flesh was hanging off it. All I had to wrap it in was a piece of tissue. The tissue drank up the blood like blotting paper. In moments it was bright red.

The incident had immobilized Caro. She had one hand over her mouth, and her legs were crossed. It was the same when she was at school. Whenever she saw something really violent, her clitoris started to twitch. I don't know how common this is. Perhaps all women get clit-ache when they see blood. Maybe public executions once secretly unleashed mass orgasms. It is not an attractive thought.

"Not exactly Francis of Assisi, are you?" said Caro. She removed the scarf that she was wearing and wrapped it around my thumb.

We walked for a while, then went for coffee in the orangery café. The café was big and cavernous, echoing with the rattle of cutlery and the polite chink-chink of cups and saucers. My thumb stung like hell, but I didn't mention it in case I came across as a crybaby.

"What happened to all those songs you used to write?" she asked me. "I thought you were going to be a rock star."

"I could never find the right people to be in a band with," I said. "They either hated my ideas or they never got out of bed."

"So now you're twenty-three and you feel your life is pretty much fucked. Well, join the club."

"I know I must be getting older," I said, "because when I turn on the TV and see a band, even bands I like, they just look like a bunch of stupid little tossers striking poses. There's no one to look up to anymore. All the best people are dead. I think Kurt Cobain was the last great rock spirit."

"Who would you say were the top five rock and roll suicides?" she asked me casually.

Without thinking, I said, "Good question. Not counting accidents?"

"No."

"Okay. Number five, Brian Epstein. Number four, Michael Hutchence. Number three, Ian Curtis. Number two, Nick Drake. Number one, Kurt Cobain."

"Got you." She started laughing. "Another list."

She went to the counter and borrowed a pen and a scrap of paper. Then she sat down again, scribbled a few lines, and passed them to me. There were three names on it.

1. MY FATHER
2. WARREN
3. JESUS

"What's this?" I said.

"I made a list of my own," said Caro. "It's a list of the people I want you to kill for me."

I laughed. She didn't.

"You claim to love me, but when I ask you to do the simplest thing it's suddenly too much trouble. What kind of love is that? Do you think Heathcliff wouldn't have killed for Cathy?"

I was silent for a long time. "Are you serious? Are you honestly suggesting that I kill people? That I kill your own father?"

She nodded slowly, her pale blue eyes fixed on mine.

"Some hit man I'd be," I said, holding up my injured hand. "Even squirrels come off better in a fight."

Caro spoke as if she hadn't heard me. "It can't be me, you see, because I've got a good reason for killing all of them. That's obvious."

"What's obvious," I said, "is that you're not really thinking about what you're saying."

She tutted, just as girls used to tut when I was thirteen and I asked them what menstruation felt like. We remained silent as we walked into the gardens behind Kew Palace and sat on the wall by the fountain that never founts.

"Why ask me, anyway?" I said. "I think we've both established that I'm too nice."

"That's why you'd be perfect. You haven't got a record. No one would suspect you."

"Caro, my life's bad enough as it is. I'm not going to prison for you or anyone else."

"So it's not that you don't think there are people who deserve to be murdered," she said scornfully. "You're just scared of going to prison."

"That's right."

"That's a bit spineless, isn't it?"

"It's not about courage," I said. "It's common sense. Whatever direction my life takes, I don't want to be shitting and pissing into a bucket with my cellmate watching."

"Mark, you want me, don't you?"

"You know I do."

"I would give myself to you," she said, thrusting herself up against me. "I'd give you that eighteen months I owe you. You could do anything you liked to me, as often as you wanted."

I looked at her for a long time. "Wow, you really are cracked."

"No." She colored slightly. "Most people could name at least half a dozen people they'd like to see dead. The only difference is, I've got the guts to admit it. The world's a bad place, Mark.

Good people starve and die while bad people thrive and get richer. You think it's bad karma to kill a few bastards? I don't. I think God and all the angels sing for joy every time another bastard dies. How about it? Don't you want to make God happy?"

"I don't see how killing Jesus would make God happy."

Caro didn't laugh.

I could tell she was disappointed. So was I. I had rather hoped she might have matured since school, developed a little more empathy for the suffering souls around her. Instead, she was the same old bitch, but with larger breasts. With sourness hanging between us like a plague of flies, we walked out of the Lion Gate and turned right. Outside her home, she grabbed me, kissed me once on the mouth, and wished me a happy life.

I drove home through the horrible, dense traffic, feeling what I'd felt so many times before, that Caro was unbalanced and unpredictable and not worth bothering with.

But as I sat down to my lonely tea, a boiled egg with toast soldiers, I found I could barely swallow. I was shivering, even though it wasn't cold. When I studied my bruised forehead in the bathroom mirror, my eyes glittered with an energy I didn't feel. I knew these symptoms well.

My love for Caro was obsessive. It had to be, to have lasted so long. Despite her lack of basic human goodness (or perhaps because of it), no woman had ever excited me more. But what was clear to me was that I hardly excited Caro at all. I was just someone she had slept with, one more sap in a cast of thousands, undistinguished by personality, good looks, or sexual prowess. A boy from her past, a naive boy who entered her life as a virgin and left as a trembling, white-faced cuckold.

* * *

To console myself, I went to see Lisa. She was about ten years older than me. Lisa and I were in a relationship that that was going nowhere, which is why I hadn't bothered mentioning her to Caro. The lack of direction was entirely my fault. Lisa, a dimpled single mother, lived in New Eltham.

It was Harry Potter that brought us together. Lisa realized, quite rightly, that unless J. K. Rowling was suddenly discovered to be the leader of a child porn network, her books were destined to appreciate in value. Lisa had a fourteen-year-old son. His name was Elliot. Lisa started buying signed Harry Potter first editions from me, knowing that if she kept them in fine condition, she could eventually sell them at a vast profit and, with the proceeds, put Elliot through college.

On first learning that Lisa had a son, I was intrigued. So far, I'd been a romantic failure, an anally retentive jerk, and a decent fair-minded bloke trying to make his fair-minded way through a confusing world. But becoming a surrogate father to a boy who missed having a man in his life was the one Nick Hornby cliché I hadn't tried. Unfortunately, Elliot had other ideas.

Tonight, when I rang the bell, Elliot opened the door. When he saw me, he turned his face away as if I were a particularly nasty road accident. "Oh, shit."

"Hi, Elliot," I said brightly, switching on the unflappable charm that was my only way of dealing with the unfriendly little bastard.

"What do you want?" he said.

I'd been seeing Lisa for seven months, and apart from the occasional gloomy half-day truce, my dealings with her son had been unsatisfactory from the outset. Tonight, I gave him my warmest fake smile. "Listen," I said. "I know you're having problems at school. I understand that you miss your real father, and

I swear I'm not trying to replace him. I may be a disappointment to you. Sometimes, I must admit, I'm a disappointment to myself. But Elliot, there's no reason why we can't be friends. That's all I want. Just to be friends."

"Fuck off, you simpering twat," said Elliot.

He was bright, I could see that. Most fourteen-year-olds would never use a word like "simpering." Before I had formulated a mature response, Elliot had swung the door toward me and walked off. Choosing to view this as progress—he usually slammed it shut—I peered through the crack into the hall. "Hello? Lisa?"

After about a minute, it became apparent that Elliot hadn't told his mother I was here. He had no intention of doing or saying anything that might make our relationship easier. I walked into the house. The brat was in the living room, watching TV. From upstairs came the annoying whine of a hair dryer, an appliance that Lisa wielded with depressing dexterity. She was a mobile hairdresser.

I hovered in the kitchen until she came down. She beamed when she saw me, showing her dimples, a girlish woman in her thirties who revealed her inherent sweetness and lack of formal education every time she smiled. She had long hair, bleached canary blonde with extravagant waves, a prime example of a hairdresser who needed a hairdresser. "Oh, I didn't hear the door," she said, kissing me lightly on the cheek. "Did Elliot let you in?"

I half-nodded. She made an I'm-pleasantly-surprised noise, as if this proved that my relationship with her beloved only child was progressing at a breakneck pace. Lisa preferred to ignore the fact that her son would have cheered if my genitals were bitten off by a rabid dog.

Before I left with Lisa for our statutory ninety minutes at the pub, she asked her son if she could do anything for him. "Yes," he said, his eyes not leaving the telly. "You can get rid of that cunt standing next to you."

* * *

I'D SEEN a lot of Wallace since his marriage failed. During my time at university, Wallace had got himself a job, a wife, and two children. He worked in IT, managing an office full of computer nerds. Then, after a one-night stand with a young programmer, he made the disastrous mistake of telling his wife. As a reward for his honesty, she asked him to leave. Now he was living in a depressing complex called Sheen Court, where the walls were so thin you could hear people breaking wind in the adjoining flats.

We took to going out for a drink about twice a week. Tonight we visited a little pub called the Wheatsheaf, just around the corner from Sheen Common Drive, where Caro used to live. It was a small pub in an almost exclusively middle-class area, the last place you'd anticipate trouble. The mood was relaxed. The landlord, Phil, always wore his carpet slippers.

Wallace seemed relieved and encouraged that my night out with Caro had resulted in nothing more physical than a brick on the head. I realized that the end of his marriage and the failure of his one-night stand to extend to two nights had damaged his confidence. He was my age but felt old. Seeing his children only on weekends had hit him hard, and now, rather too late, he recognized that he'd fucked up a happy marriage for the sake of five sticky minutes in a dark stockroom.

"Okay," I said. "In ascending order, list the top five women who'd never want to fuck you."

This was how we spent our evenings.

"Why bother to make a list?" said Wallace. "Why not save ourselves the effort by admitting that all the women in the world have reached the unanimous verdict that I am deeply unattractive?"

"Because it wouldn't be true," I said. "Come on. The top five women who would take one look at you and turn you down."

Wallace thought about it. "In fifth place," he said, "Princess Diana."

"She's dead. Corpses don't count."

"You never said they couldn't be dead," argued Wallace.

"No, but dead kind of ruins the game. If someone's dead, of course you stand no chance with them."

"That's a matter of opinion."

"Besides, Diana might have considered you," I said. "She had very dodgy taste. I'm talking about women who, if you were rich enough, even if you could move in their circles and eat in the same restaurants, they'd still turn you down. Women who wouldn't be tempted even if you were naked in bed with them and you were the last man on earth."

"That's still every woman alive."

"No, it isn't. You suffer from low self-esteem, you know that?"

"In that case," he said, "number five is that actress who was in *Pirates of the Caribbean*. I know she wouldn't fuck me. In fourth place, who's that tall Russian tennis player who wouldn't fuck me?"

"Sharapova?"

"Yeah. I'd stand no chance whatsover there. As for third place, my number three woman who I'd like to fuck but who wouldn't countenance it is probably your mother."

"My mother? My own mother?"

"Yeah. Sorry. Did I never tell you she was sexy?"

"You're disgusting."

"Yes, I am. Which is why, despite the fact that you once skidded down that poor woman's birth canal, Mrs. Madden is definitely at number three. On some days, in her nurse's uniform, she might even make it to second place."

"You'd stand no chance with my mother. No chance at all."

"Exactly," said Wallace wearily. "Which is why she's on a list of women who wouldn't fuck me."

I sighed. "You know something? We need to get out more. Our vital forces are ebbing away."

"What vital forces?"

"You know what they say in Tahiti? 'Eat life or life will eat you.'"

"What does that mean?"

"Well. Look at us. We do the same things night after night. We even have the same conversations."

Wallace swallowed his drink and watched the suds sliding down the inside of his beer glass. "I suppose we could be a little more spontaneous than we are. But you can't be spontaneous just like that."

Wallace went for a piss while I bought the next round. On his return, Wallace nudged me. "Don't look now—I said *don't look*— but there's this right evil-looking bastard behind us who looks like he wants to kill you."

I turned round. There, sitting at a table under the window, was Wuffer. His hair was neatly brushed back from his one inch forehead, and a little golden medallion dangled from his neck. Although it was winter, his prehistoric arms protruded menacingly from a short-sleeved Hawaiian shirt. He was sitting perfectly still, a cigarette in one hand and a pint of beer in front of him. Next to him was a big greasy woman with red streaks in her hair and a face that seemed to have been cast in concrete. This had to be his wife. She and Wuffer were made for each other.

Wuffer was indeed staring at me as if he wanted to kill me. So was his wife.

"Oh, fucking hell," I said to Wallace.

"What?"

"That's the guy I told you about."

"The one who threw a brick at your bonce?"

"No."

"The one who burned your book?"

"No. This is the one who hit me for stopping his son from beating up some kid."

"I'll say this for you," said Wallace. "You're a popular guy."

I tried to attract the attention of Phil, the landlord, but he was too busy trying to impress a young barmaid.

"Anyway, now's your chance," said Wallace.

"My chance for what?"

"You said he surprised you last time. Now you can surprise him. Go over and punch the bastard."

"Wallace, he's looking right at me. What kind of surprise would that be?"

"It was just a suggestion."

"Here's another. Drink up. We're leaving."

As we walked out the door, Wuffer and his wife walked after us. Wuffer's wife shook her fist at Wallace. "Lay anuver fin on ma kid and arl fucking twad yer."

"I beg your pardon?" said Wallace.

That was all it took. Bingo wings quivering, Wuffer's wife grabbed his hair and started hitting him. Wallace had to use all his strength to break away. Wuffer was laughing, his pistachio teeth glistening with beer and spit. "Yer god the ronwon, yer bent cun," he said to his wife, then pointed at me. "Him. Heed the nob-end wot clogged are Darren."

But Wuffer's wife wasn't fussy about who she attacked. Wallace started to run, and she began to chase after him, her belly lurching up and down inside a dress that resembled an orange tent. In a genteel suburban street lined with desirable prewar dwellings, it was a truly surreal sight.

Wuffer snarled at me. "You ger in mah fuckin drinker agin an arl slice yer fuckin bans off." He lunged forward, and I stepped backward so suddenly that I staggered. "Ah," said Wuffer, triumph in his eyes. "Nah yer get ooze fucking boss, yer can. Nah yer fuckin dinch."

I ran after Wallace. Wuffer's fat wife had him in a headlock and was trying to wrestle him to the ground. He punched her. She lost her balance, tottered, and lurched over a garden wall. I looked back and saw Wuffer charging toward us, screaming. Wallace and I started to run.

Wallace was heavier and less fit than me, which was presumably why flabby Mrs. Wuffer managed to catch him in the first place. As we reached the passage at the end of the road, Wuffer, who was in worse shape than either of us, briefly caught up with him. Wuffer thumped Wallace once before relinquishing the chase and doubling up in a cigarette wheeze. Only when we were about four streets away did we stop to draw breath. Wallace started giggling, and I joined in. It wasn't that we saw the funny side of what had happened. There was no funny side. Ours was the hollow, joyless laughter of the truly unmanned.

In the light of a streetlamp, surrounded by nice middle-class houses, I glanced back and noticed a trail of dark spots on the pavement behind us. It looked as if one of us had trodden in oil.

Then I looked at Wallace, saw him falter, and realized the oil was leaking out of his side.

*   *   *

WALLACE HAD been stabbed above the right hip, probably with a small kitchen knife. It was only a flesh wound, but it required seven stitches. Early in the morning, when we were riding back from Casualty in a taxi, Wallace made a somber announcement. "I don't think we should go out for a while," he said.

"That's crazy," I said. "Something like this happens, you need to get out again at the first opportunity."

"I agree," said Wallace. "I just don't want to go anywhere with you."

"You're joking."

"No," said Wallace. "I don't like being around you, Mark. I think you're unlucky. In fact, I think you're probably cursed."

*   *   *

THE NEXT day was a Sunday. I had lunch with my parents. They still lived on the wrong side of Kew Bridge, in the house I'd grown up in, with my father's huge white refrigerated van parked outside to annoy the neighbors. There was always a good roast dinner on Sundays because Dad owns a food store in Twickenham called Madden Foods. When I turned up at one, my mother kissed me affectionately, but my father and Tom, already seated at the table, merely grunted. Tom, my brother, is my junior by two years. We like each other but have never found much to talk about. Tom works for Dad—works long hours, his heart already set on taking over the business when Dad retires.

They asked where I'd got the bruises. I told them about Wuffer, but not about Caro. Mum and Dad had never quite forgiven her for fucking up my exams. When I described how unhelpful the police constable had been, Dad started jeering. "What were you hoping for? A big wet French one?" To illustrate his point, Dad stuck his tongue out and wriggled it about obscenely.

"Maurice!" said my mother reprovingly.

"Well," said Dad, nodding to me. "He doesn't seem to know what being a man entails."

(It seems unlikely that a working-class Londoner like my father would use a word like "entail," yet he did. He was full of surprises.)

"Let me guess," said my brother, raking roast potatoes onto his plate. "You're about to tell him."

Dad launched into a familiar speech. "Well, he's got to learn. Someone hits you, you hit 'em right back. There's no point crying to the law. What did the law ever do?"

Ever since I discovered Nick Hornby as a teenager, it had been my desire to bond with my father. So far, it hadn't happened. He didn't understand why I wanted to sell rare books, just as I didn't understand why he had devoted his life to sausages.

As I held out my plate for more roast beef, I spilled gravy in my lap. My brother laughed. "Fingers!" That was his nickname for me, having observed at an early age that I was accident prone. Eighteen months ago, without telling anyone, I attempted to tackle the problem through therapy. My therapist told me the clumsiness came from a deep-seated feeling of unworthiness, dating back to childhood, when my newborn brother had usurped my place in my mother's affections. This may have been true, but knowing it made no difference. I was still a clumsy bastard.

"You've got to fight your own battles in this life," said Dad. "The only man you can depend on is you. Your grandfather worked in the stone quarries down at Weymouth. Day after day, a dozen blokes breaking rocks with bloody big hammers. Now, they were hard men. There weren't any women there, women couldn't have done the job. You wouldn't have got Granddad talking about his feelings. He may have cried sometimes. If he did, he kept it to himself. That's what a man does. He does what he has to do. He keeps his head down and gets the bloody job done."

* * *

TAKING MY father's advice to heart, I enrolled in a karate class. Although the idea of learning to fight had appealed to me for some time, I might never have been prompted into action had it not been for my recent humiliations. The instructor was called Lenny Furey. The poster outside Hammersmith tube station said he was a member of the national Shotokan karate squad. I didn't know whether this was good or bad.

I took the train to Hammersmith and walked to the sweaty gym where the class was held. The first session didn't quite live up to expectations. I'd been hoping for a touch of Eastern mysticism, but there was none to be found. Just a lot of stamping, kicking, and grunting. Lenny was a coarse-looking guy of about my height. He had big ears and a stupid-shaped head. Instead of intoning, "The pebble in the pond spreads out ripples; so, too, may the spirit of a warrior radiate ripples of honor," he barked out orders like "You, straighten your leg!" or "You, give me ten push-ups, starting now!"

In the changing room after the session, Lenny called me over. He sounded like he'd smoked three hundred a day since the age of three. "You. Your sense of balance is shite. Would you agree?"

"Yeah," I said.

"Your punches and blocks are okay, but your kicks are fucking useless. Yes or no?"

"You could be right."

"I am right. You've got next to no coordination. Has anyone ever told you that?"

I nodded. "How long will it be before I start getting good?"

"You personally? Maybe two years. And that's only if you practice until you're blue in the face. Understand? That's your only chance of getting better. Because you've got absolutely no natural ability. None whatsoever. Would you agree?"

I looked at him. "Are you trying to get rid of me?"

"No. The opposite. I seen those bruises on your fucking bonce, my son. And something tells me you came here on a mission. Someone's been smacking you about, am I right?"

I nodded meekly.

"It's happened more than once. Yeah?" Lenny regarded me with fractionally more sympathy. "Thought so. I can usually tell."

"I need to be able to learn to look after myself," I said. "I need to do it now. I haven't got two years."

Lenny leaned closer and lowered his voice. "I can give you private lessons. How does fifty quid an hour sound?"

"Expensive."

He shrugged. "I could settle for forty. It'd be fucking worth it."

"When do we start?"

"How about now?" he said. "I've booked this place till ten."

"I'm tired," I said.

"That's no excuse."

*   *   *

FOR THE next hour, Lenny made me do push-ups and sit-ups and run around the gym. After twenty minutes, I had to go out to throw up. On my return, Lenny showed me absolutely no sympathy. He led me over to a punching bag and told me to hit it.

"A karate punch?"

"What do you think this is? The fucking *Karate Kid?* Kick like a ballerina and you're just gonna fall over. I'm teaching you how to fight. Real street fighting's got fuck-all to do with karate."

"That's strange coming from a karate black belt."

"Just hit the fucking thing, will ya?"

I slammed my fist into the bag. My fist came off worse. Lenny tutted and sighed, then showed me how to move with the punch so that it carried my body weight, not just the weight of my knuckles. After a few minutes, he advised me to hit him instead.

"Where?"

"In the belly. Don't hold back. Hit me with everything you've got."

Lenny tensed his muscles, and I slammed my fist into his midriff. It was like hitting a Henry Moore sculpture, but not as enjoyable. By the time the hour was up and I handed over the money, all I wanted to do was go home to bed.

* * *

WHEN I left the gym, it was pissing with rain and I was very depressed. I knew that if I trained hard, never losing sight of my goal, then in five years' time I might be capable of felling a very old woman with a single blow.

I had no umbrella, so I jogged through the backstreets, my rucksack bobbing up and down annoyingly on my back. I thought I heard footsteps, so I glanced over my shoulder. There was a guy in a pullover, quietly jogging behind me.

When I reached Hammersmith station, I looked back again, but there was no trace of him. The sullen guard standing at the barrier barely glanced at my ticket. As I crossed the bridge, there was a train approaching. I hurried down the steps, but when I reached the platform I saw the train was bound for Ealing Broadway.

I bought a bar of chocolate from a vending machine and paced up and down the platform. The chocolate tasted like it had been placed beside the mummified body of Ramses III in 1163 B.C., but I was so hungry I ate it anyway.

The next train was destined for Wimbledon, the next for Ealing Broadway. Just when I'd given up hope, the message on the board flashed NEXT TRAIN RICHMOND. There were three other people on the platform, a fat woman in a fake fur and miniskirt and a nervous teenage boy who seemed embarrassed by the attentions of his girlfriend.

It was then that I felt a stinging blow on the back of my head. At first, I thought the fat woman had seen me staring in disbelief at her badly-packed-sausage legs. I turned and saw the man with the pullover standing behind me, his hood up, raindrops all over his face. "Hey. Shitface. Stay away from her," he said.

It was only then that I realized I was looking at Warren, Caro's most recent victim.

As always when faced with the threat of violence, I decided to try the reasonable approach. It had never succeeded yet, but there is always a first time. "Warren, isn't it?" I held out my hand. He ignored it. "I'm Mark."

This time, Warren jabbed me in the chest with his knuckles. "Stay away from my fucking girlfriend, you stupid-looking wimp, or I will pull your arms out by the fucking stumps."

"Warren, I'm not even going out with her. Come on. You know what a bitch she is. She's even less interested in me than she is in you."

He grabbed my coat with both hands and swung me round so that we were both parallel to the track. Warren was a lot stronger than me. I was vaguely aware of the other passengers on the platform, slowly backing away. Behind me, I could hear the spit-and-rattle of the Richmond train entering the station. I thrust both my hands up through Warren's arms and punched sideways, breaking his hold on me. Contrary to what my instructor believed, I had picked up one or two tricks in my karate class.

I tried to walk away from him, but he grabbed my shoulders and forced me to look into his dead, dull eyes. I couldn't tell whether he was drugged or as miserable as hell. Probably both. "Fucking leave her!" he shouted.

"All right," I said. "Message understood."

As if he hadn't heard, he edged us to the very brink of the platform. The train was close, its yellow lights glimmering on the wet track. It was only then that I understood how desperate and confused he was. He didn't have a plan. All he was trying to do was ease his own grief.

With a huge effort, I broke free again, and as I turned to get past him, my rucksack whacked Warren in the chest and he fell off the platform. The only sound he made was a grunt. Then he hit the track, just in time to be cut in half by the wheels of the train. The train didn't brake; it was already braking. Blood sprayed everywhere. I felt my face burning. With shame? With embarrassment? I wasn't sure. As I walked away, I heard a woman screaming and a man shouting, but I didn't look back. I just kept walking. I'd already seen too much. I didn't want to see any more.

*   *   *

It was after midnight by the time I turned up at Caro's house. I'd been wandering the streets for hours, feeling drunk with shock and fear and appalling guilt. I knew I had to go to the police, but I was worried about how they might react. I don't know why I walked away, I truly don't. As soon as I'd done that, the whole complexion of the incident changed. Innocent people don't tend to flee the scene of a crime.

There was a light shining in the living room window of Caro's flat, so I rang the bell until she responded. She finally pushed up a sash window and called out, "Warren, fuck off!"

"It isn't Warren. It's Mark," I shouted.

She leaned out of the window and peered down at me. "Well, you can fuck off, too."

"I need to talk to you."

"Jesus Christ. Now I've got two of them," she said despairingly. She meant there were now two lovesick morons who hammered on her door at night. With noticeable aggression, she slammed down the window. Minutes later, when she deigned to come to the door, the light from the hall shone on my face and her attitude changed instantly. "Fuck. What is it? What's happened?"

I didn't say anything at first. I was staring at the purple and brown bruise over her left eye. "Yeah," she said. "Would you believe that bastard Warren? He punched me in the face."

"Well, he won't do it again," I said. I was finding it hard to think, let alone talk. Rather than deliver the fuck-off-out-of-my-life speech she had planned, she seized my arm and pulled me into the grimly, dimly lit hallway.

I swayed drunkenly, and she hooked her arm under mine with a sudden show of tenderness. She was perfectly capable of tenderness, by the way. I wouldn't want you to think she was just some slick, callous bitch who only ever thought about herself.

Moving like a very old man on his afternoon out from the rest home, I allowed her to guide me up the communal stairs that stank of dust and antique semen. Once inside the flat, I followed her into the kitchen. Pasta sauce was cooking in a large pan. "Now tell me," she said.

I looked at the dark red sauce and saw Warren's dark red blood exploding upward from the wheels of the train. Convinced that I was about to throw up, I brushed past Caro and rushed to the bathroom. It was a false alarm. I looked in the bathroom mirror and saw that my face and jacket were speckled with dried blood. I had just walked all the way from Hammersmith to Kew, looking exactly like someone who had just committed a murder.

After washing my face, I went to sit on her sofa, so stunned that I wasn't even aware that I was crying until Caro pointed it out. She opened a cigar box, took out a ready-made joint, and passed it to me.

"I'm not in the mood for dope," I said.

"It isn't dope," she said. "It's crystal. The best."

"I thought you didn't do drugs anymore?"

"I lied."

I took a blast and felt nothing, took another and felt my soul rise up inside me like a stallion rearing. "Fuck," I said. "That's good."

"Now tell me," she said, eyes searching my face. "Tell me."

"It's Warren," I managed to say. "He had an accident."

She drew back. "You're joking."

"No."

"Is he all right?"

"I shouldn't think so. He got run over by a train."

"You mean he killed himself?"

"No. I knocked the poor bastard onto the track. He got sawn in half."

Her eyes appeared to double in size. "You saw it happen?"

"No, no." Despite myself, I started to laugh. The meth was making the room rush toward me. "No, I only saw the blood."

Caro's eyes filled with tears. For a moment, I thought she was mourning the loss of a man who had meant something to her. Then she leaned forward and started to kiss my face. "So *you* killed him?"

I shrugged and nodded. It was pretty much the truth. "And I'm not proud of the fact."

Caro's icy-blue eyes were shining. "But you should be. You're an amazing person, you know that?" She threw her arms around me so tightly that I almost stopped shaking. Then she began to kiss my face and neck. "No one . . . but no one . . . has ever done anything like that for me before."

She guided my hand between her legs. She was soaking wet. Her clitoris felt like a bullet.

"Just tell me one thing," I said as she unzipped my trousers. "Did you ever call me Madeline?"

Caro shook her head, being far too polite to speak with her mouth full.

CHAPTER 4

ABOUT A BASTARD

I TOOK no pleasure in Warren's death, but Caro seemed to. As far as she was concerned, I'd performed a selfless public service. All night she showed me just how grateful she was. She told me I was beautiful and potent. I almost believed her. We went to sleep at about four and didn't wake until after eleven. By then, the thought of phoning the police seemed even stupider than it had seemed the night before.

We had breakfast at the kitchen table while the planes roared over on their way to Heathrow. This morning, radiating light, Caro looked happier than I had ever seen her. "Last night was great. I thought you were never going to stop."

I didn't bother explaining that the only reason I'd appeared insatiable was that I hadn't had real sex since she'd dumped me five years ago. Yes, I'd engaged in copulation. I'd made the right noises and kissed the right places. But I'd only ever experienced real sex with Caro. Dirty, filthy, beautiful fucking that obliterates the world and everyone in it.

"You know the only thing that might fuck us up?" (Overnight, Warren's death had become *our* crime, *our* shared triumph.) "CCTV. If the cameras were working, then they might have got footage of you pushing him off the platform."

"Maybe," I said.

"But it was night, and the picture quality on those cheapo cameras is piss-poor. You know what? It's going to look like two badly drawn cartoons that a little kid has scribbled over."

"Maybe we shouldn't see each other for a couple of weeks," I said, surprised by how cool I sounded.

I could see that Caro was surprised, too. Nodding humbly, she reached over the table and patted my hand. "Good idea. And if the police come round, I won't mention you."

She had made up her mind. I was her medieval champion. In her imagination, I had committed justifiable homicide on the westbound platform of Hammersmith station.

I could have made it absolutely clear, there and then, that I had not murderered poor Warren, that he had merely suffered a fatal mishap after picking a fight with the clumsiest bastard in Richmond-Upon-Thames, that if she wanted to show her gratitude to Warren's killer, she should have had sex with my rucksack. But I didn't say a thing, because this morning Caro was looking at me exactly like she used to look at me.

Caro opened a kitchen drawer and placed a black shiny object on the table in front of me. I blinked a few times before I could accept what I was looking at. It was a handgun. "What's this?" I asked her.

"It's Warren's gun," she said. "I need you to hide it for me."

"Warren had a gun?"

"He hung around with some pretty dodgy people."

I stared at her. "How dodgy?"

"The kind of people who kill their enemies and grind them up for dog food."

* * *

As soon as I arrived at the flat above my shop, I got out the gun and studied it. I found the inscription *Custom TLERL II* on the breech and looked it up on the Internet. On a site called Safe Shooter (*We look forward to serving all your firearm needs*) I found Warren's gun. It was a Kimber Swat, as used and abused by the Los Angeles Police Department. Altogether the Kimber carried eight shots, seven in the magazine and one in the breech. The gun was fully loaded. The black rubber grip seemed to sit perfectly in my hand, and the weapon was so light and well crafted that it was hard to believe it was designed solely to maim and kill.

My instincts told me to drop the gun in the Thames. Yet Caro had asked me to hide the weapon, not get rid of it. She trusted me and at the moment, incredible as it seemed, actively admired me. I had no desire to dampen her enthusiasm, but this wasn't my only reason for following her instructions. The gun was *sexy*. My God, I thought fine first editions were attractive enough, but knowing I was holding something that the L.A. cops used to shoot holes in innocent bystanders thrilled me beyond reason.

Desperate to find out if the gun worked, I aimed at a book-case and squeezed the trigger. There was a deafening explosion that made the door to the street shudder in its frame. The air was full of smoke, smoke that smelled of childhood. The shot had been so loud that I expected people to come running, but the only passerby was an unimpressed overalled workman, chewing a burger made from a cow's arsehole.

Then I noticed I'd blown a smoking hole right through a signed copy of *Not a Penny More, Not a Penny Less.* I cursed my misfortune. It was better than the book deserved, but that shot had cost me one hundred and twenty-five pounds.

Calling myself some well-chosen names, I laid the gun in my favorite hiding place, a hollowed-out copy of an old Arthur Mee *Children's Encylopedia.* Years before, while living with my parents, this book had concealed my dope stash and the tran-quilizers I'd stolen from my mother and saved up for special occasions.

*   *   *

I DIDN'T open for business that day. At lunchtime, I watched the local news report. There was a story about a man who'd gone hunting with a shotgun in a tower block in Mile End. A traffic warden in Epping had been set alight by angry motorists. There was no mention of a murder committed at Hammersmith station.

I needed a drink. In the fridge there was a bottle of gin and two cans of tonic water. I drank gin and tonic with ice until the tonic had gone, then I drank neat gin. By about two o'clock I could barely see the room in front of me and finally understood the meaning of "blind drunk." I staggered up to bed, lay down in the darkness, and spun.

When I'd puked for about the third time, the phone rang. I heard my own voice deliver the answering machine message. I sounded middle-class, friendly, and faintly ridiculous. Then I heard Caro talking. Her voice was husky and womanly and at least ten thousand times more confident than mine. I staggered into the next room and picked up the phone.

"Hello?"

"What's wrong?" she said. "Your voice is all funny."

"Why are you calling?"

"I was missing you."

"Where are you?"

"Standing outside your front door."

* * *

CARO STAYED with me all night, nursing me and cleaning up after me. There was no fornication. I was far too ill for that. I lay like a white-faced corpse, and Caro, lying beside me, spoke softly to me and brought me glasses of water.

In the early morning, she went out to a drug store and returned with some powders that were supposed to replace all the minerals I'd lost through vomiting. She emptied a sachet into a glass of water and forced me to drink it. About twenty minutes later, I started to feel better. Caro brought me some toast and a glass of milk, sitting on the bed to talk to me while I ate and drank.

"Why did you do that to yourself? Because of Warren?"

"I suppose so."

"He isn't worth it," she said.

"Was there anything about him in the *Standard*?"

"Don't be silly. This wasn't a child or a famous person falling in front of a train. It was Warren." She squeezed my arm. "That idea of yours, about us staying apart for a while. I don't think I can do it."

"Why not?"

"Because I don't want to be apart from you. I have feelings for you."

"What kind of feelings?"

She shrugged and lowered her gaze. "I think we could be a couple."

"A couple of what?"

"A couple of people who don't ask each other stupid questions."

*   *   *

WE SPENT the day together, me feeling frail and sipping herbal tea, Caro browsing through all the books in the shop with a silent concentration that made me suspicious. If I'd owned a security camera, I'd definitely have filmed her. We had a minor disagreement when she attempted to skim through a Wessex edition of Hardy's *Under the Greenwood Tree* while drinking a cup of hot chocolate and eating a croissant.

"It's just a book," she complained when I'd snatched it away from her. "Books are meant to be read."

"Not that book," I told her.

She got up and peered into my Masculinity case at my mint Nick Hornby first editions, their flawless dust jackets protected in plastic. "You know what you do?" said Caro. "You collect books about what it's like to be a man, written by men who don't know."

* * *

JUST AS I sometimes was quite unable to resist a first edition, whatever its cost, so was I quite unable to resist Caro. When we were in a room together and she wasn't looking at me, I was miserable. To me, one little kiss from this bed-swerving bitch was worth a thousand fucks from any God-fearing Christian woman. (Not that I'd ever slept with one.)

Caro couldn't walk across a room without dragging my entrails behind her. Her presence gave me a primordial, unwholesome hunger for warm flesh. If I appear to be overstating my case, I apologize. I just want you to understand why I accompanied her to her father's house and even bothered to listen to her ridiculous plan.

It wasn't far to Chez Gordon, so we walked. That lunchtime, Caro had returned from an illicit stroll in Kew Gardens to find her car missing from the drive.

"Did you call the police?"

"It was repossessed, you idiot."

"They repossessed your car?"

"Yeah. Just because I didn't keep up the payments. Isn't that the unfairest thing you ever heard? That's why we're going to see my dad."

"Your father repossessed your car?"

"Ha. Funny. No, but he's got money. Enough to buy me a new one."

"You're going to steal from your own father?"

"No. First I'm going to ask nicely. When he says no, that's when I'm going to steal."

It was a cool, crisp night with bright stars overhead and a thin coating of frost on the ground. The thrill of walking beside Caro combined with the way our breath flew before us reminded me of being thirteen, when I roved the streets with my friends because we had nothing to do and nowhere to go. In those days, just being seen with a girl like Caro would have been considered a sublime accomplishment.

"What is it you've got against your dad?" I asked her. "I mean, I know he's mad, but what else?"

"You seem to be fond of lists. I'll give you one. His mad eyes. The way he scowls when things aren't going his way. His horrible high voice, his smell. The way he tries to kiss me. His gray hands. His very small feet. His dirty hair. His awful dick."

"His *what?*"

"He was talking to me once in his pajamas. He leaned forward and his dick fell out. It looked like a scalded frankfurter."

"Thank you for sharing. Anything else?"

"His clutter. He was always an untidy bastard, but at least he used to keep his mess in his own room. Now it fills the house. I hate him. The way he shrieks when he can't get the lid off a jar of marmalade. The sight of his bristles in the sink when he's trimmed his beard. The way he eats, like a monkey cramming food into its mouth before a bigger monkey can take it off him. Ugh." She shuddered. "He disgusts me."

"Have you finished?" I said.

"I haven't even started. He's mean, he's selfish, he's rude to strangers. He's a bully and a coward. He has to sleep with a night-light like a fucking baby. His politics stink. He claims to be left-wing, but he thinks women in the third world should be forcibly sterilized to keep down the population."

"Maybe he's left-wing like Lenin," I said.

"And he's pretentious. One week he thinks he's a historian, then he's a sailor. Last I heard, he was a poet. Although I've yet to see a single line the fat cunt has written." She kicked a parked car as she passed it. "And his driving? Christ almighty. He drives like a drag racer but without the skill. I used to dread going on vacation as a child. He risked my life every time he got behind the wheel. We were always getting pulled over by the police because he was speeding on the wrong side of the road. He thinks the point of driving is to get away from the car behind him and to overtake the car in front."

"The guy is a hundred percent knob-cheese," I admitted, "but he *is* your father. There must be something about him you like."

"I like his heart condition."

"Jesus, Caro."

"Yeah, well. Congestive heart failure. It's incurable. The doctor gave him two years to live, but that was four years ago. I pray and I pray, but he just doesn't seem to get any worse. Now he's got his lady friend to make sure he takes his pills."

"One question. If he's so awful, why are you asking him for money?"

"What else has he ever given me?"

* * *

AFTER THEIR daughter left home, Caro's parents moved from Sheen Common Drive to a larger house near Richmond Park. Caro claimed it was worth six million. It was certainly big enough. There were stone lions on the gateposts, and the house had a terrible name. It was called Seaworthy, and in the back garden was a huge yacht. Gordon fancied himself as a mariner, although he had never successfully controlled a dinghy, let alone a yacht. Now he was too sick and old to even try, but selling the boat would have been an admission of his own decrepitude, so he simply left it to rot.

We passed across the porch, and Caro rang the bell. The sound echoed through the house beyond, giving a clear idea of its cavernous dimensions. We heard the sound of approaching footsteps, and the door opened to reveal a coarse-faced middle-aged woman with a blonde rinse and the demeanor of an embittered barmaid. She was wearing extremely high heels like a drag queen. "Oh, it's you, Caroline," she said without enthusiasm. "I do wish you'd warn us when you're coming."

"I thought it'd be a nice surprise for you." Caro gave the woman a lethal smile. "This is Mark, by the way."

"You've got so many men on the go I lose track." With this, the coarse woman walked away, leaving the door to swing on its hinges. I'm no snob, but this struck me as extraordinary behavior for a common servant. "It's your daughter!" she bellowed, and flounced off down the plum-carpeted hall.

"Who's that?" I said.

"That's Eileen," said Caro. "The wicked stepmother."

Caro's father was upstairs in his malodorous study, using a magnifying glass to peer at the small print in a book. A radio was blaring out the news at a volume that a rock festival audience would have found intrusive. Gordon was surrounded by books, not in bookcases but all over the floor and the furniture.

Whatever Caro said, Gordon didn't look at all well. With his gray face, bloodshot eyes, white beard, and enormous paunch, he looked the way Santa Claus must look when he arrives home on Christmas morning. We stood in the doorway for a few moments without attracting his attention. Then Caro walked over to him and kissed him briefly on the face.

"Oh, hello, darling," he said.

He looked genuinely pleased to see her. She nodded over to me. "Dad, do you know who this is? He was my boyfriend at school."

Gordon stared at me for a few seconds, looking thoroughly bewildered. Then he started clicking his fingers. "Oh, of course. John . . . Jim . . . Jason! You owned a Chinese takeout."

"Dad? Does he look Chinese? No, Dad. This is Mark. Mark Madden."

Gordon frowned and shook his head. "No. Doesn't ring a bell."

Caro signaled for me to go away and closed the door quietly behind her. I walked up and down the corridor. The house was freezing cold, although the radiators were on full.

I walked into a front room, where there was a framed photograph of a younger, dark-haired Gordon digging in a garden. He was smoking a pipe, and beside him, holding up a trowel for the camera, was a pudgy blonde girl-child with a familiar frown on her pale baby face. She must have been about four when the picture was taken. It looked like any happy family snapshot.

I crossed the room to Gordon's bookshelf to see if there was anything worth stealing. All I found were shoddy book club editions of the wrong books by the right people. The one exception, amazingly, was a UK first edition of *A Clockwork Orange*, without a dust jacket. I had never seen the novel in hardback and sat down on the sofa to inspect it.

I felt someone watching me and looked up to see Eileen standing in the doorway. "Don't walk away with that. That's what Caroline does, you know. Every time she comes here, something goes missing." Eileen brought in a tea tray, which she placed on a rickety table. "I'll leave this here. Best not to disturb them."

"Oh. Thanks."

She smiled to show she hadn't meant the remark about book stealing, when we both knew perfectly well she had. "Drink it while it's hot," she said as she left the room, somehow managing to inject this homely advice with frosty disapproval.

I poured myself some tea and was settling down to drink it when a door slammed and I heard someone running. Then Caro walked in. She was crying. I put down my cup and held her. "He's a fucking bastard," she said. "I hate him."

*　　*　　*

SHE KEPT me up for most of the night, fretting about her inheritance when I just wanted to sleep. I tried to be sympathetic, but she wouldn't shut up.

"Just because he wouldn't give you money doesn't mean he's cut you out of his will," I told her.

"It does. I know it does. He's usually given me money before. Suddenly, now that he's marrying that awful woman, it's 'Sorry, dear, but we're saving for the wedding.' She's got her claws into him, Mark. I won't get a penny."

"Money isn't everything."

"Since when?"

"It's unlucky, Caro. Sitting around waiting for people to die, that's what vultures do."

She sat up in bed. When she spoke again, I could tell she was getting tearful. "I know that, but I'm terrified all the time, never having enough money. Just once I'd like him to be a father to me and look after me."

"Okay," I said softly. "I can understand that."

"So will you kill him for me? Please?"

I was glad I was at her flat, because that meant I could leave. I got up and put my jacket on while the first plane of the morning rumbled over Kew Gardens on its way to Heathrow. I expected her to try to stop me, but she just lay there with her arms folded, shadows round her eyes and her mouth like a purple gash. I walked out of the flat and out of her life.

CHAPTER 5

MY MURDEROUS GIRLFRIEND

I KNEW I'd die if I didn't go out, so I phoned Lisa and asked if she was free that evening. She said yes, although I thought I detected a faint note of suspicion in her voice. I picked her up at eight, Elliot giving me the rude finger from the front bedroom, and we went tenpin bowling. Bowling was Lisa's idea of a good time.

As we were waiting for a lane, I caught her staring at me.

"Okay, what is it?" she said.

"What's what?"

"You're crying. What's the matter?"

I touched my face. Sure enough, drops of moisture came off on my fingertips. "Oh," I said. "Maybe I've got some kind of eye infection. Crying? Of course I'm not crying!" I gave an unconvincing stage laugh. "What have I got to cry about?"

Later, I drove her home. Elliot had gone to bed. This was always our cue to do dirty things to each other. We tried to have sex, but I was too sad to get a hard-on. "All right," she said, rolling off me and leaning on a pillow to study my heartbreaking profile. "Who is she?"

"Who's who?"

"Is a big book about famous people," she said. For a hairdresser, she could be pretty sharp. "I want to know who you've been seeing."

"Okay," I said. "I did see someone, but it's over, and we didn't have sex."

"Is that what you were crying about?"

"What? Cry about not having sex? What do you take me for? A baby?"

"No. More like a small boy who's keeping secrets from his mother."

"What's your point?" I said irritably.

"Well, you obviously love this person, Mark. It's written all over you. Your eyes are shining. You keep drifting off when I try to talk to you. And now you can't get a hard-on, not even when I'm being Gestapo lady."

Don't ask.

"There is someone, but it's nothing, it's purely platonic," I said.

"What does that mean?"

"It means that my attraction to her isn't really sexual. She's just someone on my wavelength, someone I can talk to about any-thing."

"Well, that's worse! That's much worse than just sleeping with her," said Lisa. I could see she was getting angry. "I suppose I'm too bloody stupid to talk to?"

"No, you're very bright," I said, trying to smooth things over. "You can't help being uneducated."

Lisa threw the pillow at me and called me a number of inter-esting names, some of which I'm convinced she invented on the spot. I got out of bed and got dressed, feeling more relieved than anything. When I got to the foot of the stairs, Elliot was waiting for me. He was in his pajamas. He looked pale and shocked.

"Has something happened?" he said.

"Your dreams have come true, Elliot. Your mum and I have split up."

"God," said Elliot. "I'm really sorry."

I was touched. All the abuse the boy had hurled at me came from pain. Deep down, he had grown attached to me. "Much appreciated," I said, squeezing his shoulder.

"It'll be strange not seeing you," said the boy.

"Thanks, Elliot," I said as I opened the front door. "You look after yourself. Okay?"

He nodded. The cold, damp air from the street came as a shock after the warmth of the house. I walked out onto the path and looked back. Elliot was still standing there. "I'll miss you," he said, his voice suddenly small and childlike.

I nodded back at him, too choked to answer.

"I'll miss laughing at you, you pathetic cunt!" shouted Elliot, before slamming the door behind me. I stood there for a few seconds, stunned. Elliot cackled in triumph. Then I heard his feet clumping rapidly up and down. I could swear he was dancing for joy.

*   *   *

WHEN I got home, I checked my Web site and found an abusive message. The sender had taken the trouble to register as IhateMarkMadden@fastweb.co.uk.

The message was very long and repetitive. The first paragraph should suffice:

I hope you know what a talentless, pitiful piece of shit you are. Who would want to buy books after you've touched them? You filthy hermaphrodite. I walk past that shop and I can smell your armpits and your shitty arse, even through a closed door. Very soon you will die of cancer. Your brain will increase in size until your eyes explode. Then you will go to hell where all weak, grimy, ugly, smelly homosexuals go.

I had received abusive e-mails before, but only from a witch, angry because the *Book of Shadows* I'd sold her didn't have any shadows in it. My immediate impulse was to answer the e-mail. Then I remembered how my carefully worded replies to the witch had merely led to longer and more deranged e-mails, culminating in threats of a curse that would blight me and all my descendants. I blocked the anonymous sender, hoping to God it wasn't Caro, tipped over the edge from strangeness into outright insanity.

* * *

I LASTED for thirty-two hours. During that time I came close to phoning Caro seven times and once, Warren-like, even walked round to her flat to stare wistfully up at the window. I had never known a pain like it. I wanted Caro so badly that I couldn't stop shaking. The slightest thing would make me cry.

I turned on the TV to watch the morning shite. A working-class man was claiming his working-class wife had tricked him into marriage by passing off her tits as real, when he believed them to be silicone implants. Despite his suspicions, the wife insisted that her tits were real, so the working-class studio audience took a vote on it. A massive majority, 96 percent of the audience, decided the working-class tits were fake. Then it was revealed that the husband and the audience were right. The wife was a big-titted cheat!

In the next part, two more women were arguing about whether a man with half his skull missing should be playing around. One was his working-class girlfriend; the other was his working-class wife. The implication seemed to be that this man shouldn't be fucking two women when any decent half-headed person would be too filled with self-loathing to leave the house.

While the women debated this important issue, the man with half a head was smiling contentedly, just happy to be on TV. The guy's wife started talking about how awful it was when this guy took the steel plate off his skull and exposed his brain while they were making love, but she still wanted him and hoped the baby was his.

"What baby?" said the girlfriend. It was the first she'd heard of any baby. She started crying. The wife looked triumphant. The guy lifted the steel plate off his skull and showed the audience his brain. The audience gasped.

Then it was time for the news. The main story was that a correspondent who worked for ITN had been accidentally killed while filming in the Middle East. For some reason, we were expected to value this man's life over the lives of millions of Arab civilians who had also been killed accidentally, the implication being that brown-skinned foreigners are expendable but white, well-fed journalists are selfless heroes who live only to bring us the truth. As I sat there, consumed by bitterness, I could hear Caro's voice inside my head. Now I was thinking her thoughts.

* * *

IN THE hope of getting some Valium, I made an appointment with a doctor. The GP was a nice fatherly old man, close to retirement. He wore a jacket in a quiet hounds tooth, and his salt-and-pepper hair was neatly parted to the left. He probably hadn't changed his hairstyle or his suit since his student days.

"What seems to be the matter?"

"I can't breathe."

"You must be breathing," he said. "If you weren't you'd be dead."

"I'm definitely suffering from hypertension. Hypertension can kill, can't it?"

The doctor looked at me with a wry smile on his nice old doctor's face. "Mr. Madden, have you ever heard the expression 'A little knowledge is a dangerous thing'?"

"Yes, Doctor."

"What do you think it means?"

"I think it means that people who know as little as doctors are very dangerous."

The doctor sighed. He took my blood pressure and listened to my chest. "Your heartbeat's a little rapid. Apart from that, everything seems fine. Try relaxing."

"Sorry?"

"You're sweating, you're shaking. Look at the way you're sitting. What's the matter with you?"

I shrugged. "I was hoping you'd tell me."

He looked into my eyes. "Are you on drugs?"

"No. But I'd like to be."

The doctor looked shocked. "Let me assure you, drug addiction is no picnic. Are you anxious about a woman, by any chance?"

"How the hell did you know that?"

"Let's just say I've been on this earth rather longer than you."

"Could you give me something to calm me down?"

"You're in love, my boy," said the doctor, smiling benignly. "There's no pill on earth that can help you with that. Have you tried talking to her?"

"Yes. But it doesn't do any good." (He was already nodding as if he'd known this all along.) "She makes insane demands."

"All women do."

"So you think I should go back to her?"

"If it's causing you as much discomfort as this, yes."

*　*　*

CARO KNEW her father's schedule. Every Monday morning, Eileen took Gordon swimming, which his heart specialist had recommended as a gentle but beneficial form of exercise for decrepit bastards. According to Caro, all her father did during his sessions in the pool was squeeze his blubber into a rubber ring and blob around in the shallow end. But it got him out of the house.

We parked round the corner, then had to duck down in our seats when Gordon's Rover came skidding by. I caught a glimpse of Eileen, white-faced and taut in the passenger seat, and Gordon, scowling as he leaned forward at the wheel. There was a loud thud as the car passed. When I leaned out of the window to see what had happened, the wing mirror of my Fiat was lying in the road, surrounded by shards of glass.

"He knocked my fucking mirror off. And he didn't even have the decency to stop."

"If he stopped every time he knocked a wing mirror off," said Caro, "he'd never arrive anywhere."

"But we're parked on the opposite side of the fucking road. There was enough room to drive a fucking tank through. The useless bastard!"

"Now you're getting the idea," said Caro.

Once Gordon was engaged to be married, he had asked his daughter to return her door keys, claiming that now he and Eileen were a couple, they needed privacy. Caro had acquiesced, but only after duplicating the keys. Shortly before ten, we drove up to the house. First Caro unlocked the Chubb lock, then the Yale. The front door opened, and the burglar alarm commenced its prescreech countdown. Caro stormed down the hall to the cupboard where the alarm was housed and tapped in the code. Then we were in.

We went straight upstairs to Gordon's study. The room smelled like its owner, an odd chemical odor with a faint dash of bile, like a science lab that someone has puked in. The shelves were crammed with books on sailing, exploring, archaeology, climbing, and outdoor survival. Gordon, the archetypal armchair adventurer, had never actually done any of these things, although he did once set off for a solo camping trip to Devon, only to return three hours later on the feeble pretext that he'd forgotten a can of soup.

We were searching for a last will and testament. I opened a drawer in the desk and found a neat black notebook with a sticky label attached to its cover. The label read STORY IDEAS. "Look at this," I said. "Your dad's a budding author."

"Oh, no," said Caro, sniggering over my shoulder. "Now he thinks he's a writer."

The book had been filled with short, scribbled plot summaries. Glimpsing an unsavory sentence, I tried to shove the book back in the drawer before Caro could see it, but I was too late. She snatched the sordid volume from my grasp and leafed through it, her amusement slowly giving way to bilious rage. "The dirty fucking bastard!"

The story ideas all shared a common theme.

Man, daughter, remote cottage. Incest?

Man, daughter, walking holiday. Incest?

Man, daughter, desert island. Incest?

Man, daughter, phone booth. Incest?

"He's been fantasizing about shagging me. My own father. Ugh. All that time I was growing up, the disgusting bastard wanted to stick his filthy old organ in me."

"We don't know that."

"I think we fucking do."

She emptied the drawer and found a short story in a knackered old binder. The story was called "First and Last Love." Caro insisted on reading it aloud. It was the touching tale of a man with a wooden leg. One day the man was hobbling past his daughter's bedroom when he accidentally saw her tits. The man with the wooden leg was embarrassed, but his daughter called him into the room and asked if he'd like to commit incest. "Would I!" said the old man. Seven fucks later, the old man wakes up in a mental hospital. It had all been a wonderful dream!

"I feel sick," said Caro.

As we turned to leave, a rare flash of inspiration made me check Gordon's calendar, which was hanging on the wall above his desk. In the square for Friday, February 13, were the words GRAEME & MERCER, 2PM.

Caro looked up Graeme & Mercer in the phone book. They were a firm of solicitors with plush premises on Richmond Green.

"That's this Friday," she said, clutching my arm. "That's when they're going to change the will." She looked at me earnestly. "My dad hates giving money to professionals. He wouldn't be going to a solicitor without a good reason. That only gives us four days. We've got four days to kill him."

CHAPTER 6

THE WAY OF THE WORRIER

WE WENT to Kew Gardens and sat among the pine trees, smoking the last of our skunk and trying to think of a way to bring Gordon's life to a swift conclusion without incriminating ourselves. Caro suggested scaring him to death. "He's got congestive heart failure," she said. "A sudden shock could kill him."

"If seeing Eileen naked hasn't finished him off, nothing will."

"There must be something you could do."

"Something I can do? You're the one who wants him dead."

"You could hide behind his car and jump out at him. Or set a firework off under his bedroom window."

Christ, she would not let it go.

"Caro, he's your father. You don't want that on your conscience."

"Conscience doesn't come into it," she said. "Some people are so awful and useless that by killing them, you're doing a service to the world."

"I don't agree with capital punishment," I told her.

"Me neither," said Caro. "Capital punishment only kills people who can't afford lawyers. What we're doing is getting rid of people like my father. People who poison the lives of those around them and never do anything useful."

"He did one useful thing. He provided the sperm that fertilized the egg that turned into you."

Caro punched me in the arm. "Don't be *disgusting*."

The dope made Caro desperate for something sweet, but she was too stoned to move. I volunteered to walk over to the café to buy some cakes. When I got back, Caro had company.

A very tall, charismatic man with a beard was standing in front of her, holding her up against a tree. His left hand gripped her chin so firmly that she couldn't move her head. I knew this guy; we'd met before. It was the Jesus look-alike who had set fire to my book. Behind him, watching and smoking, stood the young guy with face studs who had accompanied him to the shop and a heavy, bearded guy in his forties who looked like a jazz trumpeter.

When Jesus saw me, he released Caro. He stepped back and leered at me.

"Hello, hello. You must be Killer." Absolutely no trace of recognition in his face.

I said nothing. I was too scared to talk.

"Caroline here says you're dangerous. You don't *look* dangerous. Then again, I look like the Prince of Peace. Appearances can be deceptive." Jesus nodded at the pastries in my hand. "Aw. Look. He bought us some cakies."

Jesus reached for the bag. I snatched it away. "What's this about?"

"Ask her," said Jesus.

Caro just glared at me.

"I didn't get my wedge this month," said Jesus. "Payment was due five days ago."

Caro said, "You'll get the money in a few days. In full."

"Yeah? Expecting a windfall, are we?" Jesus stepped round and looked at me, head tilted to one side. "Do I know you from somewhere, sonny?"

I didn't answer. Jesus returned his attention to Caro. "How come you're wasting your time on this chump?" he said.

"We love each other."

Jesus nodded and smiled. "Do you really? Well, that's very touching. That's what I tell people they should do. Love one another. Isn't that right, Pete?"

The guy with the face studs grinned and nodded.

"You better stay away from this woman," declared Jesus. "Every time you touch her, you lose a little bit of your soul. This wo-man will only bring you woe, man."

Jesus, Face Studs, and the Jazzman had a nice little chuckle together. Caro stared down at the ground.

Jesus put his arm around the studded guy. "This is Pete," explained Jesus. "He's my little brother. I call him Rock. Peter the Rock."

Rock took a bow.

"Okay," said Jesus to Caro. "I'm adding another five thousand to the total. It's gone up because of the disrespect you've both shown for me, your benefactor, by not even bothering to tell me where my money is and when I'll see the next installment."

"The end of the month, I promise," said Caro.

"Your promises are worth shit." The Jazzman grabbed Caro while Jesus searched her bag. There must have been about twenty credit cards in there. He sorted through them, tossing them on the ground as he came to them. "AmEx, Egg, Alliance and Leicester for the smarter investor . . . I bet you've got about a hundred and fifty grand's worth of credit here. You can draw cash with these fuckers and use it to pay me. And I still want this week's interest."

Jesus glanced at me, waiting for a reaction. I didn't say anything, but I took a step forward. Instantly Rock slipped a hand inside his jacket. Jesus stopped him with a look and a shake of the head.

"I don't want to see you again," Jesus told me. Turning to Caro, he clicked his fingers and pointed at her. "*You*, I want to see again."

Jesus, his brother, and the Jazzman laughed as they walked away.

*   *   *

"His real name's Victor Callaghan, but everyone calls him Bad Jesus. He was on that list I gave you."

"I thought that was a joke."

We were drinking Southern Comfort at Caro's favorite pub by the river in Richmond. It was pissing down, the raindrops hitting the Thames like arrowheads. "You haven't heard of Bad Jesus? I thought everyone knew him." She looked at me sideways. "Not very streetwise, are you?"

"I think that's well established."

"Jesus is the reason I need my dad's cash."

"Go on."

Caro put down her glass and looked out at the lights on the water. She was solemn and silent for a long time. When she spoke again her voice was quiet and dead-sounding. "I met him through Warren. Warren used to work for him. I got in bad trouble with a credit card scam."

"How bad?"

"I was running up debts under an assumed name. The police had all they needed to put me away. Warren said he knew a man who could sort out my problems. That's how I came to know Bad Jesus. I met him in a pub in Eltham, and he told me that he'd get me out of trouble for a price. The price was twenty thousand, which I didn't have. Jesus said he knew it was a lot of money, so I could pay him back in monthly installments. It seemed like an amazing deal. So I took it. Two weeks later, I got word that all charges against me had been dropped. I couldn't believe it. I was overjoyed."

"You mean the guy's a loan shark?"

"Among other things, yeah."

"You borrowed twenty thousand from a loan shark? Caro, that's insanity."

"It runs in the family," she said bitterly. "Jesus seemed okay at the time. It was only later that I found out what kind of sick monster he was."

"What's the debt now?"

"It's hard to say. Maybe about a hundred and twenty grand."

"God almighty!"

"Yeah . . . you see, the interest doubles every month. And then there are the unpredictable extras like today's five grand!"

"You'll have to do something about this."

"Like what?"

"Let's go to the Citizens Advice Bureau."

She thought this was so funny that she laughed, spraying me with liqueur-whiskey.

"So what made him come to my shop?" I said.

"He probably knows you never stopped loving me."

"Why? Have you told him?"

"No way."

"So how would he know?"

"Jesus sees everything."

"What you're telling me doesn't add up, Caro. Why would a loan shark worry about your ex-boyfriends?"

"I don't know."

A thought occurred to me. "I've been getting anonymous e-mails. Pretty sick stuff. Could they have come from him?"

Caro shook her head. "Guys like Jesus never write anything

down. If he wanted to make someone feel bad, he'd be more likely to drag him behind a car at high speed until his head fell off."

I sipped my drink, trying not to ask a question but failing. "You and Jesus," I said, "you haven't . . . ?"

"*No!*"

I sighed with relief like a very bad actor. "But I must say, Caro, for an intelligent person you've behaved very, very foolishly."

"I know. But I kept thinking, *I'm my dad's next of kin. One day I'll inherit the house and the money and pay Jesus off*." Her eyes filled with tears. "Mark, have you any idea how frightened I am?"

She didn't look particularly frightened. A little drunk, maybe. "What did Bad Jesus mean about interest?" I asked her.

She only hesitated for a second. "How should I know? The guy's a prick. He just opens his mouth and shit pours out."

"He said he hadn't had any interest this week. How could you have been paying interest? You haven't got any money."

"I've given him a couple of hundred quid now and then," she said, pressing her face against my shoulder. "Just to keep him off my back."

* * *

THAT NIGHT, I returned to my one-to-one unarmed combat class, realizing that I might need to be fit for whatever lay ahead. Again, Lenny insisted that I punch him in the stomach as hard as I could.

"Isn't this the way Houdini died?" I asked him.

"How the hell should I know?"

That was the frightening thing about Lenny. He was a world-class exponent of karate, but he had no interest whatsoever in

Japan or Zen or Shaolin monks. His areas of expertise were drinking, putting out fires, and causing grievous bodily harm.

As a firefighter, he had cut people from wreckage and walked into burning buildings, yet the only anecdote he had to offer involved giving a fireman's lift to a naked eighteen-year-old. "She had the biggest pair of knockers you've ever seen in your life."

Obeying orders, I drew back and hit him in the stomach as hard as I could. Lenny let out an angry yell.

"Sorry," I said, surprised by my own strength.

"I'm not shouting 'cause you hurt me. You daft prick. I was using . . . what's it fucking called? Chi. Spirit. If you cry out when you're hit, it limits the damage your opponent can do to you. It's like I'm directing all my resistance here." He patted his solar plexus. "Hit me again."

I whacked his belly a few more times. Each time, he roared defiance. Then it was my turn. "But you're a black belt third dan," I objected.

"Yeah?"

"You could cause me permanent damage."

"Don't worry. I'll hold back a bit."

I braced myself, and as his fist flew forward I summoned all the chi at my disposal and yelled. A few seconds later, I was lying on my back on the floor of the gym.

"Fucking hell," I said, rubbing my aching gut.

"No," said Lenny. "That was good. You showed good spirit."

He made me stand up while he hit me again. After the third time, I started to feel a little pissed off. When it was my turn to hit Lenny again, I summoned all my strength, yelling as well as punching. This time, the blow contained all my accumulated pain and embarrassment, and when it connected, Lenny rocked slightly on his heels. At that point, he beamed. "I'll tell you what, my son," he said. "That was a fucking beauty. Keep punching like that and you'll have no problems whatsoever."

Later, in the shower, Lenny made me an opportunistic offer. "Listen, I've been thinking," he said. "You know that little chat we had about your kicks? How I said there was room for improvement?"

"If I recall, you described me as 'fucking useless.'"

"Did I? Well, listen. I've got something that might help you. A set of leg stretchers."

"Leg stretchers?"

"Yeah. They're yours for forty quid."

We went out to Lenny's little white van, and he produced two long movable metal bars joined by a handle. The idea was that you held the device between your ankles and pressed down on the handle until the bars forced your legs apart.

"Do they work?" I said.

"Yeah," said Lenny. "How do you think I got to be so supple?"

I didn't really want the stupid contraption but thought that buying it might further my relationship with my karate tutor. "Okay, you're on," I said. "But could you give me a lift home? This thing's a bit heavy."

"Deal," said Lenny, and we shook on it.

So he drove me all the way to East Sheen, saving me a tedious bus journey. On the way, I asked him to tell me a few firefighter's jokes. He didn't know any. "There is one thing we say. Some of the houses we go to are so filthy that we have to remember to wipe our feet on the way out."

I forced a laugh. Lenny asked me what I did for a living. I told him. He nodded. "And business is bad, is it?"

"How did you know?"

"Because you worry a lot. I can see it. You got frown lines on your forehead." Lenny cackled, having thought of a joke. "You're s'posed to be following the way of the warrior. Not the way of the worrier."

Lenny took a look at my book collection while I went upstairs to get his money. Without much hope, I suggested that if he found a nice book he wanted, we might be able to arrange a trade. Lenny found this hilarious. "A book that's worth forty quid? There's no such thing."

While I was taking a piss, I heard a knock at the door. I assumed it was Caro, or someone complaining about the way Lenny had parked the van on the pavement. The lavatory window was open, and I peered down into the street. I heard Lenny answer the door; then came the sound of shouting and scuffling. A moment later I leaned forward to peer through the window and saw three shapes spinning about in the darkness.

I cut my piss short and ran down to see what was happening. Lenny was standing on the pavement, looking down. A large man was lying on his back in the gutter, illegally parked on the double yellow lines. The big man was gripping a baseball bat that had obviously not done him much good. His face looked like a strawberry flan that someone had trampled on.

"What happened?" I said.

"I opened the door and this idiot took a swing at me," said Lenny incredulously. "There were two of 'em. The other one legged it."

The guy on the ground, all two hundred and fifty pounds of him, coughed and blew out a huge bubble of blood.

"Fuck," I said. "What did you do to him?"

"Simple block, then elbow strike to the face," said Lenny. "The elbow's one of the deadliest parts of the body."

"What about that speech you give us about how it's always safer to run away?"

"I didn't have time to run." He eyed me warily. "I got the impression they thought I was you. Is that possible?"

I looked at Lenny. I hated to admit it, but we were the same height, with similar haircuts and similar sticky-out ears. I'd swear I was far more handsome, but maybe not.

"All right," he said. "Do you mind telling me what you've been doing to bring fellas with baseball bats down on you?"

I chose to ignore the question. "We better call an ambulance."

"You call the ambulance. I need to run some cold water over this elbow."

Lenny went up to the bathroom. Before dialing 999, I went out to see what Lenny's victim was doing. He wasn't doing anything. He'd gone, leaving a trail of blood that stretched all the way to High Street.

CHAPTER 7

AND WHEN DID YOU LAST
KILL YOUR FATHER?

THE NEXT day started promisingly enough. I opened the shop just before nine. There was the usual crowd of people standing outside, none of them wanting to come in. But then I logged on to my Web site to learn that someone had ordered my most valuable book, a very good first edition of *Casino Royale* without a dust jacket, price three thousand pounds. I was elated and went to the case to remove the book, only to find it wasn't there.

I wasn't unduly concerned. I tended to mislay books all the time. I had a habit of taking the finest copies off display, subjecting them to lingering adoration, then putting them down somewhere stupid. When a book was lost in this way, I found that a frantic search never helped. It was always best to take time out, go for a walk, do something else. As long as I remained reasonably relaxed, my unconscious mind could usually be relied upon to lead me to the missing volume.

So I locked up and went across the road to Jeff's café. I ordered pancakes and hot chocolate and waited for my unconscious to do its thing. Jeff, who had bought a few gardening books from me, wandered over to discuss the worsening international situation. "What about the Middle East, eh? Wouldn't want to go there for me holidays, would you? And what about them United Nations? Eh? Eh? Name me one bloody nation they ever united. Just one . . ."

When I left I saw two teenaged boys coming out of a local driving school called the Passmore School of Motoring. I didn't pay much attention, but as I was unlocking the shop, one of the boys spoke to me. He was about sixteen, tall and wiry with a complexion like a fully detonated mine field. Although I couldn't understand a word Spotty was saying, something about his diction was horribly familiar. "You torch ma bruddy agen yera ded man."

"I beg your pardon?"

I looked around and saw that the spotty kid was standing next to Hitler Youth, son of Wuffer. "Yeh? Yeh?" taunted Spotty. He and Hitler Youth were evidently brothers.

I entered the shop as quickly as possible and closed the door behind me. The boys pressed their faces against the window, scowling and pointing. Then, abruptly, they got bored and walked away. I waited a while, then checked up and down the road. The two brothers were nowhere to be seen.

I went back inside but, as a precaution, locked the door. I sat down at my desk, logged on to the Madden Books Web site, and trawled through the orders and inquiries. After about ten minutes, someone hammered belligerently on the door. The two boys had returned with their father.

Wuffer, face pressed to the shop window, pointed in turn at me and his feet, inviting me to venture outside for a confrontation. What deterred me, apart from common sense, was that Wuffer was holding a loaded crossbow.

Seeing that I was unwilling to accept the challenge, Wuffer tried the door again, confirming that it was indeed locked. Then he and his sons embarked on a truly bizarre war dance. They started prancing and jumping past the window. Wuffer took off his T-shirt, exposing a torso that was the color and texture of lard. He bounded back and forth past the window, flexing his biceps, shouting and pointing. His sons imitated him, spitting on the window and beating their chests.

This went on for about fifteen minues. Finally, slowly, my tormentors moved off down the road, still pointing, shouting, and dancing.

*   *   *

No sooner had I washed the spit off the window than Caro turned up. She was extremely agitated. Two police officers had been round to see her about Warren. Someone had reported seeing him being pushed off the platform into the path of the train that had killed him. There was even a likeness of the suspect, which looked so unlike me that Caro had been able to say, quite truthfully, that she had never seen the man in the picture before. But the experience had shaken her up quite badly.

"Did they act like they suspected you?" I said.

"No."

"Did you tell them Warren had been hounding you?"

"No." She looked at me with contempt. "Of course I fucking didn't!"

"So they don't know anything. What are you in such a state about?"

"I didn't like the way they looked at me."

I closed the shop for lunch. Holding hands, we walked into Sheen, not because we wanted to or because there was anything in Sheen worth seeing, but because walking helped me to think. We sat on a bench outside Woolworth's, watching the filthy traffic roar by.

"I've been thinking about what my own dad would do," I said.

"I remember your dad," said Caro. "He's handsome, isn't he?"

"No! My dad? Absolutely no way. You must be thinking of someone else. One thing he is, though, he's strong and solid. He never gives up until he's found a way through a problem."

"And?" said Caro, meaning when was I going to stop making speeches and get to the point.

If I weren't such a reasonable, fair-minded everyday Nick Hornby kind of guy, I would have split her lip.

"I'm going to do what my own dad would do," I said. "I'm going to go and talk to Gordon, man to man. I'm going to try to put things right."

She sat up straight and linked her arm in mine all cynicism gone. "You really think you can?" she said.

"Yes," I said. "Whether he's a prick or not, I saw the way he looked at you. The old guy obviously adores you. I'll tell him the truth, that you're worried he's going to disinherit you, that you've got into serious financial trouble but you're too proud to tell him yourself."

"That's good," said Caro. "I like that a lot."

"I'll tell him it's not just the money. You need to feel he loves you."

"But don't mention Bad Jesus," she said. "Tell him I made some bad investments."

"Okay," I said.

"Tomorrow night," said Caro.

"What about tomorrow night?"

"Eileen is a spiritualist. That's her night for communing with the dead. Dad'll be alone all evening."

* * *

I took Warren's gun, tucked into the waistband of my trousers. The gun wasn't for Gordon's benefit. I was planning to talk to the old man, not murder him. But recent events had made me wary of making journeys in the dark—even a journey as short as this one.

Lenny always said that in a real fight, running away was the best defense. *These days, any stupid little jerk could be carrying a knife. No matter how skilled you are, someone can always run up behind you and stab you. You might hate yourself for running, but it's better than making your wife a widow and your kids fatherless.*

But now I didn't need to run. If I bumped into Bad Jesus or he bumped into me, I would have the perfect reply to his supercilious remarks. The most eloquent answer of all.

Someone was walking behind me. Wondering if I was being followed, I slipped through a gate bearing a sign that read NO HAWKERS. I waited in a garden until the stranger passed by. It was a white-haired old man in a raincoat, leaning on a walking stick.

At twenty past eight, I rang the doorbell of Gordon's comfortable residence. It was a windy night, and the trees in the drive strained and swayed. You could almost smell the money blowing through the gardens of the rich houses. Bright, welcoming lights twinkled in the neighboring drive. I heard a car pull up, its tires stirring gravel, followed by words of welcome. Someone was arriving for a dinner party. There was the gentle *thwuk!* of an expensive car door closing—the doors of the cars I drove never sounded remotely like that. A woman laughed, and the confident, twittering voices faded away.

It finally struck me why Caro was so angry about everything. Her father was loaded. This house, a stroll away from Richmond Park, may not have been able to compete with Dickie Attenborough's home on Richmond Green or the Jagger residence on Richmond Hill, but Gordon obviously didn't have to scrape by on his old-age pension. While other offspring from similar backgrounds were living on generous allowances in well-appointed flats, Gordon's only daughter was surviving on benefits and fraud, living in a run-down hovel with bailiffs queueing at the door.

Gordon didn't answer, so I leaned on the bell and gave it a trick-or-treat ring. There was movement in the hall, then another long pause, as if someone were listening. Eventually, a thin, high, womanly voice said, *"Who's there?"*

"It's Mark," I said brightly. "Caroline's boyfriend. We met the other day."

There was another pause, as if Gordon believed me but was not convinced I merited the enormous effort of opening the door. "What do you want?"

"Just a friendly visit."

"Why?"

"Friendliness."

I heard sighs and grumbles. A key turned, and the door opened to reveal Gordon, in his dressing gown and slippers. His bare ankles were snow-blindingly white, and he was wearing a particularly unlovely pair of green paisley pajamas, in a material that I believe is known as winceyette. For a man who couldn't punch his way out of a colostomy bag, Gordon glared at me with considerable hostility. When he saw I was uncowed, he backed down a little and tilted his head to one side like a drooping lily. "Well, look. I was about to watch a television program, so this isn't the best time."

"Can't you record it?"

"Well, no, you see. I'm recording something on the other channel."

"What time's the program on?"

"Nine o'clock."

"But that's forty minutes away."

"I know. But I need to make a cup of coffee and find the *Radio Times.*"

"And that'll take you forty minutes?"

Experiencing a rare moment of self-awareness, Gordon gave a high-pitched laugh. "No. I suppose not. You awkward sod!" Then he stepped back to let me into the hall, already hatching a contingency plan. "I suppose I could always make the coffee now, to save time."

I followed him into the kitchen, passing the living room, where a television blared at geriatric volume. Gordon's idea of making coffee was turning on the kettle and spooning brown granules into a mug. In the middle of this exacting task, he heaved himself onto a stool and sat there, panting.

"Are you okay?" I said.

He nodded and waved his hand to indicate that for the next few moments, he would rather breathe than talk.

"Well, what it is," I said, coming straight to the point, "is that Caro has no money and she's worried that your marriage to Eileen will affect her future."

When Gordon nodded and smiled, I thought my charm offensive was working. I was mistaken. "Oh," he said, "She is, is she? Well, why won't she tell me this herself?"

"She's too proud," I said. "You know how it is with families. Simple things aren't said, then as time passes they become complicated things that are more or less impossible to say."

Gordon stared at me as if I were talking utter bollocks. He may have had a point.

"Now, listen, Rodney," he said, waving his forefinger like a conductor's baton.

"Who's Rodney?"

But Gordon was too busy talking to listen. "My daughter hasn't been as hard-done-to as all that. I don't suppose she's ever mentioned her trust fund to you?"

"No."

"Well, when Caroline was twenty-one, a trust fund we'd set up for her matured. Since her birth, we'd been paying in so much a year, I forget the exact sum. It was around four thousand per annum. So when she came of age, what did Caroline do? She cashed in her trust fund and got a lump sum of about eighty-five thousand pounds. Now, she could have used this as a down payment on a flat or a small house. After all, she had a good job at the time, so repaying a small mortgage would have been perfectly within her means.

"Instead, what does she do? She resigns from her position at the magazine, travels round the world, buys a new car, treats herself to new clothes. In six months, all the cash had gone. Not a penny left. All right, you might argue that what Caroline does with her money is her own affair. Fine. But by the same token, what I do with my money is mine."

I was surprised by his story but tried not to show it. "Okay," I said. "I admit it was a shame for Caroline to squander her trust fund. But come on, most twenty-one-year-olds would do the same. What does anyone know at that age? She's still your daughter. I don't see what point you're making."

"My point is this," said Gordon, slopping hot water into his mug. "Caroline is an adult, and she hasn't exactly made a success of her life. I regret that, of course, but fail to see that it's any of my doing. I'm seventy-three, and at a time of my life when a man couldn't reasonably expect further happiness, I find I'm about to be married to a wonderful lady. Caroline isn't here to look after me when I feel ill, Eileen is. My only real responsibility is to my wife and myself."

"So Caro's right, then? You don't intend to leave her the house. How would her mother have felt about that?"

"I don't think that's any of your business. Or hers."

"You can't see why Caro would find your attitude hurtful?"

"I'll tell you what's hurtful, shall I? My daughter's attitude to me. When I was young, I didn't expect my parents to leave me a house."

"Did they have a house to leave?"

"No. But that's beside the point!" Gordon was getting cross. "When I was a student at the LSE, there was a fellow called Dimbo Witters. His name wasn't Witters, nor was it Dimbo, but that's what we called him. Poor old Witters. His one topic of conversation was how his mother had remarried and Dimbo had been done out of his inheritance. Well, I always thought it was terrible to be so bitter. It's not how I want Caroline to feel."

"You mean you're going to make sure she's provided for?"

"I mean I don't want her to feel slighted when she isn't." He glanced at his watch and rose from his seat. "Now, if you'll excuse me, my program will be on shortly. I've watched the whole series, and I don't want to miss it."

I gave Gordon a long, slow appraisal. With his white hair and neat maritime beard, he ought to have been a handsome old man. The raw materials were there. Had a different spirit inhabited that promising frame, the effect might have been pleasing. As it was, Caro was right. All the old man radiated was selfishness, negativity, and slow, brooding madness. Not content with disinheriting his only child, most definitely against the wishes of his dear departed wife, Gordon actually expected to be loved for this most unfatherly act.

"And the loan for a new car is definitely out, is it?"

"Loan, my foot!" said Gordon. "We both know I'd never see a penny of that money again."

It was time to leave. Gordon was beginning to grate on me. In the hall, I turned to deliver a parting shot. "Oh, by the way," I said. "You broke off my car's wing mirror."

"I beg your pardon?"

I explained what had happened. He denied it. I informed him that Caro was a witness. "It's not a big deal," I said. "If you pay for a new mirror, I'll be happy and you needn't lose your no-claims bonus."

"No! No!" said Gordon. "I won't be pushed around. I refuse to be pushed around." And he started walking up and down the hall with his hands behind his back, rather like the duke of Edinburgh on a Commonwealth tour, confronted by a particularly monotonous display of tribal dancing.

"I'm not pushing you around," I said patiently. "You're moving all by yourself."

Gordon turned to look at me, his eyes slits of malice. "Listen, you arrogant, self-opinionated little bastard. You come here, playing the little-man-about-town, telling me what I should do with my own house and my own money. When that fails, you try to squeeze money out of me by blaming me for something you know perfectly well I had absolutely nothing to do with. Well, you can just piss off back to whatever housing project you crawled out of . . ."

As he delivered this speech, Gordon's face changed color three times. Red, dark purple then a deep pace. When he finished speaking he looked like a portrait by Francis Bacon. Then Gordon staggered and fell over backward. He landed heavily, with a great *whumph*, sending a cloud of dust into the air. The dust came from Gordon, not the carpet.

I took a few moments to react. Then I shocked myself by

laughing. It was a completely spontaneous laugh of childish jubilation for which I refuse to accept responsibility.

Gordon remained motionless on his back, his beard tilted at the ceiling and one slipper hanging off its foot. His eyes were closed, so I leaned over to tap his face. "Gordon? Gordon?" I slapped his face a little harder. "Gordon? Are you all right?"

He made a faint rattling in the back of his throat. Then he was silent. I felt for a pulse in his neck, found none. Caro's father was dead.

I rushed through the house, searching frantically for a phone. I found a cordless in the kitchen, picked it up, and prepared to dial 999. Then I considered. If I called an ambulance, the paramedics might save his life. Caro would never forgive me. I would never forgive myself.

So I replaced the phone on the kitchen table. I walked down the hall, stepped over the old man on the floor, and quietly let myself out.

CHAPTER 8

MAN AND WHORE

WHEN CARO eventually answered the door of her flat, she was all smily and off balance. That afternoon, she had treated herself to some Liquid X. Now, five hours later, she was serenely blasted. Dazedly, I told her the news about her father. She clutched my jacket and kissed me. "Really? You really think he might be dead?"

"He didn't look too well when I left him."

I argued, told her it was ludicrous, but Caro insisted on seeing the body. "I have to be sure. That sack of shit has ruined my life."

I drove back to Gordon's house with Caro beside me, giggling inanely whenever we passed over a bump in the road. We parked a few doors away and walked to the front door. Caro was about to use her illicit door key when I seized her arm. "What if Eileen's home?" I said.

"Nah. She'll be raising the dead till the early hours."

"What if she isn't?"

"Mark, relax. She isn't here. Do you see a car in the drive? Fucking stop it."

"I think we should ring the doorbell. Just in case."

Caro made an elaborate show of impatience but pressed the bell anyway. After a sensible interval, she inserted her key and opened the door. That was when we had our first surprise. The hall was empty.

"I thought you said he was lying on the floor?"

"He was."

"Well, where is he?"

The television was still roaring at deaf-bastard volume. Caro tiptoed down the hall, peered stealthily into the living room, and then pulled back sharply, her back against the wall. She beckoned to me. I walked over and glanced through the doorway. Gordon was sitting in front of the television, watching a comedy program.

His feet were propped up on a low stool and he had a plate of cookies in his lap. While the canned laughter thundered, Gordon munched cookies and cackled at the screen. As I watched, he raised one gray haunch and emitted a leisurely fart.

* * *

THE SHOCK of seeing her father alive canceled out the effect of the X, bringing Caro miserably down to earth. On the way to my flat, she was inconsolable. "He isn't dead," she lamented, weeping against the car window. "You promised me he was dead and he isn't. What kind of unfeeling bastard are you?"

"Caro, I swear he was dead. He didn't have a pulse. You can't get much deader than that."

Driving down Sheen Lane, we found our way blocked by a police barricade. There were lights flashing ahead. A column of pale gray smoke climbed the sky. At the barricade, a uniformed constable stepped over to the car and leaned into my window. "You'll have to turn round, sir."

"Has there been a bomb?"

The officer didn't answer, just repeated what he'd said.

"But I live here," I protested.

"Sorry." (He wasn't.) "You'll just have to park as close as you can and walk back."

We did what I was told, leaving the car in a narrow street of terraced houses and walking back to Sheen Lane. There were two fire engines parked outside my shop. It took me a few seconds to appreciate what this meant. I left Caro behind and started to run. Even from fifty yards away, the heat was insufferable. Bright flames roared through the broken windows and the blistering eaves. Even the sign that said MARK MADDEN RARE BOOKS above the door was on fire. Many of the letters had been obliterated, so that it now read MAD ARE BOOKS.

Caro caught up with me and squeezed my arm.

"Oh, no. Oh, no," she said.

My love understood what I had lost. My home and business. All my beautiful first editions gone. My whole life, turned to cinders and ash. It was all my life deserved.

* * *

A CONSTABLE questioned me briefly, finding me so stunned and tongue-tied that he had to ask Caro if there was anyone who could stay with me. Caro volunteered herself for the job, but the constable, perhaps seeing that Caro was in as bad shape as I was, wasn't satisfied with this. He phoned my dad, who came to collect us in his refrigerated van and drive us back to the family home. Dad was very quiet and reflective, reminding me that the business and the premises were insured so that I'd be fully compensated.

Caro sat next to me at the kitchen table. My mum gave us both brandy and hot water and told us not to worry. "The most important thing is that you're both safe. Yes, you've lost all those books and you've lost a home. But what if it'd burned down while you were in there? It doesn't bear thinking about."

Mum, always the nurse, was constantly looking for the positive side to any situation. I could imagine her cheering up patients who had suffered grave misfortunes in the same warm, brisk manner. *Yes, you've lost all your limbs in an accident. But at least you've got all your own teeth.*

My father, stuck for anything to say, offered to make us a curry. It was the only meal he could cook. Neither of us had eaten, so we said yes. Dad looked grateful.

"You'll have to stay here," said Mum. "I know it's a mess, but you can have your own room back."

"It's all right," said Caro. She reached over to take my hand. "Mark can live with me. I want him to." She suddenly smiled ecstatically, in that crazed way she sometimes had. "In fact, hasn't he told you?"

"Told us what?" said my parents in unison, like characters in a very bad play.

"We're getting married," said Caro.

"Are you?" said my mother, then had to sit down.

"His house has burned down and you're getting married?" repeated my dad. "I'm sorry, but the timing doesn't feel quite right, to me."

Caro's announcement had left me more surprised than my parents. Mum and Dad looked at me, eager for my comments. I didn't know what to say. What can you say when you're in love with a mad person?

*   *   *

IN THE morning, Caro and I had breakfast at Jeff's café, gazing across the road at the smoldering shell that had been my home and business. There were black charred fragments scattered all the way up Sheen Lane, all that remained of my precious books.

Caro, muching Melba toast, tried to cheer me up. "Did you know that Melba toast was discovered by Dame Nelly Melba when she accidentally caught her piss flaps in a toaster?"

"Yes," I said gloomily. "I already knew that."

Jeff felt so bad about the tragedy that he gave us breakfast free of charge. "I remember my dad telling me about the blitz in the war," said Jeff. "People losing everything they'd ever worked for in a single night. Terrible thing."

Over fried potatoes, mushrooms, and bacon, Caro explained the marriage idea. "The last twenty-four hours have probably been the worst of our lives. My father didn't die and you lost everything you own. So I suddenly thought, *How do we salvage something from this? How do we save our lives from being a total disaster?* And straight away, the answer came to me. *We'll get married.*"

"So you love me?"

"I'm not going to lie to you," she said. "I'm not sure I love anyone. But, on the plus side, you're probably the least vile person I've ever known."

"Oh, *thanks.*"

"We could give it a try. We might be lucky for each other."

"We haven't been very fucking lucky so far."

"So you don't want to marry me?"

"Yes," I said. "I do. But just for future reference, it's customary to tell the other person before you announce your engagement."

* * *

On Thursday, Caro refused to get out of bed. She was too depressed, knowing that in twenty-four hours her father would officially write her out of his will. In my own heart, soaring happiness warred with the powerful suspicion that the world was a seething ball of worm-ridden excrement.

The girl I'd worshipped since school wanted to marry me. On the other hand—the hand with no fingers—I'd lost my house and business, and until the insurance settlement came through, I had absolutely no means of financial support.

I was sitting in the front room of the flat, listening to the planes flying over, when the intercom buzzed. I answered it, and a man's voice said, "Hello, I'd very much like to speak to Miss Bigun."

"There's no one of that name here," I said.

He immediately sounded disheartened. "She doesn't live here anymore?" "No," I said.

By the phone lay a stack of bills and final demands, all addressed to either Ivy Bigun or someone called Chile Concarne. It was obvious to me that Caro hadn't learned her lesson and was still obtaining credit cards in false names simply because she could.

I went to the window and saw the caller, who looked far too old to be a bailiff, returning to his car. He sat outside the house for a few minutes, watching the windows. Then he drove away.

My mobile phone rang. I picked it up and a deep, officious-sounding voice said, "Mr. Madden?"

The caller identified himself as Detective Constable Flett. He had a few routine questions to ask me about the fire at my shop. Would it be convenient for me to call in at the Richmond police station that afternoon?

"Is something wrong?" I said.

"It'll be easier to tell you about it face-to-face," said Flett coldly.

"Easier for who?" I asked.

"*Whom*," said Flett.

* * *

I WALKED into Richmond and entered the police station. When I told the desk sergeant I'd come in to talk to Flett, he tried to put me off. "He's very busy. I'm sure he'll pop round to talk to you in due course, sir."

"No," I insisted. "You don't understand. Mr. Flett specifically asked me to come in. He wanted to talk to me about something."

I was placed in a queue, next to minor drug offenders and a madman whose pushbike had been stolen. I didn't realize he was mad until he told me how he'd been robbed. "I was riding through Kew when a man ran up to me and pushed me off the bike. Then he took it off me."

"Have you got a description?"

"Yes. He was a centaur."

"Half man, half horse?"

"Exactly."

"A centaur rode off on your bike?"

"Don't be ridiculous," said the madman indignantly. "Of course he didn't ride it. He pushed it. Who ever heard of a centaur riding a bike?"

A sandy-haired CID man called me into a small interview room. This was Detective Constable Flett. I smiled at him. He didn't smile back. Nor did he offer to shake my hand.

Flett was probably in his early thirties, already paunchy and dead-eyed. His off-white shirt had sweat stains under the arms. His tie hung loose, and to add insult to sartorial injury, his fly was undone. I didn't bother telling him about his fly in case he took offence. As a rule, people don't like having attention drawn to their little blunders and imperfections.

"I thought I'd give you an update on the fire at your shop on Sheen Lane," he said, making it sound as if I'd owned a whole chain of incinerated stores.

"Yes?" I said.

"I can confirm that it looks like arson."

"How do you know?"

"We found the remains of a Home Fire Log in the debris."

"What's a Home Fire Log?"

"It's basically a lazy way of starting a real fire. You know how people who have real fires in the grate sometimes find it hard to start them? Well, these logs mean you needn't bother with fire lighters and rolled-up newspaper and all that stuff. Home Fire Logs. They're made by Bryant & May, the same company that makes the matches.

"What we're looking at here is basically a small log, coated in wax, which lights easily. It comes wrapped in highly inflammable paper. You light the paper at either end and pretty soon you've got a decent fire. It looks as if our arsonist lit one of these logs and used it like a brick, smashing your shop window and setting fire to everything inside. Not exactly subtle, and in a bookshop, guaranteed to incinerate the building and everything in it."

"Fuck," I said.

"I beg your pardon?" said Flett, obviously indignant that I'd used an expletive.

To take his mind off my swearing, I told him about the abusive e-mail.

"Have you still got it?" said Flett.

"Yep."

"Could you possibly forward it to me? We might be able to find out where it came from."

"So someone must really hate me," I said. It wasn't a question.

"It looks like it," said Flett, looking at me sideways as if he weren't particularly surprised. "Does anyone spring to mind?"

"It could be practically anyone," I said.

There's something about the police that makes me nervous. When I get nervous, I talk too much and always end up saying more than I need to. When I was nine and my bike had been stolen, the policeman who took down my details made me feel so guilty I told him I'd stolen a Mars Bar from the shop down the road. He said the Mars Bar didn't really matter, and I said no, but the fact that I'd set off a firework under my neighbor's window did. Then I started crying.

It was the same with DC Flett, minus the tears. I ended up saying far too much. I told him how Bad Jesus had visited my shop to vandalize a valuable book. Then I realized that Bad Jesus might kill me if I made a complaint about him, so I changed my tack, chronicling Wuffer's hate campaign against me. Flett seemed to be familiar with both of my persecutors. "I don't think Barker would be clever enough to buy a Home Fire Log," said Flett. "As for Victor Callaghan, it's far too amateurish a job for a man like that."

"Well, who did it?" I said. "Any ideas?"

"Don't be impudent, Mr. Madden."

"What? What've I said?"

Flett stared at me coldly. Then he got up from his desk. "Could you wait here a moment, Mr. Madden?"

He left the room, and I looked at the posters on the wall. Under the words HAVE YOU SEEN THIS MAN? there was a grotesquely unlikely photofit of a homicidal lunatic with cropped hair and staring eyes. Under this were the words "White Caucasian, aged 25–30, approximately 5 feet 10 inches tall, average build. Wanted in connection with a serious incident at Hammersmith station on Sunday, October 9, at 9:00 P.M. Were you there?" *Did you see a stupid-looking twat with a rucksack?*

Although the image on the poster looked more like a brain-damaged Fred Flintstone in a rain hood, I was tempted to flee the police station. Then Flett returned with a thinner, older man who announced himself as Detective Sergeant Bromley. Despite his seniority, Bromley was friendlier than Flett, offering me a choice of tea, hot chocolate, or coffee. I opted for the chocolate, and while Flett went out to fetch it, I repeated my theories for Bromley's benefit.

When I'd finished, Flett returned with my hot chocolate and some greasy tea for Bromley. Flett hovered by the door like a waiter who wants to go home, while Bromley sat at the desk with his arms folded as if he was posing for a football team photo. "All right, Mark," said Bromley in a friendly voice. But it wasn't a normal sort of friendliness, more like the bogus bonhomie of a skilled salesman. "We can't prove it, but we think you burned down your own shop."

"That's outrageous!"

"I agree," said Flett. "So why did you do it?"

"Do you really think I'd be that stupid?"

"Yes," said Bromley, "and what's more, we both think there's something horribly familiar about you."

Flett nodded in agreement. I just stared at them, terrified that if I shifted my gaze, I might inadvertently draw their attention to the wanted poster on the wall.

"Now, we could be wrong," Bromley continued. "Maybe you didn't start the fire. But we can tell just by looking at you that you're guilty of something."

"That's right," agreed Flett.

"And what's more," added Bromley, "We don't fucking like you."

"Why?" I said.

"*Why?*" said Flett, mimicking me in a whiny voice.

* * *

I COULDN'T face telling Caro what had just happened. I got into the car and went for a drive. I stopped in Richmond Park and just sat there in the car, looking at my deluded-by-love eyes in the mirror, wondering whether I was cursed or just stupid.

I read somewhere that what we believe about the world and other people dictates the pattern of our lives. Meaning that a good-natured person who looks for the best in others will invariably find it, just as a misanthrope will always find ample proof of the inherent rottenness of others.

This rule didn't apply to me. I was raised by loving, easygoing parents and always expected my life to be pleasant. Now it was filled with tattooed thugs, malevolent policemen, and butchers who looked like Jesus Christ.

While I was sitting there, aching with hurt, confusion, and self-pity, my cell phone rang. It was my dad. I was really surprised to hear from him. He never made phone calls unless he had to and any letters or cards that needed to be sent were always sent by Mum.

"What is it?" I asked him.

"I just wondered how you were feeling," said my dad gruffly.

"Not great," I confessed.

I heard his brain ticking over. "We've been worrying about you."

I reassured him that I was all right. There was a significant pause. "You still there?" I said.

Dad cleared his throat. "Is it true, then? You and Caroline are really engaged?"

"As far as I know," I answered cautiously.

"Only, I hope you haven't forgotten the way she treated you when you were at school."

"No, Dad."

"She messed you about then, didn't she? Got you in a right state. Who's to say she won't do it again?"

"Come on. She was seventeen. Who knows what they're doing at seventeen?"

"Your mother was seventeen when she got engaged to me."

"I rest my case."

"Oi. That's enough of that." There was a spectacularly long pause. "All right. I just want you to know that if you're in trouble or you need anything, we're here. That's what mums and dads are for, you know."

"Yes, Dad," I said, hanging up. There were tears in my eyes. Mainly tears of shame, because I was technically an adult and my dad was still trying to look after me. My big, rough, working-class dad, who didn't really understand me, who didn't really understand anything apart from the off-side rule in football.

It started to rain. I switched on the engine and drove back through the park gates. I was passing Gordon's house when his battle-scarred Rover swerved out of the drive, shooting right in front of me so that I was forced to brake sharply. Gordon was at the wheel, out to knock off a few more wing mirrors.

After the phone call from Dad, Gordon's sudden appearance was like a lucid communication from the timeless ones who preside over mortal affairs. It was as if they were saying, *We've just shown you what a father should be. And here, by way of contrast, is a complete and utter bastard.*

I was so incensed by Gordon's maneuver that I accelerated sharply, instantly overtaking his car. Gordon, who never used his mirrors, had no idea what was happening until it was too late. I caught a blurred impression of his hideous gray head as I swept past and cut in front of him. Now it was Gordon's turn to brake.

Like all selfish drivers, Gordon could hand it out but he couldn't take it. He gave his horn a protracted blast. I glanced in the mirror to see him alone at the wheel, making elaborate obscene gestures with his left hand. His headlights flashed in rebuke.

Relishing my petty revenge, I signaled left and turned into Sheen Common Drive to let the wanker pass. I was a little surprised when the Rover screeched after me. Gordon gave his horn another stab, and I realized with awe that the father of my intended had turned off without needing to, had actually *gone out of his way* to pursue me. I had overtaken Gordon. Now, according to his demented logic, Gordon could only reassert his manhood by overtaking me in turn.

At any other time, I would have let him pass. Today, I felt too angry and sad to capitulate to his bullying craziness. I moved out into the center of the road to prevent the Rover from passing me. I also slowed down, a perfectly legitimate action as the limit was ten miles an hour and there were speed bumps every fifty yards or so.

I looked in the rearview mirror and saw that Gordon had gone apeshit. He had removed his hands from the wheel to shake both fists at me, and I could see his mouth, twisted in hatred, spewing out a stream of insults.

So I slowed down even more, crawling forward at about three miles an hour. Gordon was now twitching and jolting uncontrollably like a Pentecostalist possessed by the Holy Spirit. He looked like such a prick, and I laughed with cruel delight. Then I came to a bend in the road so, for safety's sake, moved over to the left. As glorious as it was to goad Gordon, I had no wish to cause an accident.

Instantly, Gordon stepped on the gas and surged forward. His car was faster than mine. He overtook me with arrogant ease. As I turned the corner, I heard the baritone blast of a powerful horn. A large truck was coming the other way. I saw smoke rising from Gordon's wheels as he tried to brake, then heard the deafening crunch of the collision. The truck quaked with the impact, its driver jerking about violently in his seat.

Gordon rocketed through the Rover's windshield in a torrent of blood and glass. Hurtling headfirst, he hit the truck and dropped onto the squashed and tangled hood of his own car. The truck driver remained in his cabin, safe but shaken, rubbing his neck, veiled by a tower of hot steam that emanated from the Rover's radiator. Tingling with unholy glee, I executed a perfect three-point turn and drove off in the opposite direction.

I returned to Caro's flat. She was still in bed but awake and listening to music. I didn't dare tell her about Gordon's accident in case he wasn't dead. I feared the bitter disappointment of her father surviving death a second time might be too much for her. At about five o'clock, the phone rang. It was Eileen, sounding reassuringly tearful. She asked to speak to Caro.

"Is anything wrong?" I asked her.

"I need to speak to Caroline in person," repeated Eileen, not quite capable of being grief-stricken and charming at the same time.

"No," I urged. "She's not feeling well. Give me the message and I'll pass it on to her."

Gordon had died of his injuries on his way to the hospital.

I went in to Caro and quietly told her what had happened. Using the remote, she turned off the stereo, then sat up in bed and stared at me. "How do I know he's really dead?"

"They want you to go to the mortuary and identify him. You're the next of kin."

Caro grabbed my hand, her eyes ablaze with startled joy. "He's really gone?"

I described the crash to her. When I got to the part about him flying through the windshield, she got out of bed and danced for joy. "God, I wish I'd seen that."

"It was very satisfying," I admitted.

She followed me into the kitchen. "How the hell did you arrange it?"

Before I could explain that I had arranged nothing, that Gordon had virtually committed suicide, Caro stopped me. "No, better not. If I know what you've done and don't report you, then legally I'm an accessory. It's better that I don't know anything."

"Okay. If you say so."

"I *do* say so." Caro started to cry. "You look after me. You're about the only fucker who ever did. And I take back what I said about not loving anyone. At this moment, I love you, Mark Madden. More than anything on earth."

Now we were both crying.

"You killed my fat-bastard father," continued Caro. "Tomorrow he would have gone to his solicitor and written me out of his will. Okay, you cut it a bit fine, but in the end, as always, you delivered. We're going to be rich. We'll never need to steal or claim benefits again. And it's all because of you. You are such a wonderful bastard."

She demonstrated precisely how wonderful right there and then, on the kitchen floor. I was intoxicated by the fumes of hell. After twenty-three years of denial, I was finally owning up. *My name is Mark Madden, and I derive deep and lasting satisfaction from the deaths of people I don't like.*

* * *

GORDON HAD his faults, and he may have lived his entire life without making meaningful contact with a single human being, but at least he had made a will. By some sardonic quirk of fate, his final will was signed and witnessed in the same month in which Caro and I had become high school sweethearts. The will was a simple document, in which Gordon left everything he owned to his wife and, in the event of her death, to their only child, Caroline Rose. Eileen, his common girlfriend, hadn't even made the small print.

Another very useful aspect of Gordon's will was its stipulation that he be given no funeral service. A lifelong atheist, he had instructed that no undertaker should profit from his corpse, no priest intone pious platitudes over it. Gordon wished only for his body to be placed in the cheapest available coffin and unceremoniously burned. His ashes were to be taken to Harwich, where his boat had once been moored, there to be strewn on the sea—the sea that he had never once managed to sail on.

The lack of a funeral service was particularly useful to us, because it meant that Caro wasn't obliged to make a public pretense of grief. This was a great relief to me, as it had been hard enough to prevent her from laughing when she'd identified her father's body.

Not that Caro's attitude to Gordon was entirely callous. She did shed tears for her father, not so much crying for what she'd lost but for what she never had.

The most astounding result of Gordon's violent death was that it had left Caro financially secure. She had his house valued and found it was worth six and a half million. Gordon's other assets amounted to four million in various savings accounts and insurance policies and three-quarters of a million in stocks and shares. Even if the taxes she would have to pay sliced the fortune in half, she would be left with about five million. Unless she invested all her assets in luminous earmuffs, Caro would never have to defraud a credit card company again.

*   *   *

OUR FUTURE assured, we got married at the Richmond registry office on a sunny Saturday. It was a drab occasion, despite the unseasonal sunshine. Only my immediate family were in attendance. My mother wept through the ceremony, and not because she was happy; Mum had never liked Caro and thought I was making a serious mistake.

With something of a shock, Caro and I realized we didn't have any friends. Literally no one to invite. I asked Wallace, but he couldn't come because it was a Saturday and his kids were staying with him for the weekend. "Bring them along," I urged him.

"I really don't think Caro's suitable for children," he answered.

Afterward, we'd booked a champagne buffet aboard a Thames pleasure cruiser. I think the only person who enjoyed the trip was my brother, who had brought along his new girlfriend, a teenaged shopgirl called Marina who laughed at all his jokes.

My father got tipsy and amiable, flirting with Caro, whom he'd obviously always fancied. My mother told Dad to act his age. Dad's response, although not ill-intentioned, was not helpful. "It's not my fault, my voluptuous darling, that she's younger and thinner than you are."

By the time we docked at Hampton Court, we were all so drunk that we couldn't be bothered to disembark, so we asked the crew to turn the boat around. The moon and stars began to show in the late afternoon sky. As the boat sailed under Richmond Bridge, Caro took me aside and threw her arms around me. "After all these years, I can't believe I finally married my Madeline."

"So you admit it!"

"It was meant as a compliment."

"That's not what Andy Wallace told me."

"Andy Wallace is a simpleton. When I called you Madeline, it was a reference to your strongly developed feminine side."

Before I could protest, my dad came over to tell us both a joke. It was the one about the echo. (I'd heard it before.) My attention wandered to the bank, and I noticed a gray-haired man sitting alone on a bench, staring straight ahead and sobbing as we glided past. Something about his appearance seemed unsettlingly familiar, as if I were seeing an apparition of myself in forty years' time.

*   *   *

FOR THE first time in our lives, Caro and I borrowed money we would actually be able to repay. We spent three weeks in Europe. It was our first holiday together. We visited Florence, where we saw Michelangelo's David glaring at the Medicis to distract attention from his uncommonly small penis. Then on to Venice, where we searched in vain for female dwarfs in scarlet duffel coats. We passed our time sightseeing, eating, and screwing, splendidly drunk on fuck-the-world elation.

The last week was spent at Euro Disney. It was Caro's idea, not mine. Frankly, it didn't matter to me where we were. That holiday was the highlight of our entire lives and possibly the only time either of us had ever been truly happy.

When we got back, I logged on to my old Web site to sort through the countless complaints from customers who'd ordered books and not received them. I'd posted a personal announcement on the Web site, stating that my business had been razed to the ground and that anyone who'd purchased an item that no longer existed would be fully refunded, but I was still getting abuse from people who hadn't read the message and thought I was the laziest bookseller in the universe.

Among these loving epistles was an e-mail from someone at Hotmail who called himself Guy Montag. As soon as I opened it, I saw it was another blaze of goodwill from my anonymous hater.

> You are such a pathetic excuse for a man. Do you really think she loves you? Do you really think she wants your miserable, undersized cock in her face? She will use you and discard you but you deserve it because you are too weak and pitiful

I stopped reading, partly because I didn't want these sick ramblings in my head, but mainly because I'd remembered that Guy Montag was the hero of Ray Bradbury's *Fahrenheit 451,* a futuristic fireman whose full-time occupation is burning books.

* * *

WE'D DECIDED to be careful with our money. Having sampled dire poverty, we had no desire to go back there. But Caro had to allow herself one luxury. She went out and bought herself a secondhand BMW Sportster like the one that had been repossessed. Her present to me, to my astonishment, was a fine copy of "*Casino Royale.*"

"How did you get this?"

"It's yours. I stole it from your shop just before the fire," admitted Caro coyly. "But aren't you glad that I did?"

* * *

CARO REFUSED to move into Gordon's house. She felt that everything her father had touched was cursed and infected. She was physically unable to sit in a chair that he had occupied, and the mere thought of his underpants could launch her into hysterics.

It therefore goes without saying that she had no desire to keep her father's ashes. As a joke, she offered them to Eileen. Neither one of us was particularly surprised when Eileen turned them down. The vulgar woman hadn't really wanted Gordon in his original state, so what possible appeal could the incinerated version hold for her? As a conciliatory gesture, Caro called Eileen to the house, inviting her to help herself to a memento, any object that reminded her of Gordon. Eileen chose the Sony plasma-screen television.

"So that reminds you of my dad, does it?" said Caro cynically.

"Why not?" said Eileen. "He spent enough time watching it."

"You couldn't find anything worth less than four and a half thousand quid that was vaguely reminiscent of him?"

"Your father, young lady, was about to share all his wordly goods with me," said Eileen. "He would not have begrudged me a television set."

I gave Caro a look, and she appeared to relent. Eileen's son walked in to take the TV away. He was slightly younger than me, but pudgy with a bright pink face. I couldn't help thinking he found the situation embarrassing. He tried to lift the television, but it was too heavy. I had to help him carry it out to a van parked in the drive.

Eileen stood in the porch, watching us struggling. I heard her say to Caro, "I suppose you've got what you want now?"

"I can't complain," said Caro.

"Yes, it all seems to have worked out very convenient for you," continued Eileen. "Some would say almost *too* convenient."

"Firstly," retorted Caro, "the word you're searching for is 'conveniently.' And secondly, *Mark, bring back that telly!*"

"Caro, let it go," I said.

"No!" Caro sprinted down the drive, and while Mr. Pink Boy and I were lifting the Sony into the back of the van, she launched a roundhouse kick that Lenny could not have bettered and put her foot through the TV screen.

CHAPTER 9

HI, INFIDELITY

THE WEEKS passed, but there was still no sign of Caro's riches. It was a stressful time for us, suspended as we were between outrageous wish fulfillment and the crippling possibility that our life was about to turn into an Ealing comedy. *(Mark and Caro are forced to embark on a new killing spree when Caroline's solicitor discovers that she is adopted and that the Caroline Sewell referred to in the will is actually Gordon's first daughter, the illegitimate heir to his millions.)*

Caro's bank manager, all smiles, had offered her a generous overdraft. But she didn't want the bank's money. She wanted her own.

Most days, we walked in Kew Gardens, talking about all the things we were going to do with our wealth. It was my plan to behave like the reformed Scrooge, giving my brother and my parents ten thousand each. Caro thought this was a bad idea. "Whatever you give them won't be enough. If you give them ten thousand and they know you've got a million, they'll still think you're a mean bastard."

* * *

ON THE evening of my class with Lenny, I placed the Kimber handgun at the bottom of my rucksack and covered it with my karate suit. At the door, I kissed Caro good-bye. Five minutes later, I returned to the flat.

"What's the matter?" she said, her face noticeably paler than usual.

"I don't know whether I can be bothered with all this self-defense shit anymore. We'll soon be able to hire a bodyguard."

"No, you've got to learn how to look after yourself." Caro virtually pushed me out of the door. "I want you to protect me."

"So you're saying I've *got* to go?"

"It's for your own good."

I knew then that something was wrong.

At the noisy, yobby pub next to Kew station, I bought a horrible warm pint of bitter and drank it at a table outside, my breath turning to mist in the cold. After ten minutes of refrigerating my sphincter, I decided I was being paranoid and caught the next train to Hammersmith. I got off at Baron's Court, meaning to walk to Hammersmith. Instead, I switched platforms and caught the next train back to Kew.

It was only a ten-minute walk from the station to Caro's flat, but I made it last longer by walking as slowly as I could. I reached the house to find a pastel blue Porsche with a familiar registration plate parked in the drive. Trembling, I unlocked the front door and stepped into the nasty communal hall. I could smell fried garlic.

Opposite me stood the door to the ground-floor flat, silent and dark, permanently unoccupied. The landlady preserved it as a shrine to her son, who once owned the entire house but died tragically young.

A supernaturally well behaved New Zealand couple occupied the top floor. The only time we were aware of their presence was at weekends, when they acted as hosts to an endless trail of backpacker Kiwis in search of free accommodation.

The smell of garlic emanated from Caro's flat. I climbed the stairs and turned my key in the lock. The door to Caro's flat didn't open. It was bolted on the inside. I hammered on the door with my fist, shouting Caro's name. "Is that fucking biblical bastard in there with you?"

After a few minutes, I heard Caro's voice. "Mark, go away. Please."

"You're my wife," I said. "What are you doing?"

"Trying to keep us alive."

"You're fucking him. You are, aren't you? Answer me!" I punched and kicked the door, but it held fast. "You're my *wife*, you fucking bitch!"

On the other side of the door, Caro pleaded with me. "Mark. *Please*. Don't make it worse than it already is."

I was about to ask her how it could be worse when I remembered the gun. I rushed down the stairs and out of the front door.

A narrow passage ran alongside the house, ending in a gate that led to the back garden. I passed through the gate and stood among the rank, overgrown weeds. A light shone in our bedroom window. Almost vomiting with jealousy, I took the Kimber out of my bag and aimed it at the window. I didn't hear the first shot because a plane was flying over, its landing lights as big as saucers. The second shot hit one of the windowpanes, blasting an enormous jagged hole through the glass. Dread filled me at the thought that I might have hurt Caro. I stopped firing.

After about five minutes, the gate creaked softly. Something pale and vaguely luminous drifted into sight, and I heard a man's voice. "Killer?"

It was Jesus.

"What?" I said.

"Are you all right?" He sounded friendly, almost gentle.

Gentle Jesus.

As he drew closer, he held up his hands. "Listen, if you want to shoot me, you better do it. But I'd rather you heard what I have to say. Okay?"

I didn't answer. It was dark, and he couldn't possibly have seen the expression on my face or where the gun was pointing. But, exhibiting the kind of wild courage that had established his reputation, he walked straight over to me and placed a hand on my shoulder.

"Listen, man," he said quietly. "It seems I owe you an apology. Until just now, I didn't even know you and Caro got married. I mean, she never told me. She doesn't wear a ring or anything. I thought you were just another punk, one of the hundreds of thousands of filthy punks who chase her pussy every day. When I sent those guys to bat you around, I just didn't appreciate what was going down between you and her."

"So you admit it, then? You tried to cripple me?"

"Well, how was I to know you were the most important thing in her life? Anyway, it backfired. My boys were the ones who got crippled. What have you got to be pissed about?"

"You've been fucking my wife."

"Oh, yeah. Sorry about that."

"Yeah," I said. "I bet your heart bleeds for me."

"No," said Bad Jesus, letting his hand fall to his side. "It doesn't bleed for anyone. But I care about marriage, all right? I was married once. My wife screwed another guy when my little boy was in the house, so I know how that feels. I know the pain you're feeling. So come on. Let's go for a spin."

"What?"

"Have you ever been in a Porsche before? Let's just go for a ride. We can talk as we drive along. And you won't be needing this. Don't you know these things are dangerous?"

Jesus took the gun from my hand. Nearby was a dilapidated garden shed with broken windows. The shed had a hole in its base that rats used as their own private entrance. Jesus stooped low to shove the weapon through the hole.

"Okay, let's go," he said.

"I'd better tell Caro."

"She already knows."

"What did she say?"

"She didn't believe me. She thinks I'm going to cut off your balls with piano wire." Then he laughed.

* * *

CONSIDERING WHAT the Porsche must have cost, it seemed mean and cramped inside, with only two small bucket seats. A fat bastard wouldn't have fitted in the car.

"So is this the part of the story where you drive me off to a warehouse and impale me on a butcher's hook?" I said.

"No," said Jesus. "It's the moment when you catch the superstar criminal off guard, when he shows his more natural side to the camera. The warm, lovable side that until now you didn't know existed."

"Tell me something," I said. "When you saw me in Kew Gardens, did you recognize me?"

"Sure. You were the guy whose book I burned."

"So that was just coincidence?"

"No. I made the bitch give me a list of all the scum that had ever fucked her. Fucking long list. Then I went round to humiliate you all."

"Why bother?"

"Until tonight, I thought she was mine." Jesus sighed. "I really fucking did."

He turned on the engine, released the brake, and reversed into the path of a black cab. The cabbie, showing remarkable restraint, braked and waited. Then Jesus pressed down his foot and drove on, surging past the gardens. I could smell his pine-based cologne, heavy and sweet, redolent of first love and beauty and obscene wealth. The car was spotlessly clean. I suddenly found I was enjoying the surreal experience of being luxuriously chauffeured by a homicidal Christ look-alike.

"How's your heart feeling?" he asked me. Neither mocking nor remorseful, just interested.

"How do you think?" I said.

"Bad," he said. He reached into the glove compartment and passed me a silver flask. "That's women, you see. Take a woman too seriously, won't be long before you find teethmarks on your dick. Have a drink, buddy. You look like you could use one."

I opened the flask and sniffed it. It was cognac. I took a big swig and felt my insides light up. "So when I started shooting, how come you didn't shoot back?"

Jesus shrugged. "Violence doesn't thrill me as much as you might think. You see, Killer, there's a lot of theater in what I do. The men who follow me need to be scared of me, so I have to do frightening things. You can't be a successful criminal unless you inspire fear. It's a strange way to make a living."

"Then why do it?"

"Boredom. I'm serious. Anything remotely normal bores the shit out of me."

"Give me an example."

"The moon," he said.

We were following the Thames east, heading for the city. A big full moon accompanied us all the way, now skimming on the water, now vanishing only to be glimpsed moments later in the branches of a tree.

"You don't think it's beautiful?"

"A long time ago, maybe," said Jesus. "But now I've seen it too many times. It always does the same things. I find the moon depressingly predictable." He lit a cigarette from the dashboard. "I was a bright child. Have you heard of the Mary Swallow School for Gifted Children?"

"No."

"No? Well, you're an ignorant slob. It's a famous school, and I won a scholarship to go there. But they kicked me out. They said I was ungovernable. That was their word for it."

"Why are you telling me this?"

"Just trying to explain. I was hyperactive before people knew what the word meant. There's this restlessness in me that makes me smash things. Even when I don't want to."

"Have you read an Edgar Allan Poe story called 'The Imp of the Perverse'?" I said.

"Do I look like I've read an Edgar Allan Poe story called 'The Imp of the Perverse'?"

"No. But then you don't look like a man who went to a school for gifted children."

About fifty yards away, a male pedestrian in his twenties crossed the road in front of us, walking with exaggerated slowness to demonstrate how cool and unafraid he was. Jesus checked his mirror. There was nothing behind us.

To avoid a collision, Jesus needed to brake. Instead, he sped up and knocked the pedestrian over. The hood slammed into his legs and he flew sideways, bouncing across the road like a rubber ball. Jesus laughed but he didn't stop. I glanced back to see the pedestrian writhing in the gutter.

"You ran him down," I pointed out helpfully.

"That's right," said Jesus. "Did you see how he was swaggering, daring us to hit him? The pathetic little worm. He dared the wrong man, didn't he? Man, I love my life." Then he laughed again, hard and loud.

"Maybe we better go back?"

"Yeah. He was still alive, wasn't he? Maybe we should go back and run over him again?" He tutted. "What kind of world do you think you're living in, Killer?"

"A bad one."

"That's right. People don't like each other enough. I like my kid, but I can't say it goes any further, 'cause I never see him. I only truly love two people. My kid brother and myself. And I'd say I was fairly typical."

"You think it's typical to run someone over and not stop?"

"Yeah. And don't try and tell me you've never done it."

"Did you burn my shop down?"

"What?"

"I asked you a question. Someone set fire to my shop. Was it you?"

"No. Like I said, I did send some guys round to paste you. That's as far as I got."

Victoria Embankment rushed by on our left. By Cleopatra's Needle, a real London bobby was giving directions to some tourists.

"Look. A child's view of London," sneered Jesus. "All we need is a red London bus going by."

Right on cue, a red London bus passed by.

Jesus laughed delightedly. "What did I tell you? Now we need Hugh Grant running up out of breath to tell Julia Roberts he loves her and wants to spend the rest of his life with her. You know what I'd like to see? A film where Hugh Grant runs up at the end and Julia Roberts throws acid in his face."

"Uh, that doesn't sound very commercial," I said.

"Well, I'd pay to see it," said Jesus.

I took another swig of the brandy. Then an image of Caro being fucked by Jesus drifted into my mind. I covered my face and sighed like a Hampton Court ghost.

"Don't go on about the wife-fucking," said Jesus. "I've already apologized about that."

"Okay," I said, speaking through my hand.

"And the reason why I was hostile to you, I don't like anyone going near the women I'm doing it with. It's just a rule I have. But if I'd known you were married, I wouldn't have fucked her. I'm a reasonable man."

"What about the money you're charging Caro? She only borrowed twenty grand and you're asking for—what? One-thirty? What's reasonable about that?"

Bad Jesus sighed. "I'll cut the debt in half. Okay? Sixty-five thousand."

"Thirty."

"Eighty-five," said Jesus.

I looked at him. "Now you're going higher. What are you going higher for?"

"Because, my friend, you tried to take advantage. Bad mistake. Never try to take advantage of a maniac who's doing you a favor."

"I just don't think we can find sixty-five."

"Yes, you can. And you pay me in full on Friday, understand?"

"I thought we were friends."

"Are we fuck? Friends? Why are we friends? Because I gave you a ride in my car?"

"You're acting friendly."

"Oh, *acting*. Sure, I'm great at acting. But I don't do friendship. Nothing against you, you could be the nicest guy in the world, it'd make no difference. I don't feel what other people feel. That's why I'm rich. So don't flatter yourself. You get on the wrong side of me, you'll soon find out how friendly I am."

I must still have looked unhappy, because he added, "But look, if it makes you feel any better, C and me didn't fuck tonight. I couldn't face all those loud noises she makes. All she did was give me a hand job while I ate my dinner."

At Victoria, Jesus parked his smart little car in a square and asked me to get out.

"Why?"

"Don't be so suspicious all the time. I want you to see something."

We cut through an alley and walked past a burger restaurant and there was Victoria Cathedral in all its gloomy glory. The building was closing, and a steward at the door prepared to bar our way, but when he looked up at Jesus his mouth dropped open and he stepped to one side. "God be with you," said Bad Jesus. Then he turned to me and grinned.

* * *

ON THE way home, Jesus was in such a good mood that he let me drive his car. Until now, I had always ridiculed Porsches because of the kind of people who own them. Yet the Son of God's car was a beautiful machine, and driving it felt like gliding through space.

Jesus wanted me to go to a drinking club in South London with him. I told him I needed to get back.

"Why?"

"Caro'll wonder where I am."

"Here's my phone. Call her."

"I've got my own phone."

"Why are you in such a hurry to get back to a woman who's been fucking another man?"

"Well, given the choice, she wouldn't have done that."

Bad Jesus was incredulous. "You honestly believe that? Let me tell you about me and women. I could walk into any bar and within ten minutes, three ordinary whores would walk up to me and beg me, literally *beg* me, to mistreat them. Do you doubt that?"

"No."

"Women like to be told they're ugly. Once in a while, they like to be punched and kicked. They particularly like to crawl naked on their hands and knees before a dirty murderer who looks like Jesus Christ. Caroline is no different."

I felt I was in no position to argue.

"And now you know what a liar she is," said Jesus, "are you still eager to hurry home to her?"

I nodded. He blew out his breath despairingly as if he'd never heard anything so stupid. When we were passing through Barnes, a shiny four-wheel-drive overtook us. The guy in the front passenger seat leaned out of the window and swore at us. Then the car sped off, tearing crazily round the narrow bend and out of sight.

"See that?" said Jesus. "Standards are declining everywhere. How old would you say that guy was? Forty? Forty-five?"

"Yeah. About that."

"He's probably somebody's father. Why was he shouting? Where's his dignity?"

"Dunno."

"See his face? He was fat and soft. It's amazing how many weak, cowardly bastards act brave when they're behind the wheel of a car."

"But he wasn't behind the wheel."

"Yeah, okay, but you know what I mean. He felt safe in his metal box. Maybe he'd got that false sense of security that guys get after a few drinks. Also, perhaps he was irritated because this car's better than his, so he thinks he has the right to insult us. Or maybe he hasn't got a car. Maybe his friend who was driving is the only one with a car. I'm serious. We live in a very petty world."

Jesus lit a cigarette from the dashboard. A little later, we passed the same car, parked on the pavement outside an off-license. Two well-scrubbed middle-class men were getting out, laughing and joking, big bellies bursting over their trouser belts.

"Stop the car," said Jesus.

"Why?" I said, already doing what I was told. I mean, it was his car.

"I just want to talk to them."

I pulled up, and Jesus got out and walked over to the two nice middle-class men. I followed him, afraid that the situation might be about to turn nasty.

"Excuse me? What did you shout at us just now?" said Jesus to the passenger. He had plump, shiny red cheeks. His friend, the driver, wore glasses and had sleek white hair with a boyish fringe. You could tell that neither of them had had to worry about money in his entire life.

"You were driving in the middle of the road," declared the driver, in a self-satisfied, plummy voice. He had that kind of re-pulsive confidence that people get from living in a place like Barnes, earning too much money and eating like pigs.

"I didn't ask you," said Jesus.

The driver huffed and puffed. His friend said, "Now, come on, it's hardly something to get heated about."

"You called my friend here a bad word," said Jesus.

"Did I? I really don't remember."

"Are you saying you don't think he can drive? He's a martial arts expert. He could hurt you very badly."

The passenger was trying to edge away. "Well, I dare say he could. But the fact remains, he was in the middle of the road."

"He was keeping left, like all good motorists," said Jesus.

"Well, that's your perspective," said the passenger, with a tight little sneer. "It certainly isn't mine."

Before I could react, Bad Jesus grabbed the passenger's ears, dug his thumbs into the man's eye sockets, and flicked his eyeballs out onto the pavement. The victim screamed and put his hands to his face. Blood burst through his fingers in sad, thin little spurts.

"What's your perspective now?" said Jesus, drawing a dainty little revolver with a golden handle.

Then he turned to the driver, who was backing away. "See that?" said Jesus, pointing down at the two bloody staring eyes on the pavement. "That's what happens to people like you."

"Bastard!" said the driver.

Jesus waved the gun at him, and the driver turned to flee, but he ran straight into a litter bin, hitting it so hard that he doubled up in pain. His blind friend continued to squeal, staggering around in circles, treading his own eyes into the pavement. It was a scene from hell, yet I was curiously reluctant to leave it.

Jesus was obliged to take my arm, drag me to the Porsche, and push me in. Then he got behind the wheel and drove away, keeping his lights off until we were out of sight in case some good citizen made a note of the registration.

Jesus snatched a tissue from a box in the glove compartment and wiped his fingers as he drove along. I watched him for any signs of emotion, but there weren't any. He wasn't even flustered. He might as well have swatted a couple of flies.

"Why the fuck did you do that?" I said.

"They'll live. What are you worried about?" Bad Jesus grinned at me. "I wanted to show you something. Caro tells me you're dangerous. A real killer. Maybe so. But you're nowhere near as dangerous as me. No one is."

"I still don't know why you did it."

"Didn't you see the looks on their faces? They thought they were *right*. Men like that spend their whole lives being right. They go to the right schools, marry the right women, their politics lean to the right. Believe me, Killer, I've done those guys a real favor. Now they'll spend the rest of their lives thinking about the day they were wrong."

* * *

CARO RAN to the door and threw herself into my arms. She was crying. "I didn't think I'd see you again," she sobbed.

I held her for a long time, still numb from what I'd just witnessed. She asked me what had happened. I told her. She nodded gravely.

"You don't seem very surprised," I said.

"Why would I be? That's what he did to Warren."

"He gouged Warren's eye out?"

"Yeah. Warren made a joke about Jesus in front of one of Jesus' girlfriends. Jesus reached over and flicked out Warren's eye with his thumb. Apparently it's one of his favorite tricks. The real Jesus made the blind see. Bad Jesus does the opposite."

"The guy put out Warren's eye? And Warren still carried on working for him?"

"He didn't have much choice," explained Caro. "He didn't want to lose the other eye."

When we got into bed she kissed me and turned over on her side. With her back to me, she said, "I only lied to protect you."

I lay there in silence, having made my mind up to avoid the usual jealous-lover questions. I didn't want to know whether Jesus had an enormous cock or whether Caro had ever reached orgasm during their weekly encounters. I knew, from personal experience, that such questions seldom have helpful answers.

I decided that Caro's behavior couldn't be classed strictly as unfaithfulness. She'd been in a war zone like France during the Nazi occupation. The SS had forced her to work as a sex slave, but soon the war would be over. After liberation, it would be my sacred duty as a loving husband to do the only decent thing.

I was going to pretend that none of it had ever happened.

* * *

IN THE morning, while Caro was in the bath, I gave her the good news.

"A discount? From Bad Jesus?" she marveled. "What happened? Does he fancy you?"

"Even if he does, I doubt he values my arse cheeks at sixty-five grand."

"Bad Jesus doesn't let anyone off anything. It's unheard of."

"I suppose even the worst people like to be nice once in a while."

When Caro was dressed, a miracle took place. She logged on to her online bank account to find just over three million sitting there. Caro arranged there and then for half the money to be transferred to my account. I couldn't believe it. No one had ever given me one and a half million pounds before.

"I wouldn't have a penny without you," said Caro," so even if we split up you'll have enough to live on."

"What about the proceeds of the house sale?"

"The same. From now on, we share everything fifty-fifty."

This was good news for me, because my income, never impressive, had sunk to zero. The fire brigade had confirmed that the fire at my shop had been the result of arson, which meant that the insurance company, suspecting me of torching my own ailing business, was a little wary of paying up.

Enjoying my amazement, Caro grabbed me by the shoulders. "Now. What are we going to spend it on?"

My face became mock stern. "First of all, I think we should take care of all our debts. Which includes the debts of Miss Chile Concarne and Ms. Ivy Bigun. We don't always want to be in the position of hiding every time we hear a knock on the door."

"I'll sort it out today," she promised.

* * *

FRIDAY MORNING was cold and misty, like a picture postcard of winter. At nine o'clock, as arranged, we walked into the bank to collect sixty-five thousand pounds in cash. The assistant manager called us into her office, and an underling brought in Jesus' money on a tray, in bundles of fifty-pound notes. The bank helpfully provided us with a special zip-up bag to carry it in so that any muggers would immediately know we were worth bludgeoning to death.

By ten minutes to ten, we were waiting among the pine trees in Kew Gardens. The mist hadn't lifted, and the deserted gardens seemed to be floating in a gray dream. It was freezing cold, but that wasn't why we were shivering.

I'd intended to take Warren's loaded gun, just in case Jesus had wanted our money *and* our lives. Caro had begged me not to. "Even with a gun, you wouldn't stand a chance in hell against these people. Can you shoot straight? No. If Jesus finds out you're armed, he'll think you were planning something. Mark, for God's sake, leave the fucking thing behind."

So I did.

At five past ten, Peter the Rock turned up with another guy who looked like a bailiff, a little square head on big square shoulders in a cheap square suit. Caro and I were both relieved. Without his brother around, Rock was noticeably more relaxed, clearly regarding neither Caro nor me as a serious threat. Rock even apologized for the way Jesus had set two thugs on me. "He gets like that," he explained. "He's even like it with me. Nice and friendly one minute, next minute he goes off like a fucking rocket." Then he introduced his companion. "This is Cancer Boy. He kind of grows on you."

Caro placed the money bag on a bench, and Cancer Boy unzipped it. His eyes glistened as he reached in and withdrew a bundle of fifty-pound notes.

"Brilliant," said Rock, laughing boyishly. "It's all here?"

"Sixty-five thousand," I said. "As agreed."

"That is just great." Rock shook his head." I have to admit, I didn't expect you to deliver. I'd have taken bets on it."

"So can we go now?" said Caro.

Rock shook his head. "Gotta frisk you."

"Why bother?" said Caro pleasantly.

"I know, it's shit, it's boring," said Rock, "but Jesus told me to check you weren't wired." He shook his head apologetically.

With brisk efficiency, Cancer Boy patted us down and declared us both clean. "Okay," said Rock. "Now here's the bit I don't like. Jesus says we gotta add an extra two grand onto the debt."

"*What?*" said Caro and I in unison.

"Don't blame me," said Rock. "You know what he's like."

Cancer Boy shook his head dolefully as if he didn't agree with it either.

"Why should we pay an extra two thousand?" I said.

"Jesus says it's a disappointment fine," explained Rock.

"A what?" said Caro.

"A disappointment fine." Rock nodded to me. "He's disappointed in your man here—what's his name?"

"Mark," volunteered Caro.

"Yeah," said Rock. "Seems Jesus let Mark drive his car the other night. Then some knobhead called him a name and Jesus was forced to punish him. Seems Mark here didn't show much gratitude. In fact, according to Jesus, he acted like he *disapproved.* So that's what the fine's about. It's a penalty for disappointing Jesus. You hurt his feelings, man."

"Oh, that's bullshit," I said.

I could see that Rock was about to disagree. Then he changed his mind and nodded. "You think I don't know? Jesus drives me insane. But he's my brother, you know. I'm stuck with the crazy fuck. Hey, that rhymes."

"Couldn't you just say we paid the extra two thou even though we didn't?"

"Er, no. I'm afraid Jesus is a highly numerate kind of guy."

"What if we refuse to pay?" I said.

Cancer Boy spat on the ground. "Then it all starts again," said Rock. "Jesus hounds you for the two thousand, doubles your debt every month until you owe him a stupid fucking fortune all over again." He shrugged. "It's up to you, man, but I know what I'd do."

I thought for a moment. "I've got a car that's worth a few grand. A Fiat Uno. You could have that."

"A fucking Fiat Uno? That's an old lady's car. Why are you driving around in a piece of shit like that?"

Cancer Boy laughed silently, his big shoulders moving up and down.

I felt myself blushing. "It's not so bad," I said.

"How old is it?" said Rock.

"A couple of years."

"And I could take it away with me now, yeah?"

"Why not?"

Rock decided this was a reasonable solution. So Cancer Boy departed to drive back alone while the Rock, carrying the money, strolled back with us to Caro's flat, where the Fiat was parked.

"Before I forget," said Rock, as we passed through the Lion Gate. "Either of you seen this before?"

Casually, he passed a crumpled note over to me. It was an e-mail printout. The sender was jesusisapansy@netscape.com. By the first sentence, I knew the message had been written by the same freak that had been spamming me.

```
Who do you think you are, you filthy homosexual coward? Do
you think a single woman would ever look at you if you
weren't pointing a gun at them? You hideous glob of pu-
trescence, I would like to remove your eyelids with a
blunt razor, whip your genitals with barbed wire, and then
pour kerosene onto the wounds. You couldn't satisfy a sex-
starved mongrel, let alone a woman.
```

"Yes? No?" inquired Rock languidly.

"Yeah," I said. "I've had a hundred e-mails just like it."

"So have we," said Rock. "We checked—they all come from libraries or Internet cafés."

I passed it to Caro. "As they coincided with me getting back together with Caro, I even wondered if Jesus was sending them."

Rock shook his head. "My brother doesn't type. Doesn't write as far as I know. I don't mean he's illiterate. He's a very bright guy. But if he wanted to hurt your feelings he'd use a pair of pliers." His eyes narrowed as he assessed us. "You really didn't send it?"

"No," said Caro. "He didn't."

Rock glanced at her sharply. "Did you?"

She shook her head. Rock smiled in acceptance. Apart from criminality, he appeared to have little in common with his sinister sibling.

The Fiat was parked on the drive. Rock walked round the car, decided it was worth at least three grand, and asked for the keys. I handed them over.

"You're doing the right thing," said Rock. "You really don't want my big brother breathing down your neck."

We watched from the porch as Rock unlocked the Fiat, placed the money bag on the passenger seat, and locked himself in. Then he nodded to us, grinned, and turned the key in the ignition.

There was a blinding flash, followed by a blistering wind that hurled us against the front door. A second later, the car and the air around it were ripped apart by a vicious explosion. Caro's BMW, which had been parked beside my car, was blasted to the other side of the drive. Metal, glass, and gobs of oily red meat rained down on the porch, the drive, and the passing cars. And overhead, fifty-pound notes were sprouting from the branches of the trees.

PART 2

BADDER

CHAPTER 10

HAPPINESS IN SEVEN DAYS

OUR GOOD friends Detective Sergeant Bromley and Detective Constable Flett held Caro and me for forty-eight hours, interviewing us in strict rotation to see if they could catch us out. As she and I had already decided to tell the truth, or at least part of it, this wasn't likely to happen.

"So, Mark," said Flett, the tape running as he grilled me for the fourth time. "When did you decide to murder Mr. Callaghan?"

"I didn't. He was Bad Jesus' brother. No one in their right mind would have murdered him."

"So why did you offer him your car? You knew there was a bomb underneath it. You knew because it was you who planted the car bomb. We're here to help you, Mark. Why don't you tell us what happened?"

"Firstly," I said, "I haven't a clue how to make a bomb. Secondly, why would I blow up sixty-five thousand pounds of my own money?"

"Because you're stupid?"

"That's very funny."

"Mark, if you didn't plant the bomb that killed Mr. Callaghan, who did?"

"I have no idea."

Then Bromley took over, still smiling and avuncular. "Mark, what would you say if we told you we know everything? That your lady friend has already spilled the beans?"

"I'd say you talk in clichés, officer. And that you've run out of ideas, in fact never had any ideas in the first place. And that you're now resorting to a desperate bluff in the hope of securing a confession."

The expressions on their faces were eloquent. Fortunately for me, the interview was being videotaped. Otherwise, I'm fairly certain that Bromley would have held me down while Flett kicked my teeth down my throat.

* * *

OUR CAPTORS let us go, their disappointment palpable, their small eyes dark with resentment. We were released without charge, which meant that our house and clothes had been scoured for forensic evidence and found wanting. It was official: We weren't bombers, just arseholes. The police search could not have been particularly thorough. I found the Kimber handgun where Jesus had left it, in the rat run under the garden shed. I was happy to be reunited with Warren's old handgun. Something told me we were going to need it.

Bromley confiscated our passports while the investigation continued, but Caro and I knew it would be suicidal to remain in London. Bad Jesus was sure to hold us responsible for his brother's death. We had given Rock the keys to the car that killed him. *I only truly love two people. My kid brother and myself.* If Jesus could blind a motorist for shouting abuse, what would he be prepared to do to Pete's killers? We had no intention of hanging around to find out.

Caro had the bright idea of driving to the east coast. Both our cars had been written off by the explosion, so we hired an inoffensive gray Audi and set off for a small resort in Norfolk. I told no one but my brother where we were going, swearing him to secrecy and making him promise to tell my parents that I loved them if anything should happen to me.

The resort—a last resort, if ever there was one—was called Holeness, a name that seemed to belong in a dirty limerick. Throughout her childhood, Caro had spent many happy holidays in Holeness, staying with her grandparents, who had once run the post office and general store. She had enjoyed her first sexual experience there at the age of thirteen. So although the village was completely devoid of culture and charm, Caro had grown to associate it with freedom and pleasantly moist panties.

The seafront consisted of a café, a souvenir shop, an amusement arcade, and a crazy golf course. The café played loud music constantly, presumably to muffle the agonized groans of the customers who'd eaten there. After school, the teenagers of the town congregated outside the café and the arcade, the kebabs, slot machines, and flashing lights being the closest thing to excitement they could find.

After viewing all the sights, I gave Caro a cool, objective evaluation of the resort. "This place stinks," I said.

"I agree," said Caro. "But that's why we'll be safe here. I don't think Jesus would ever think of looking for us here. Why would anyone in their right minds come to such a shithole?"

We took out a six-month lease on a house in Prospect Square on the west cliff. Ours was the end terrace in a row of three. The house was called the Prospect, but our only prospect was the village hall, a squat wooden box poised on the edge of the cliff. Thanks to this monstrosity, we could only see the sea from the back garden, unless you counted the thin blue strip visible from the attic window.

A brass plate above the entrance to the village hall was engraved with the following:

This plaque was presented by the Village Hall Committee to
Janet and Philip Mather on December 11, 1999, in appreci-
atian of all their efforts on behalf of Holeness Village Hall.

When we read the plaque, we sniggered at the spelling mistake.

In front of the hall stretched a vast private parking lot. In the far corner of the parking lot lay an ornamental garden with a bench at its center. The bench faced our house, affording anyone who cared to sit there a perfect view of us sneering down at them from our bedroom in the attic.

*   *   *

THE PROSPECT, a five-bedroom house, was let furnished. It had once been a guesthouse, and the bedroom doors were still numbered. Downstairs, in the long dining room, were five circular tables, each covered with a white linen tablecloth. The lounge, so obviously a "guests' lounge," smelled of tomato soup, had a ghastly carpet, and was filled with plump flowery chairs. You could almost imagine the previous guests making conversation before the gong was struck for dinner.

Well, tomorrow we thought we'd drive along the coast to visit Cromer.

Yes, it's very nice. We went there today. Tomorrow we're going to Walsingham to pray for a miracle.

How lovely. What kind of miracle are you praying for?

That God will make us interesting people.

Now, that really would be a miracle.

On a small table in the hall lay a book called *Things to Do in Norfolk and Suffolk*. It was a rather slender volume. The original dinner gong still stood on a ledge outside the kitchen. Caro thought it was great fun to beat it before meals. On our first evening, hearing the gong, I walked into the dining room to find a place set for one and a half-eaten bag of chips on the table.

Later, when we were lying in the attic room we'd chosen as our own, I admitted to finding the house a little sinister.

"I don't agree," said Caro.

"But what about all the empty bedrooms underneath us?" I said.

"So? Pretend there are people sleeping in them."

"That's even worse."

"Come on," said Caro drowsily. "It's not as if we've bought the place. We're just on holiday."

"Caro, we are not on holiday. We are fleeing for our fucking lives."

But Caro was already asleep. I lay beside her, drowsy but unable to sleep, listening to the sea. I heard footsteps on gravel and a man singing. He sounded drunk. Then there was a prolonged rattling sound, as if someone incompetent or incapable was attempting to insert a key in a lock. A door slammed, and all was quiet.

After a few minutes I noticed another sound, a sharp scratching noise that seemed to be coming from beneath the floorboards. I sat up in bed and listened intently, but the scratching had stopped. I was now wide awake.

Some time after three, I got up again to peer through the bedroom curtains. There were no streetlights, but a bright waning moon cast a pale glow over the square. Immediately I saw that there was someone sitting on the bench on the far side of the parking lot. At that hour and distance, it was impossible to tell whether it was a man or woman. Whoever it was kept perfectly still. It crossed my mind that it might be one of the Mathers, keeping watch over their beloved village hall.

As I watched, the figure seemed to move away from the bench and glide behind the village hall, its progress so slow and stealthy that I came to believe that I wasn't watching a human being at all but a shadow cast by the moon.

* * *

HOLENESS WASN'T a complete disaster. It had a handsome, award-winning beach, overlooked by a row of identical beach huts, neatly painted in pastel shades. Desperate to please me, Caro rented a yellow beach hut, ours until the spring. It came with deck chairs, pots and pans, and a little Calor Gas stove. "If you don't want to go on the beach," said Caro, "you can sit in the beach hut and take drugs and sulk."

It never came to that. As I surrendered myself to aimless loafing, the sea and the sky and the complete lack of responsibility began to work on me. My initial boredom and resentment faded, and I began to experience a glow I hadn't felt since losing my virginity to Caro. It was a sensation that combined relief and optimism with a curious faith in the basic goodness of people and things.

Even Holeness itself started to seem charming. There was something jolly about being the laziest couple in a drab little village. We watched the sea, played crazy golf, and fed money into the slot machines. In the amusement arcade, I discovered an interesting fact about gambling. The less I cared about winning, the more I won. It gave me a childish thrill to quit while I was ahead, then spend my pitiful winnings on a newspaper or a chocolate bar.

I told Caro how I was feeling on our third afternoon, when

we were taking our daily walk along the beach. It was windy but dry, the North Sea worshipping at our feet. "The only thing that puzzles me," I said, "is that I haven't suffered the slightest bit of remorse about Warren or your dad. I thought we'd be like the couple in *Therese Raquin*, haunted by conscience. But I haven't had the slightest twinge of guilt."

"That's because they deserved to die," said Caro airily. "It's like I told you. We shouldn't go into mourning when bastards perish. Having said that, I don't think we should be glad, either."

"I beg your pardon?! You were jumping up and down when you heard your dad had croaked."

"Yeah, well. Since then, I've had time to think about it. The main feeling I have about him now is a kind of regret. He didn't have the faintest idea how to relate to other people. The saddest thing is, he never made another person happy. And he knew it."

"He made you happy enough when he died," I said.

"No, Marky," she said, kissing my hand. "You're the only one who's ever made me happy."

On our way back, we stopped at the fortune-telling machine outside the amusement arcade. Caro slotted in a coin, and out popped a card that was supposed to tell the future.

You may have a lovers' tiff later this week. You'll have a lot to say, but may not find the right person to say it to. Social events are highlighted, and there will be a family celebration of some kind. You'll be good at starting projects, but not so good at finishing them. Never mind.

It was the "never mind" that got me. I laughed out loud. Caro didn't even smile. "I hope you don't take that shit seriously?" I said.

"Of course not," she answered. "But I believe that some things are preordained."

"Then you must believe that I came back into your life to save you."

"That's right. Without you, my dad would have married that fat chip-eating bitch. I'd have been destitute, and Bad Jesus would have screwed my arse until there was nothing left of it."

I stopped walking and looked at her. "Is that what he used to do to you?"

Until that point, my battle to keep sexual jealousy at bay had been largely successful. Now Caro had presented me with a lurid image that would haunt me for the rest of my life. She saw my face and realized what she'd said. "I'm sorry."

"I should have killed him, too," I said between clenched teeth. "I had the chance. I could have blown his head off."

Caro defused my futile rage by singing to me. It was an old David Bowie song about filling your heart with love and not worrying about what happened in the past. I looked at her with her colorless hair and pale eyes. The girl that I'd dated in school had grown into a screen goddess. And I threw my arms around her so violently I almost broke her back.

We walked back, arm in arm. I had never felt as close to anyone before. Maybe it was the same for Caro. I didn't ask in case she contradicted me.

Caro told me about the self-help book she'd been reading. It was called *Happiness in Seven Days*.

"That must be one of the world's worst titles," I said.

"What are the others?"

I shrugged. "Who cares?"

Caro laughed delightedly. "I don't believe it. You had the chance to make a list and you turned it down. That's a very good sign, Mark. According to my book, it means you're feeling happier in the present. People who make lists are clinging to the past, just like people who collect things."

"I'm not going to give up rare books."

"But I notice you haven't bought a book since your shop burned down."

"There's no hurry."

She told me about this awful crap she was reading. "Each chapter takes you through a different day. Day one is about forgiving yourself. Day two is about forgiving other people."

"Forgiving them for what?" I said.

"Being morons," said Caro.

When we'd stopped laughing, she added, "But the very fact that we find that so funny shows where you and I have gone wrong. We go about expecting people to be lousy, so we're on the lookout for their worst faults. This book says you can transform your luck by changing your attitude to others."

"But hang on," I said. "Our luck changed when your dad died. We didn't change our attitude to him. I didn't like him, and you hated the bugger."

"Okay," she said. "But what about when you went out for a drive with Jesus? That's a better example. You did a mad thing. You went out in a car with a notorious psycho. You gave him a chance to prove he wasn't all bad. And what was your reward? You got a discount. A fifty percent discount. From a *loan shark*."

"And then I was nice to his brother," I said. "And what was my reward? His brother blew up, and now Bad Jesus is going to kill us."

"Maybe we can stop that from happening."

"How?"

"By being nice."

"Bollocks! What about all those Christian martyrs who were hung and crushed and burned? What about that poor woman who had her tits cut off? Being nice didn't do her much good, did it?"

"You don't understand," said Caro. "If we really try to become better people, we can protect ourselves from harm. According to Cassandra Maitland, positive thoughts shield us from negative events."

"Who's Cassandra Maitland?"

"She wrote *Happiness in Seven Days*."

I groaned. Was the world's most cynical woman changing into the most gullible?

"One day," said Caro, "Cassandra shuffled her tarot cards and asked them a question. The question was 'What does God want from me?' The answer was the nine of cups. Also known as 'Happiness.' What do you think of that? What if all God wants is for human beings to be happy? Not just happy. What if his dearest wish is for all his creatures to be *ecstatic?*"

I laughed. "He must be very disappointed."

A jogger passed us, gray and ill-looking in a baggy tracksuit with a baseball cap pulled low over his eyes. He wasn't really jogging. He was skipping lopsidedly. The man looked as if he didn't have long to live, so God knows why he was wasting his time jogging. I mean, it wasn't exactly going to keep him fit. Instead of mocking him, we both directed waves of love at him. "Be ecstatic!" I commanded, addressing his retreating form.

The jogger glanced back at us and scowled.

"He probably thought you called him a spastic," said Caro.

* * *

WHILE WE were sipping tea in the kitchen, Caro demonstrated a skill I didn't know she possessed. She laid the Kimber handgun on the table and showed me how to strip, clean, and lubricate it. She did this expertly, using a bottle of solvent, oil, a rod, a dry rag, and some cotton buds. I was amazed. Caro had her own ready-prepared gun maintenance kit. "I had to do this for Warren," she said. "He was the kind of jerk who never looked after anything. But it's foolish to neglect a firearm. Respect a gun and it can save your life."

"I'm impressed."

"Don't be," she said. "This doesn't take much intelligence. I mean, how could it? Guns are mainly used by criminals, soldiers, and cops."

She lightly applied oil to the Kimber's moving parts, taking special care to grease the point where the connector meets the trigger bar. "This is the tricky bit," she commented. "Too much oil can make the gun fail just as surely as too little."

She reassembled the gun, slotting in a fresh clip that I didn't know we had but was very happy to see. Then she pointed it at the fridge and mimed a shot. "Done," she said, beaming at me.

"Caro," I said, "would you mind telling me what you've just done has got to do with transforming your attitude to others?"

She checked that the safety catches were on. "Hoping for the best from people doesn't mean you shouldn't be prepared for the worst."

There was a knock at the front door. We answered it together. It was a dumpy middle-aged woman with long, straggly brown hair. She was wearing an ungainly sweater and nasty brown slacks. Her plain, disapproving face promised few liberal sympathies. "Oh, hello," she said. "You must be the new people."

"Yes," said Caro and laughed.

"I'm Janet Mather," the visitor said, and shook our hands. Her hand was cold, dry to the point of crustiness. "I'm not being funny, but I was wondering if you could do something about your front garden?"

When people say they're not being funny, they always fucking are.

"I beg your pardon?" I said.

For the first time, I noticed that the grass of the front lawn had reached jungle height and was choked by weeds of every conceivable description, some of which appeared to be triffids.

"The house next door to you isn't occupied," said Janet Mather. She tried to smile, but it looked more as if a nasty wound had opened between her nose and chin. "Mr. Cragg, who lives next-door-but-one, keeps next-door's garden tidy as well as his own. But we can hardly expect him to do yours as well." We followed her to the front gate so that she could show us what a sterling job Mr. Cragg had done. Then she waved her arm at the wild undergrowth that started at our hedge. "So I was hoping you might tidy it up."

"Why?" I said.

She recoiled slightly.

"Well, maybe it seems like a little quirk of ours, but we members of the village hall committee take quite a pride in our hall. In 1999, we came second in the best-kept village hall competition for England and Wales. Even a piece of litter in the parking lot can create a bad impression. So we like the square to look as neat as possible for anyone who visits."

She nodded at our front door with its cracked and blistered paintwork. "I'm not asking you to decorate the house, although goodness knows it needs it. But if you could trim the grass and cut back the hedge a little, we'd all be very grateful. Or we could arrange for someone else to do it?"

I was about to explain that the terms of our lease stipulated that we leave the property in the condition that we found it, and that really what our garden looked like was none of her fat-arsed business, when my beautiful wife answered for me. "Yes, we'll do that," said Caro brightly. "It could do with a tidy-up."

I looked at Caro, waiting in vain for the lethal put-down. Caro smiled at me. It was the kind of smile you get from a devout Christian when you admit that you sometimes hum the odd hymn.

"Well, that's a weight off my mind," said Mrs. Mather, already walking away. "I would be very much obliged to you." She stopped to survey our mud-spattered car. "I don't know whether you're interested, but Dale, my son, washes cars. He's very reasonable."

"Send him along," said Caro sweetly. "I like reasonable people."

Mather gave us a smile worthy of a medieval torturer.

"Oh, by the way," said Caro, "I'm Caro. And this is Mark."

Mrs. Mather nodded curtly, as if to say "whatever," and walked over to her car. I noticed that she leaned forward as she walked as if the weight of her huge unshapely buttocks were tipping her forward. I turned to Caro, unable to digest what I'd witnessed.

"Ugh," I said.

"Ugh what?"

"That," I said, "is one horrible reactionary bitch."

"We don't know that," said Caro.

"Yes, we do. You heard what she said. You should have told her to fuck off."

"I would have done, once. But that was the old Caro. The new Caro gives people the benefit of the doubt. Just because the woman has an unfortunate manner doesn't mean she hasn't got a point. The garden *does* need a bit of work. Let's buy some gardening tools. We'll need them anyway, for when we buy a house of our own."

"I'm not going to fix the garden because that cow says so. She only mentioned her car-washing son because she didn't want our muddy car parked near her marvelous village hall."

"You may be right. Probably are. But all I'd say to you is, you don't seem to be trying very hard. I'm trying to be nice here. You could at least join in."

* * *

IN THE morning, as I was coming down for breakfast, Janet Mather's son knocked on our door. I'd only just got out of bed. The boy, Dale, was about fifteen. He was carrying a hose, a car vac, sponges, and leathers. I was discussing terms with him when Caro appeared behind me. She was dressed only in a T-shirt and panties. Dale was visibly embarrassed, but that didn't prevent him from staring down at the soft mound of Caro's crotch. Possibly inspired by the sight, Dale began to sponge down the Audi as if it were a big-breasted woman in the bath.

Later that morning, we received a phone call from James, our estate agent. James, whom I'd met in Richmond, was one of those spoiled, empty-faced young men who are only interested in money. James informed us that someone had offered six million, four hundred thousand for Gordon's house. "That's no good," said Caro. "We asked for six and a half million, and that's what we want."

Ten minutes later the estate agent rang back. The buyers had raised their offer by another fifty thousand. I would have accepted this, but Caro was having none of it. "If they can afford what they're already offering," she said, "they can afford the extra fifty thousand."

Half an hour later, the phone rang again. We'd got our six and a half. Caro hugged and kissed me. "See? It's karma. This has happened because we're being nice."

"Nice?" I said, laughing. "There was nothing nice about the way you held out for that money."

"Being nice," she said, taking a bottle of Bollinger RD out of the fridge, "does not involve letting other people trample all over you."

It was eleven-fifteen on a Monday morning. We were loaded and we were drinking icy, expensive champagne. Caro slipped a CD into the stereo and we danced around the kitchen, cheek to cheek, listening to "Way Too Black" by Bleep and Booster.

Let's not forget I was upset
And that is why I blacked your eye
You got me back and threw a knife
That missed me and impaled my wife
It served her right
She was too white
But your attack was way too black.

When we'd had two glasses of champagne each, Caro guided my right hand down her trousers. We undressed each other, and my tongue explored the area of outstanding natural beauty between her legs. We had a half-dressed leisurely fuck on the kitchen floor, and then Caro started shrieking. I felt pleased with myself, convinced that I was a thrilling lover and she was crying out in carnal bliss. Then I lifted my head and saw what was really exciting Caro. There was a mouse under the kitchen table.

*   *   *

We phoned a company called Pestkill, who sent a man around to search the house. His name was Ron. Ron didn't inspire confidence. He was disheveled and obese and he reeked of ancient sweat, so that being in close proximity to him was only marginally less distasteful than being infested by rodents.

"What did it look like?" he asked us.

Small with brown fur and little shifty eyes.

"Sounds like a field mouse," said Ron. "They come in from the fields in the winter. What they're mainly looking for is food and warmth."

Ron found mouse shit on the floorboards of the airing cupboard. "Looks like at least two mice to have made that many droppings. We could leave out poison, but if they die under the floorboards or behind a cupboard somewhere, then you've got the smell to contend with. So I'd recommend traps. Which do you want? Lethal or humane?"

"Humane," I said.

"Lethal," said Caro.

Ron showed us a lethal trap. Resembling mousetraps from Tom and Jerry cartoons, it was armed with a nail, designed to impale the mouse in case the trap didn't kill it instantly. The humane trap was like a little house with windows, only cruel if you forgot about it and went on vacation, leaving the captive mouse to starve to death.

"The idea behind the humane traps is that you take them out into the country somewhere and let the mouse go. But you have to drive at least twenty miles or they'll run straight back home again."

Caro was appalled. "You mean they *know where we live?*"

Ron chuckled.

"That's okay," I said. "I'll drive the mice wherever they want to go. I'll be their personal chauffeur."

Caro couldn't believe it. "They're vermin, Mark. I say we execute the little fuckers."

I said that was fine as long as she was the one who disposed of the cute little corpses with blood oozing from their noses and their heads hanging off.

Sullenly, Caro gave in. But when the traps were laid and Ron had left, I refilled our champagne glasses and turned to see my bloodthirsty bride staring at me. She didn't say a word, but in her pale eyes I saw the first glimmer of doubt.

*   *   *

THAT EVENING I went out alone to the nearest pub, the Jolly Sailor. I ordered a pint of bitter and was about to pay for it when the man standing beside me told the barmaid to add it to his tab.

I turned to thank the stranger. He introduced himself as Ricky Cragg, the man who lived next-door-but-one, he of the neatly manicured lawns. Ricky looked to be in his sixties, a nice old toff with slicked-back nicotine-yellow hair and a thin, spivvish mustache.

"I know you," he said genially. "You're the layabout who lives next-door-but-one. The chap with the bloody gorgeous wife. God, I do love a blonde. Wish she'd grow her hair, though. Wouldn't fancy making love to a skinhead. Already been through that with my ex-wife. How come neither of you work for a living?"

I told him we didn't have to.

"Oh, well done," he said. "Good luck to you, I say. I tried to marry a rich woman but ended up falling in love with a pauper. Now she's left me and I'm stuck in this godforsaken hole."

It was only eight o'clock, but Ricky's breath was already flammable. I realized that he was probably the merry drunk I'd heard staggering home the other night.

"You don't like it here?" I asked him.

"Good heavens, no."

"How long have you lived here?"

"Almost forty years. It was the wife's idea. She thought it'd be good for the children, you see. Growing up by the sea, fresh air and whatnot. Didn't matter to me. I was away most of the time. RAF, you see. Now I'm stranded."

"You could always sell up and move away."

"Yes, but where to?" he said, wrinkling up his nose. "At least people know me here and I know them. And to be brutally honest, I don't think I could face the strain of being uprooted at my age. They say moving house is one of the great traumas of life, don't they? Right up there with bereavement, divorce, and losing a twenty-quid note."

Warming to the old airman, I drank his health and asked him what he thought of Janet Mather.

Ricky winced as if he'd tasted something nasty. "Can't stomach her," he confided. "Bloody awful woman."

"But I thought you tidied the gardens in the square for her?"

"Is that what *she* told you? I garden because I like gardening. Not because of any fondness I have for the Mathers." He gave a convincing shudder. "Have you met Dale yet?"

"Briefly. He washed our car for us."

"Notice anything unusual about his hands?"

"No."

"The next time you see him, take a look at his right hand. It's a mass of scar tissue. Want to know how he got it?"

"I'm not sure," I admitted. I had a feeling an unpleasant anecdote was on its way.

"The boy isn't Mather's real son. I doubt she and the supremely charismatic Philip have ever had sex. They may have tried, but it'd take a very sick man indeed to be aroused by the sight of Janet Mather in the nude."

I grinned. "You know that for a fact, do you?"

"Call it an educated guess. Anyway, Dale was the Mathers' nephew. His parents died in a crash, so when he was about eight years old, he came here to live with an uncle and aunt he barely knew. The boy was disturbed, and who can blame him? Anyway, one morning he came into school with his hand all bandaged.

Naturally, his teacher wanted to know what had happened. The boy told her that Janet Mather had branded him. Well, phone calls were made. Social services were called in. It turned out young Dale was telling the truth. Because the lad was so screwed up and didn't want to be living with the bloody Mathers, he got into the habit of playing with fire. Taking live coals out of the fireplace with a pair of tongs and dropping 'em on the carpet to see what happened.

"Well, old Janet caught him at it. And she decided he needed a lesson in how dangerous fire can be. So she grabbed the boy's wrist, thrust his hand into the fire, and held it there."

"Fucking hell!" I said.

"My sentiments exactly. Anyway, the authorities investigated the matter, and nothing was done. You know what useless buggers these social workers are. No charges were brought against Mather. The bloody woman got off scot-free. A few months after the event, my wife got talking to her at some Women's Institute event. Asked her why she'd done it. Know what Mather's answer was?"

I obliged him by shaking my head.

Ricky lit a cigarette. I saw that his fingers were stained brown with nicotine. "She said, 'I couldn't think what else to do.' Now, there's imagination for you. An eight-year-old kid has lost his entire family, he's so angry and desperate for attention that he's resorted to pyromania, and all Mather could think of to do for him was burn his hand."

"The woman's a genius."

"Hanging's too good for her," said Ricky.

* * *

WHEN I opened the front door, there was Caro, pointing the Kimber handgun directly at my face. "Fuck," I said. "What're you doing?"

She lowered the weapon. "Where have you been?" she demanded. She was almost crying. "It's midnight. Where the hell have you been till this time?"

I told her. "What's the big deal?"

"I've been hearing noises."

She'd heard someone try the back door handle. Then she thought she saw something moving in the back garden. When she phoned my mobile, she found it was turned off. Unwilling to phone the police, she had resorted to sitting on the stairs, holding the gun.

"And you haven't taken anything?" I said.

"What do you mean?"

"I don't know. A pill or anything."

"You mean am I hallucinating?"

"Even weed can make you a bit paranoid."

"We're out of weed, remember. I'm clean, Mark. And I'm telling you, there was someone out there."

I took the gun and a flashlight and went out into the back garden. There was nobody there. "Look," I said. "Nothing."

"There's no one there now," she said impatiently. "There was definitely someone there before."

We went to bed, and I placed the gun on the bedside table. When the light was out, I made a clumsy attempt to seduce her. Caro took my hand off her breast and gave it back to me. "I'm scared," she said.

"What of?"

"I don't know," she said. "If anyone tried to kill me, you'd protect me. Wouldn't you?"

"With my life," I promised.

* * *

IN THE morning, we found a mouse imprisoned in one of our humane traps. Now we had to drive twenty miles to humanely release it into the wild. We stopped at a lonely spot on the coast, released the gate on the trap, and watched the little bastard scamper off toward the sand dunes.

"You know, you were right," commented Caro. "It's better to live and let live."

On the way back, Caro saw a sign for a garden center and turned off.

"There's no need to do any gardening," I said.

"What're you talking about? I told Mrs. Mather we would."

"We're not going to do anything to oblige Mrs. Mather. Not ever." With a certain sadistic glee, I told Caro about the hand-burning incident.

I could see that Caro was outraged, but she pretended not to be. "So? She did something bad and stupid. Who are you to judge anyone? You pushed somebody under a tube train."

"You want to play friendly neighbors with Vlad the Impaler? Go ahead."

"I just want the garden to look nice. I'm doing it for us, not for Mather."

At the garden center we bought a spade, a rake, a hoe, some shears, and some seeds. I couldn't believe how expensive this stuff was, but Caro said it was an investment.

"No, it's not," I argued. "An investment gathers value with the passing of time. Classic cars and rare books, they're investments. A garden rake just gets more and more worn out until its head breaks off."

Driving back, our journey was delayed by a line of funeral cars traveling at about fifteen miles an hour. Caro refused to drive past the cortege, having read somewhere that it was unlucky to overtake a corpse. We crawled through a village called Bloxham, drawing to a complete halt outside its little church. Caro waited until the flower-topped coffin had been carried into the church-yard before driving on.

* * *

IN A sudden burst of activity, Caro went out to test her new spade on the garden, digging away at the weeds like any proud householder. I made her some hot chocolate and took it out to her. While we were chatting, me leaning against the car, Caro leaning on the gate, Mrs. Mather came out of the village hall and walked over to us.

"Look," said Caro, pointing at two square feet of freshly dug soil. "I've started."

"Very good." Mather nodded and frowned. "But, you see, that's no use. You need to remove the weeds."

"Which are the weeds?"

"These," said Mather, pointing at some green things with the toe of her shoe. "All you've done so far is move the soil about. If you don't uproot the weeds, the garden will be in as bad a state as before."

"Oh," said Caro. "Thanks."

"I'll be back later to see how you're getting on," said Mather, then walked away.

"The cheeky fucking bitch," I said.

"I'm sure she means well," said Caro unconvincingly.

I lit a fire in the back room and lazed in an armchair, reading *Happiness in Seven Days* by that best-selling simpleton Cassandra Maitland. The last page of the book made me laugh out loud, and to that extent I suppose it could be said to have induced a small measure of happiness.

We tend to think of happiness as a state brought about by a series of random events. For example, I may feel happy if I like my job, if I have enough money, if I'm happy with my appearance, and I'm in a good relationship. What I'm failing to realize is that I can have none of these things and still be happy and inwardly fulfilled. Real happiness comes from within and is not determined by outside events. *A person who is impoverished or solitary or even terminally ill can experience great happiness. Conversely, we can all think of famous and successful people who never appear to have found contentment.*

To be happy, you only have to decide to be so. Can it really be that simple, I hear you ask? Yes, absolutely! Once you accept that you are an eternal and unique spirit, and that feeling love for others is the ultimate good, all the joy that God has been storing away for you shall be yours. All you have to do is ask.

No sooner had I asked God for all the joy he'd been storing away for me then the door opened and a large belly walked in, closely followed by Detective Constable Flett. Then came Caro, looking strained and unhappy, with Detective Sergeant Bromley behind her. Bromley wore his habitual irritating smile. Uninvited, Bromley and Flett settled themselves on the sofa. Caro hovered by the door, and I got up to join her.

"It was very naughty of you to come away without telling us," said Bromley. "Very naughty indeed."

"What do you want?" I said.

"Well, that's up to you," said Flett, and then he laughed. It was a harsh, unpleasant little laugh.

"It's like this," said Bromley. "We don't have any proof yet, but we've been doing some research. It seems you were telling the truth about your inheritance." He nodded at Caro. "Her father's sudden death seems to have worked out very well for you both."

"So what?" said Caro.

"Then we've got the death of Warren Jeavons," said Flett. "Pushed under a train by an unknown assailant. Now, unfortunately, the CCTV cameras at Hammersmith were down at the time of the attack. All we have is a witness who was so traumatized by the incident that she subsequently suffered a nervous breakdown. Which would, of course, make it easy for any counsel to discredit her testimony. But we have recently noted a similarity between the likeness she helped our artist to create and a certain person sitting in this room."

Caro started to swear. Bromley hushed her with a wave of his hand. "Now, we don't give a fuck about Warren or Peter Callaghan or even your dear father. But we strongly suspect that you two have been rather busy. Admittedly, most of our evidence is circumstantial. Then again, the majority of convictions are secured on the strength of circumstantial evidence. Wouldn't you say so, George?"

Flett nodded slowly. Then he licked his lips. "We could build a case against you, no problem. Or you could be nice to us. It's up to you."

Caro looked at me, then directed her attention at Flett. "You expect us to give you money?"

"It wouldn't have to be money," said Bromley, laughing amiably. "You could just let us fuck you."

"What?"

"Just a few hours of your time, every now and then," said Flett. "We wouldn't be greedy."

"You want to fuck us?" I said in amazement.

Flett tutted in disgust. "Not you, you clown. *Her.*"

"Get out," said Caro to Flett, cheeks aglow with rage. "You disgusting bastards."

Bromley chuckled. "You needn't look so shocked," he told her. "We know you used to oblige Jesus."

"Just fuck off," I said.

"All she has to do is lie down for us," said Flett. "That's not too much to ask, is it?"

Caro picked up a vase and hurled it in their direction. It shattered on the wall above the sofa. Bromley and Flett thought this was hilarious. They were both laughing as they got up. I caught the reek of alcohol as they walked past me.

"No need to decide now," said Bromley, brushing fluff off his overcoat. "We'll give you a couple of days to think about it."

The two police officers sniggered all the way to their car.

* * *

CARO WENT back to the garden. It was getting dark. A wind was stirring, a harsh wind that tasted of the sea. The lights of the village hall glowed yellow behind us as Caro angrily assaulted the earth with her new spade. For some reason she wasn't speaking to me.

"I suppose you think I should have shot them," I said.

She just carried on digging, her face paler than the moon.

"It's good news," I said. "They can't really prosecute us now, not after what they suggested. They're a pair of piss-takers, Caro. They're just trying it on. They're not going to do anything."

Silence.

"I still don't know why you're mad at me."

"No? How did they know, Mark? About me and Jesus?"

"I've no idea."

"I suppose you fucking told them."

"No. I kept to our bargain. I told them exactly what we agreed, nothing more. You untrusting cow. Anyway, if it comes to that, how did they find us here?"

An insistent bleeping sound was coming from the village hall. I turned to see Janet Mather switching off the lights and locking the building. She walked over to us, jangling her keys. It was not a good moment.

"My word, still at it?" barked Mather, grinning like a hangman. "You can come round and dig my garden if you're that keen."

Caro continued to dig without looking up.

"No," said Mather, "you're doing a good job, my dear. And on behalf of the village hall committee, I'd like to thank you."

Mather didn't seem to notice the hate radiating from Caro's back.

"Of course," she continued, surveying the house critically, "if you really want to improve the house, you could try cleaning the windows."

"Oh, *fuck off!*" snapped Caro.

Mather stepped back in astonishment. It was the kind of out-moded theatrical gesture that is now only seen in old British films like *Brief Encounter.* "I beg your pardon?" she said.

Caro turned on her. "What business is it of yours whether our windows are clean? Or whether the garden looks like shit or not? None."

"I am only trying to help," said Mather.

"You're a horrible, interfering cow. All you care about is whether the houses in the square live up to your village hall. Which, incidentally, looks like a low-grade public toilet. So fuck off!"

"You are a very rude and ignorant young woman," said Mather.

And as she turned to walk away, Caro stepped forward, swung back the spade, and slammed the flat of the blade onto Janet Mather's skull.

It was a tremendous blow. The clang of metal against bone resounded through the square. Mather's eyes rolled and her knees gave way. Then she fell facedown on the gravel before launching into an unsightly convulsion, shaking and twitching as if she'd been electrocuted. At last she lay still.

Caro burst into spontaneous, uncontrolled laughter. So did I. All she had done, after all, was what I would have done myself had I possessed the courage (and the spade).

Three seconds of silence followed. I waited for the blood to well out from the wiry lavatory-brush hair. But no blood came. Encouraged by her efforts, Caro stepped forward to strike Mrs. Mather again.

In that instant, I breathed in and seemed to smell piss, sweat, and bleach. I knew it was the smell of prison, a place I had no desire to visit. I held out my forearm to block Caro's follow-through but, with my usual lack of coordination, fully absorbed the impact rather than rotating my arm to deflect it. "Ow, fuck, shit! You stupid bitch."

"Sorry."

Now it wasn't funny anymore.

I gripped Mather's wrist, feeling for a pulse. "Why? Why did you have to do that?" I asked Caro.

Caro held her hand to her mouth and started giggling. "I couldn't think what else to do," she said.

"What?"

"That's what Mather said, isn't it? When she burned Dale? 'I didn't know what else to do.' That's what we should tell the police when they ask why we killed her," she said. Caro laughed quietly and then started sobbing.

I knelt down to look at the stricken woman's face. The eyes were wide open, but they saw nothing. The tiniest filigree thread of blood was trickling out of her left ear. Janet Mather had gone to the great village hall in the sky.

CHAPTER 11

ABOUT A CORPSE

WE DRAGGED the body into the hall and locked the door. Then we sat in the kitchen for a long time, drinking strong tea, searching for a way out.

"I was upset," said Caro helplessly. Her eyes were ringed with shadow, her face bloodless. "I didn't mean to kill her."

"Oh, that's all right, then," I said. "You mad cow."

"You've got no room to criticize me," snapped Caro. "You're the real murderer, not me. It's still 2–1 to you."

She was quite wrong, of course. It was 1–0 to Caro. I was finding my situation confusing. Having lied and dissembled to convince Caro how dangerous I was, in the end it turned out to be she who took the first life. The temptation to tell her the truth was stronger now than it had ever been, yet I feared that Caro would crumble if she knew I was not a killer. She wanted, actually *needed* me to be bad. A bad motherfucker could protect her from justice. What use could a star-crossed bibliophile be?

"Okay," I said. "She was visiting the village hall. She wasn't planning to drop in on us. She only spoke to us because we were in the garden. So if someone asks us, we never saw her. Plus we hardly knew her. What possible motive would we have for killing her? We have not seen her. Caro, listen to me. We haven't seen her. It's vital that we don't contradict each other. Do you understand?"

"But they'll see her lying in the hall," said Caro dazedly.

"No." Her state of mind was worrying me. I reached over the table and took her hand. "I'm going to move the body, Caro. I'm going to hide it."

"I'll help you," said Caro.

"No," I said. "I don't expect that."

"But I want to," she said. "I helped to kill her. She really was a vile woman. Wasn't she?" The question contained a note of desperation.

"She was a fucking nuisance," I admitted. "She's even more of a nuisance now."

"A woman who deliberately burns a child doesn't deserve to live, does she?"

"Well, I don't know about that," I said. "But she certainly deserved a bloody good kicking."

"Yeah," said Caro dreamily. "She got off lightly, really. Didn't she? She should have been burned alive with her husband's bollocks crammed down her throat. I'd have liked to have seen that."

I looked at her skeptically. "Would you really?"

She thought about it for a few seconds. "No. But I'd have liked to have seen her run over by a tractor."

I excused myself, feeling that the conversation was taking a distinctly bizarre turn.

Trying not to look at the corpse, I took the spade from the hall and went upstairs. All I could think about now was DNA. What if tiny traces of Mather's blood or skin still clung to the spade that had killed her? I took the spade into the bathroom and half-filled the bath with hot water. Then I scrubbed both sides of the blade with bleach. Sure enough, a single frizzy brown hair floated to the surface of the water. I scooped up the hair in a piece of tissue and flushed it down the lavatory.

Next, I held the blade up to the light and examined it minutely for marks that might correspond to the indentation in Mather's skull. There were none. Relief surged through me. Then I was violently, effortlessly sick.

When I went downstairs, I was hit by an unsavory smell, like brussels sprouts and overboiled cabbage. Then I noticed that the body was lying next to a hot radiator. I straddled the corpse, grabbed it under the arms, and shunted it along the floor. I looked up to see Caro standing in the kitchen doorway.

"She isn't worth going to prison for," I said.

"Who?" said Caro vaguely.

"What do you mean 'who'? Her! This woman you just killed."

I noticed that the shape of Mrs. Mather's head had altered. Her forehead appeared to have inflated, and the back of her cranium had been completely flattened. "Look at that," I said. "Look how hard you hit her."

"I don't feel very well," said Caro.

* * *

CARO RAN upstairs to the bathroom. I turned off all the lights and sat in the shadows of the front room, sipping brandy and looking out on the square. It was late and the heating had gone off, but I was sweating like a sunbather at noon. The enormity of what had occurred staggered me. I didn't want to believe that Janet Mather was lying in the hall, but every time I stepped out of the door, there she was.

The wind had grown stronger. It was playing a tune in the empty milk bottles outside. Every thirty seconds or so, the front door shuddered and a blast of icy air rattled the letterbox and washed through the hall.

Sometime after midnight, I heard unsteady footsteps on the gravel. Someone coughed. It was an old man's cough, so I guessed it was Ricky, reeling home from the pub. Silence reigned for a few moments, as if he were looking toward our house and listening. Then I heard his front door slam.

Shortly after one, headlights washed over the village hall. The Mathers' Volvo Estate sped through the parking lot and skidded to a halt. Philip Mather got out of the car, moving with some urgency, hunching forward as he hurried to the village hall and unlocked the doors.

Soon he was inside and the lights flashed on, one by one. I could picture him looking for Janet behind the stage, in the lavatories, in the kitchen, and behind the stacked chairs, unaware that all the time she was lying in our hallway, growing steadily colder and colder.

After about three minutes, the building went dark. Only the security light in the lobby remained on when Mather reappeared at the entrance. He locked the hall, walked over to the Volvo, and removed something from the trunk. He was holding a powerful flashlight, which he now shone around the square. Mather's attention was caught by a white van in the corner. Wobbling unhealthily, he aimed his beam through each of the van's windows in turn.

Then he moved off toward the hall again and vanished behind it. Now he would be searching through the bins, shining his flashlight at the coastal path, unlocking the shed where the lawn mower was kept. When that failed, I knew he would be peering down the cliff face, hoping not to see his wife lying on the concrete far below.

After another short interval, the flashlight glinted on the hood of Caro's BMW. Instinctively, I got out of my chair and sank to the floor. No sooner had I moved than a bright arc of light appeared on the wall behind me. In his zeal, Mr. Mather had shone the flashlight directly through our living room window. Two seconds passed and the light moved on. I felt a sudden stab of fear and, on my hands and knees, crawled out through the doorway into the hall.

If Mather was impertinent enough to shine a light through the window of a house, what was to stop him from aiming the flashlight through the letterbox to see his wife's body lying in the hall? My fears were well grounded. I was approaching the front door when I heard the gate creak and light flooded through the opaque oval of glass set high in the front door. I reached for the letterbox and held it shut with both hands, sensing Mather's presence on the other side of the door. I heard a sniff and the faint scuff of a heel on concrete.

For a long time, there was no other sound. I was afraid to swallow, convinced that Mather was still out there, listening intently for the merest sound. Then the Volvo's engine rumbled into life, and I heard the tires grinding gravel as the big car turned and headed out of the square.

Thirty minutes elapsed before I found the courage to stand up and peer through the glass in the door. There was no one out there. I unlocked the front door and walked to the end of the short path. All was quiet. No light shone in the windows of Ricky's house. I suddenly felt certain that this was the time, that I must act now or face evil consequences.

I turned on the landing light and went upstairs. In the airing cupboard, there were several old, dusty blankets. I removed two of them. After turning off the light, I took one out to the car and lined the trunk with it. I wrapped the other round the body and used cord to bind it tightly. I was grateful for the whine of the wind as I dragged the bundle out into the dark. It was so heavy that all I could do was grip the end and heave it forward, six inches at a time.

When the corpse was clear of the front doorstep, I closed the door behind me. I was about to open the gate when I heard a car approaching. I crouched down and peered through the gaps in the wooden gate. There was now a police patrol car outside the village hall. A lone officer got out of the car and, leaning against the hood, spoke into his radio.

Here's how it was. There was a police officer two hundred yards away and I was hiding behind a gate with the newly slaughtered body of the woman he was searching for. I had never been in such an incriminating position in my life.

Had it not been such an unpleasant night, the police officer might have been a little more conscientious. As it was, I doubt he was thinking of anything but the warm bed awaiting him at the end of his shift. Without conviction, he shone his flashlight through the windows of the village hall, walked halfway round it, and strolled back to the car. Then he leaned against the hood for a few seconds while he lit an illicit cigarette. I saw the little pinprick of light glow and fade as he drew the first blast into his lungs.

A great gust of wind raced across the square. Somewhere behind me, a shed door clattered and banged. An abandoned Coke can rattled belligerently in the village hall parking lot. That was enough for the police officer, who got back into his car to finish his cigarette.

Eventually, the car rolled forward, executed a loop, and headed slowly out of the square. When its headlights hit the gate in front of me, I flung my head earthward.

As soon as the sound of the engine had died, I opened the gate. It immediately swung shut. I found a brickbat in the front garden and used it to wedge the gate open, then heaved the body through. So intense was my guilt that I felt I was being watched and had to keep stopping to scan the dark windows of the neighboring houses. I could see no one, but my sense of public shame persisted. I had the peculiar feeling that the spirits of my forebears were looking down at me, shaking their heads in sorrow and disbelief.

The thought of my ancestors brought forth a childhood memory of my aunt Edna defending me against my mother's suspicions when my kid brother ratted on me for kicking him. *Not Mark,* she had insisted. *Mark would never do a thing like that.* My aunt's loyalty brought tears to my eyes then and did so now.

Sniffling, I unlocked the trunk of the Audi. The automatic light flashed on, unhelpfully providing illumination for anyone who wanted a grandstand view of a man in his early twenties trying to lift a dead woman into a car.

I flattered myself that I was strong, but that was before I tried to lift one hundred and fifty pounds of dead meat off the ground. The effort almost gave me a hernia, and still I got nowhere. The body on the ground made an eerie hissing noise as air escaped from it. It was as if Janet Mather were booing me from beyond the grave.

Someone tapped me on the back. Bucking like a startled cow, I spun round to see Caro standing behind me. When I'd finished swearing, she seized my shoulders and kissed my brow. "I'm feeling better now," she whispered. "I want to help."

*   *   *

TOGETHER, WE lifted Mrs. Mather into the trunk. Then we sat in the car, discussing what to do next. "What about the beach hut?" I said. "We could store her in the beach hut and throw her into the sea, a bit at a time."

"I've got a better idea," said Caro.

She fetched the spade from the house and told me to drive to Bloxham Church.

We parked the car on a dark track along the side of the church and wandered into the cemetery. Even without a flashlight, we could see where the latest arrival had been interred. There was a fresh mound on the north side of the church, made luminous by the pale flowers heaped upon it.

In the churchyard, Caro grabbed me and stuck her tongue down my throat. I wasn't remotely aroused and pushed her away.

"What do we do now?" I said.

"We dig up the grave and throw her on top of the coffin," said Caro. "Then we just fill the grave in again."

"Earlier today, you wouldn't overtake the coffin because you thought it'd look disrespectful. Now you want to dig it up."

"So?"

"Well, as hiding places go, don't you think this is a bit obvious?"

"Who to?"

"The police. Wouldn't a fresh grave be the first place they'd look?"

"You'd think so, wouldn't you?" sneered Caro. "You'd think they'd target drunk drivers by parking outside bars and waiting for the drunks to stagger out to the cars. You'd think they'd automatically issue speeding tickets to everyone who drives in the fast lane. But no. The police are the same people we laughed at at school, Mark. They couldn't pass their exams then, and they can't solve crimes now."

"But if anyone ever opens the grave, they'll find Mrs. Mather in it."

"Yeah. But she'll just be a pile of old bones by then. Even then, why would they link her to us? Unless . . ."

"What?"

"While I was lying down, you didn't fuck the body?"

"What?"

She laughed. "Just checking. Some men find dead women attractive."

"I cannot believe you," I said.

We fetched the spade and a tiny flashlight from the car. Caro shone the light at a makeshift sign that had been placed at the head of the grave in lieu of a headstone. It read ALAN BEEVIS 1963–2004. AT REST.

"Not for much longer," said Caro.

Carefully, working systematically from top to bottom, we removed the floral tributes from the grave and arranged them on an adjacent plot so that when the job was done and the hole refilled, we could return each wreath to its original position.

The digging took longer than I'd expected. The recently excavated earth was soft and yielding, but still the task was backbreaking. Caro, who was meant to be keeping watch, sat with her back against the churchyard wall, smoking. At one point, she offered to help, but then she started giggling and throwing the soil everywhere, so I had to take the spade from her.

There were no houses overlooking the churchyard. My labors were observed by no one. Our only companion was a fat hedgehog who crossed the cemetery, grumbling strangely. My mouth was dry, and I wished we'd thought to bring some bottled water. I got so hot that I took off my jacket and hung it on the branch of a young tree that stood in a corner of the cemetery.

The church clock chimed the quarters. By two-thirty I was bathed in sweat and the hole was a reasonable size. "Let's get her," I said to Caro.

"But I thought graves were meant to be six feet deep."

"Yeah, six feet is the legal depth," I snapped. "But in case you hadn't noticed, what we're doing isn't legal."

"No need to get grouchy."

"No need to get grouchy? You kill someone, I break my back and sweat buckets to hide your dirty work, and all you can do is criticize the size of the hole I've dug?"

All bickering ceased when we returned to the car to fetch Janet Mather. Numbed into silence, Caro and I each took an end and dragged the blanketed corpse through the cemetery gates. I heard a soft chink, like a small coin hitting the ground. I shone the light at the ground but could see nothing. We continued to haul our burden over the grass, brought it to the brink of the grave, and pushed it into the hole with our feet. The wind blew. The trees scraped and sighed.

At that moment it seemed as if there were no light or joy or loveliness anywhere in the world.

Then I started to shovel the dirt in. There was a snigger. I stopped digging and turned to Caro. "What's so funny?" I said.

"Nothing," she said.

"Well, what are you laughing for?"

"I didn't laugh."

We froze, watching and listening for the slightest sign of another presence. A car droned by on the main road, and the trees in the churchyard creaked. The wind played its traditional haunted-house symphony in the telephone wires overhead. Then, as a final insult, it started to rain.

I lay on my back among the rotten leaves while the rain lashed down. Caro patted the mound with the back of the spade and carefully replaced the flowers. As she labored, she passed from airheaded levity into cold determination. The only thing we couldn't do anything about was the thin layer of spilt soil around the grave. When the last resting place of Alan Beevis looked more or less pristine, she shone the light over the ground between the side gate and the grave, ensuring that we hadn't dropped anything.

Then we drove back to Holeness, our wipers set at max to combat the pounding rain.

"It's good that it's pissing it down," said Caro. "The rain'll erase our footprints."

Her coolness astonished me. "Is that all you've got to say?"

"What would you like me to say?"

"Well, you just killed somebody. I don't expect you to break down in remorse. I know you better than that. But you must feel *something*."

"Listen," said Caro. "My feelings for that woman amount to precisely nothing. With her reactionary views, her small-town self-importance, her bride-of-Frankenstein hair, and her despicable fat arse, she represented everything that makes this country second-rate. She should have been killed years ago, when she burned that kid's hand. But guess what? She got away scot-free. People can get seven years in prison for fraud, but that bitch scars a child for life and doesn't even go on trial. So I don't care. Understand? I don't care about Janet Mather. She was a piece of despicable trash. All I care about is that we don't get caught."

"What happened to being nice?"

"It was being nice that caused all this," said Caro. "Let's face it, I'm not a nice person. I'm vengeful and unforgiving. So if I pretend to be nice, all the contempt and spite I want to show has nowhere to go. It's like that poem by William Blake 'I was angry with my foe, I told him not, my wrath did grow.' So when Mather asked me to tidy the garden, I wanted to kill her.

Instead, I backed down. When I found out what she'd done to Dale I wanted to burn her hands, *then* kill her. So when I hit her with the spade, I was letting out all the festering hatred I'd stored up by being nice to her."

"That's all very interesting and highly insightful," I said. "But somehow, I don't think it'd impress a jury."

I could smell Mrs. Mather's ghastly scent on my hands. "Oh, God, Caro," I said. "Tell me something nice. Tell me something that'll make me feel the world isn't one enormous grave."

"I'm pregnant," said Caro.

"It needs to be something true," I said patiently. "Not just something you've made up to please me."

"It is true. I did a test. I'm about nine weeks gone."

"Why didn't you tell me this before?"

"I was waiting for a special occasion."

* * *

BACK IN Prospect Square, I searched in my trouser pocket for my house key but couldn't find it.

"We've got to go back," I said. "I must have dropped it in the graveyard."

"We didn't drop anything," she said. "You probably left it in the house somewhere."

We used Caro's key to open the door and went inside. The bad smell still lingered in the hall, as if Mather's ghost were invisibly glowering at us. We stuffed our muddy clothes into the washing machine and cleaned the dirt off the spade and our shoes. By the time we had showered it was after five.

When we went to bed, Caro crawled under the duvet and started playing with me. I wasn't in the mood, but she was so skilled and insistent that before long I was hard. Then she climbed aboard and screwed me. She took ages, arching her back to take me deeper inside. And as she came, shuddering with pleasure, she murmured, "We killed her, Mark. We killed the fucking bitch."

After that, I didn't feel much like sleeping. I left Caro alone and went out to clean the car.

* * *

IT WAS noon before Caro surfaced, awakened by shrieks of laughter. Out in the square, a teenaged boy was waving an air pistol at two teenaged girls. As we watched, the boy fired at one of the girls. He missed, and the shot broke the window in the door of the village hall.

"You were right about this place," said Caro, watching the spectacle disinterestedly. "It stinks. Let's go somewhere else."

"We can't," I pointed out. "If we just up and leave, it's going to look like we're running away. We might as well place an ad in the post office window. *Murderers of Janet Mather seek life imprisonment.*"

* * *

I WALKED to the village bank to withdraw some cash. As I was turning away from the ATM, I saw Philip Mather and Dale. They were on the other side of the road, deep in conversation with a middle-aged couple. I could tell by their earnest expressions that the topic under discussion was Janet. Philip looked exactly like a man who hasn't slept for thirty-six hours because his wife has gone missing. Dale looked almost as bad. I realized, with a twinge of sadness, that the boy had probably loved the woman who branded him.

I felt sorry for Dale. But like Caro, my only feeling about Janet

Mather was a quiet sense of righteousness, as if she had been an enemy soldier that we had been forced to shoot in self-defense.

Once I got home, I intended to look up the word "sociopath" in the dictionary to see if I qualified. But when I walked into the kitchen, I received a severe jolt. Caro was having tea with a shy young policewoman. The shock made my heart flutter as if I'd stepped under an icy shower.

There was no immediate cause for despair. The WPC and her colleagues were making house-to-house calls in the hope of finding someone spattered with blood to help them with their inquiries. She asked us how we'd spent the previous night. I noticed an empty champagne bottle by the sink and had an idea.

"We were celebrating," I said.

"Oh, yes?"

"I'm pregnant," explained Caro.

The police officer's face lit up. "Oh, that's lovely. My big sister's expecting. I'm dying to be an auntie."

At that moment, I knew beyond doubt that we had won the WPC over and she didn't suspect us of anything.

Toward the end of the day, Ricky Cragg dropped round to ask if I wanted to go to the pub.

"Not today," I said. "Caro's feeling a bit under the weather."

"Oh. Women's trouble, is it?" he said knowingly. "Rather you than me. I suppose you've heard about Janet Mather?"

I nodded.

His eyes twinkled mischievously. "Hope you didn't do her in and bury her under the floorboards."

"No," I said truthfully. "I didn't do that."

"Pity," said Ricky. "Then I could have danced on her grave."

There was a silence while I wondered what he knew or suspected and how much he could keep to himself.

"Apparently, the police have arrested a local man," said Ricky. He looked away, yawning and scratching the back of his neck as if the news bored him. "As the story goes, this chap once spat at Mrs. Mather when she tried to sell him some raffle tickets. God knows, the man was only doing what we'd all like to have done."

Then he winked at me.

* * *

THAT NIGHT, we kept hearing noises. Creaks and sighs, doors opening and closing. Then there would be silence for a while, and we would doze only to be reawakened by another eerie sound. Finally, we both sat up in bed with the light on, holding each other. Downstairs, the creaks and bangs continued.

I reached for the Kimber on the bedside table. The gun wasn't there.

"Did you move it?" I said.

"No."

"You must have done," I said. "It was right here when we came to bed."

"I swear I didn't touch it."

"It's her ghost," said Caro. "She doesn't know she's dead, so she's walking about downstairs."

"Bollocks," I said. "The woman didn't have a soul, so how could she haunt us?"

Together, we went downstairs to investigate. When we were on the first landing we stopped to listen. All was dark below. We inched down the stairs in the dark, and then the light came on and we saw someone sitting in the hall, back against the wall.

Caro yelled, and I jumped back so suddenly that I bashed into her, causing her to stumble. "Jesus, Mark! She came back!"

It was true. Mrs. Mather had returned from the grave. In two days, she had decomposed considerably. Her face, blackened and distended, resembled an overripe plum with skin about to burst. Her trademark frizzy hair, now caked in mud, sprang up from her skull like a cloud of petrified filth.

"Shit," I said. "Who did this?"

"Mark, what if no one did it?" She was holding the sleeve of her dressing gown over her face because of the pungent stink coming from Mather's corpse. "What if she walked from the cemetery by herself?"

"She didn't." Caro was squeezing my arm so tightly that my hand was going numb. "Someone did this. This is some sick bastard's idea of a joke."

*   *   *

WE SEARCHED the house. There was no sign of forced entry, or of the culprit. "I think I know what must have happened," I told Caro. "I dropped my house keys in the cemetery. They were found by whoever did this."

"Bad Jesus," said Caro. "It's got to be."

"Why would he bother? If he thinks we killed his brother, he's just going to come straight at us, like a rottweiler. He's not going to toy with us. He's going to torture us and kill us."

"What about Bromley and Flett?" said Caro.

"What about them?"

"You've met them. They're sick enough. If they know we've killed Mather, they've got us, Mark. They'll be able to fuck me whenever they like. I won't be able to stand it. I'll kill myself before I let them touch me."

Caro went rigid, trembling so furiously that her teeth chattered. I had to fetch a quilt from upstairs and wrap it round her, holding her firmly until her body relaxed. I left her in the kitchen with the radio on while I covered the less-than-fragrant Mrs. Mather with large plastic garden refuse sacks, dragged her carcass into the back room, and locked the door.

*   *   *

NEITHER OF us wanted to be left alone in the house with a corpse. In the morning we both walked to the shops to pick up some groceries. It was the Thursday before Easter. Easter eggs were on sale in the post office and the local convenience store. In the window of the cake shop, rows of hot cross buns, Easter Bunny cookies, and little iced chicks were proudly displayed. We might have bought some if our appetites had not been affected by the events of the previous night.

In our justifiable paranoia, it semed to us that everyone, from the bank clerk to the strangers in the street, regarded us with unusual interest. "What if they know?" whispered Caro when a telephone engineer shouted down from his pole to wish us a good morning. "What if the whole village knows what we've done?"

Walking back, we passed the smallholding owned by the Mathers. A notice at the end of the drive displayed a bad photocopy of the missing woman's face under the heading MISSING. HAVE YOU SEEN THIS WOMAN?

"Yes," commented Caro bitterly. "And I've fucking well smelled her."

*   *   *

WE WAITED all day until the darkness blew in from the sea. With the coming of night, the waves seemed to grow louder, their distant cry a steady incoherent roar that pursued us from room to room. We had searched everywhere for the gun but failed to find it, so were forced to conclude that the weapon was in the possession of our mysterious taunter. All we could do now was wait for him to show himself.

We sat in the kitchen, lit a fire, and waited. Through the open kitchen door, we had a clear view of the hall and the front door. The downside of this was that the aroma of Mrs. Mather drifted in from beneath the closed door of the back room. She now smelled strong enough to make eating impossible.

We sat by the fire, sipping vodka and ice, eyes on the clock above the door. Not having a gun was a worry, but reason told us that whoever had walked into the bedroom to steal the weapon wanted us alive.

Just before eight, several cars rolled into the parking lot. It was the monthy parish council meeting at the village hall. The cars left just after ten, and then there was only stillness and the reassuring crackle of the fire. Eleven o'clock passed, then midnight. Caro made some strong coffee to help keep us awake. We were both sweating with fear. We didn't know who was coming but sensed they would come soon.

I went upstairs to the bathroom, splashing cold water over my face to ward off the exhaustion that threatened to overwhelm me. As I turned off the landing light and was about to go down, something made me glance up at the staircase that led to the top floor. The stairs were bordered by an old wooden bannister, and through its rails I could see something glowing. It was a human face. A thin white face was peering down at me. Its owner gripped the rails with two white-knuckled hands.

I was so startled that I ran downstairs, virtually hurling myself into the hall. In the kitchen, I took a carving knife from a drawer and waited. Before Caro could ask me what was wrong, the intruder moved down the hall and stood in the kitchen doorway, pointing my own gun at me.

It was not Bad Jesus or the ghost of Mrs. Mather but someone else, someone I recognized. A traveler who had returned to port after a long, desperate voyage of love and self-hatred.

"Danny?" I said.

"Very good," he said. "It's nice to be remembered."

Danny Curran, our old art teacher. The years had been extremely unkind to him, although I daresay he deserved it. The warm, joky poseur who used to spend our art lessons lecturing us about how all truly great music ended in 1967 now looked like a remnant of that era himself. He was as leathery and gaunt as an old junkie. His complexion was dotted with tiny pockmarks as if, having run out of places to inject, he had finally resorted to jabbing the hypodermic into his own face.

"Danny?" said Caro, taking a step toward him. When she saw what her old love had turned into, her eyes softened with dismay. Danny saw the look and nodded.

"Yes," he said, looking at her tenderly. "Hard to believe, isn't it? Am I really that dashing art teacher you once professed to love? I was a bit like Lord Byron in those days. At least I thought I was. He was a cripple, too—as I'm sure you know. Now I'm a fucked-up old man. I lost my wife, my kids, everything I had because of you." He laughed uncontrollably. It was the laughter of despair, impossible to fake. "All because of you, Caro. I still love you, you know. Did you know Caro is Italian for 'dear'? And God almighty, you have cost me dear." He laughed again.

I looked down at the gun, its barrel leveled precisely at the narrow space between Caro and myself.

"If you love me," said Caro slowly, "then why bring back the body? Why do something that you know is going to hurt me?"

"I wanted you to understand," said Danny. "I've seen what you've done. I've been your neighbor, my love. I've been living next door in the house you thought was empty."

"You're going to blackmail us?" said Caro, accidentally breathing in too deeply and almost choking on the smell of death.

"Yes, she does whiff a bit," said Danny. "Let's shut the door. We can chat by the fire. It'll be nice and cozy."

A loaded gun can be very persuasive. I couldn't believe that my art teacher, the man who used to lend me his Leonard Cohen albums and tell me that war was wrong, would actually shoot either of us. But for the time being, we were at his mercy, and there was no point in antagonizing him.

We all sat down at the kitchen table.

"You've got terrible taste in men," commented Danny, sinking into a chair. "Thugs or idiots."

"No prize for guessing which heading you come under," I said.

Danny nodded in agreement. "I saw you two get married. I even saw your reception."

Then I remembered. The old man on the bench, alone and weeping. The bailiff who'd called at Caro's flat. The jogger on the beach. I realized that Danny had been pursuing Caro for five lonely years. As if he knew what I was thinking, he looked at me and said, "She took out a court order against me. Did she mention that?"

I shook my head.

"Yes," he explained. "I'm not supposed to come within a two-mile radius of her. Or was it one mile? I never could remember. It made no difference, darling." He smiled at her with genuine affection. "Look at her. Isn't she just about the most dazzling thing you've ever seen? How does she *do* that? This girl's been up most of the night waiting for a crazed gunman, and look at her.

Big eyes full of light, skin perfect. Can you blame me? Can you honestly fucking blame me?"

"I'll tell you what," I said. "Why don't I make us all a nice cup of tea?"

He nodded. "Yes," he said. "That'd be nice and civilized, wouldn't it? Very English. But don't try anything. I'd love an excuse to put a hole through your ugly fucking face."

"You don't mean that," said Caro.

"Yes, I do." Danny rattled the table and gritted his teeth like a child in a temper. "I hate his fucking guts. I hate anyone who's ever touched you. Why do you think I burned his shop down?"

I felt myself blushing with anger. At that moment I wanted to kill him. "I suppose the e-mails were from you, too?" I said.

But Danny wasn't listening. All his attention was focused on Caro. That cropped blonde head. That mouth to kill for. The rapture on his thin, tired face was explicit and profound. It was as if a humble Italian peasant had come face-to-face with the Virgin Mary.

"You were mine," he told her. From his jacket, he extracted a crumpled scrap of paper, which he slowly unfolded. "Remember this? You bought me a thesaurus for my forty-fifth birthday. This was the letter you put inside it. *Happy birthday, Danny. I will love you forever, your very own Caro. P.S. You are beloved, admired, adored, cherished, darling, dear, dearest, precious, prized, revered, sweet, treasured, worshipped.*"

I turned away to switch on the kettle and heard Caro say, "Yes, and when I wrote those words they were true."

"But you loved me." He sounded genuinely puzzled. "Love doesn't just evaporate, does it? It isn't like an electric light that you can turn off when it suits you. Is it?"

When I turned round, they were holding hands across the

table and Danny was quietly weeping. What made the scene even more surreal was that Danny was still pointing a gun at her. The sick bastard may have burned my shop down and inconvenienced me greatly by digging up Mrs. Mather, but at that moment I found him *deplorable, distressing, grievous, heart-rending, lamentable, miserable, pathetic, piteous, pitiable, sad, woeful, wretched.*

"There are thousands of women in this country alone who could make you happier than I could ever make you," said Caro.

"Oh, you are *so* right," mocked Danny. "I'm such a catch. Women round the world are just queuing up to have relationships with bitter old paupers with spastic legs."

Caro and I both laughed, recognizing a spark of the warm, self-deprecating humor that had once endeared Danny to his pupils, before he was ravaged by defeat and loneliness.

"Why don't you put the gun down, Danny?" I suggested.

The advice was well intentioned, but Danny took exception to it. "Don't you dare tell me what to do, you stinking bollockless ineffectual homosexual bastard of a gym monkey."

"Hey," I said, "you talk just like your e-mails."

This rather ineffectual remark seemed to tip Danny over the edge. As I moved toward the now boiling kettle Danny turned and fired the gun.

The bullet shattered the door of a kitchen cabinet on the wall above my head. Shards of frosted glass rained down around me. The shock waves of the explosion rattled the dirty pans and the cutlery waiting by the sink. I wasn't sure whether Danny was trying to unnerve me or actually hit me. In all the excitement, I forgot to ask.

When Danny squeezed the trigger, Caro almost fell off her chair. "Danny," she said, "don't scare me like that."

"Like what?" he retorted. "Like the way you scared me when you went off with Andy Wallace?"

"What?" I said. The shot was still clamoring in my ears. I thought I must have misheard.

Caro looked at me and kind of shrugged with her eyes.

"Oh, didn't you know?" leered Danny, showing how badly he needed a dentist. "When our relationship ran into difficulties, she sought solace in the arms of your fat friend Wallace. Over the years, she's been a very busy lady."

That was presumably why Wallace hadn't attended our wedding. He couldn't face the pain of seeing his old flame joined to me. He was yet another of the men she had loved and then dumped. How many more of us were there?

"What do you want?" Caro asked Danny.

"Ah," said Danny. "I see you haven't lost your knack of getting straight to the point. I want you, Caro. I want you all to myself. But I'm not likely to get that, am I? So, being a realist, I'm willing to share you."

"What are you talking about?" I said.

"Shut up," ordered Danny again, pointing the gun at me. I complied. He returned his attention to Caro. "I know you can't take away my pain. But you can ease it."

"Why should I?" she said.

"Because if I tell the police about that body out there, you'll both go down for a long, long time."

I poured the tea, which we sipped in silence.

"Danny, could you explain something to me?" said Caro.

"I'll try to," he answered.

"Why did you go to all the trouble of digging the body up again? If you knew what we'd done, why didn't you just tell us?"

Danny blinked in surprise. "Because I didn't think of it." He emitted a shrill laugh. "God, I really must be mad, mustn't I? I must be. It's not a problem, though. Mark can help me rebury her. No one need ever know. Not if you can bring yourself to be good to me."

I watched Caro contemplating the unsavory implications of his words. What exactly did Danny mean by "good"? That Caro could iron his clothes, make him cups of tea, darn his socks, and bake him flapjacks? Somehow, I didn't think so. Judging by the look on her face, nor did she.

"I'll tell you what's going to happen, shall I?" announced Danny. "First of all, I'm going to take a much-needed bath. Then Caro can start showing how sorry she is for ruining my life. As for you, you gutless parasite," he said, pointing the gun at my face, "you should be dead. That bomb under your car was meant for you."

"You tried to blow me up?" I said.

"Don't act so surprised. Have you any idea what you've put me through? Seeing you walking through Kew Gardens, hand in hand. Do you know how thin the walls are in these houses? While I've been living next door, I've been able to hear you two rutting. I've heard her groaning." He looked directly at me. "She used to come louder when she was with me. *Much* louder."

I nodded. Danny got up and limped across the room. "And don't either of you get any ideas," he said. He hummed a tune to himself as he went upstairs to the bathroom. It was Neil Diamond's "I'm a Believer."

* * *

WHEN WE were alone, Caro stared intently into my eyes. "You know what you've got to do, don't you?"

"Phone the army," I said wearily.

"What good would the army do? What good do they ever do?"

"They could help us fight the police," I said.

"You've got to kill Danny," said Caro. "He could ruin everything."

"Everything's already fucking ruined."

"Are you going to do it or not?" said Caro.

"Why does it have to be me who kills him?" I said.

"Because I killed the last one."

"Yes, but you didn't need to kill her. So it doesn't count."

"*Doesn't count?* What are you? Eight years old?"

The gas boiler was roaring. Danny was definitely running himself a bath. I took one of Caro's cigarettes and lit it. I didn't smoke it; I just needed to do something with my hands. "Okay," I said. "I'll do it."

She nodded darkly and waited.

"What?" I said.

She passed me a sharp knife from the kitchen drawer. I accepted it unwillingly. "Does it have to be a knife?"

"Well, I don't see any trains for you to push him under. What's the matter, Mark? First you can't bring yourself to kill a mouse, now this. Are you a killer or not?"

Tell her the truth.

No, don't. It'll ruin everything.

Everything is already ruined. Look around you. There's a rotting corpse in the next room and a naked blackmailer upstairs.

"I . . ."

"What?" said Caro.

"I'll do it now," I said.

CHAPTER 12

FATHER FIGURE

I WALKED through into the stinking hall, the soles of my shoes sticking on the fluid that had oozed out of Mrs. Mather's body. The landing light lit my way as I slowly climbed the stairs. When I was halfway up, I stopped and listened. I could hear water running in the bathroom. I looked down at the knife in my hand. The blade was about six inches long, and both its edges were sharp. I wasn't sure what it had been designed to cut. All I knew was that it would make quite a mess of my old art teacher. I held the knife upended in my hand, the flat of the blade hidden behind my wrist.

The bathroom door was half open. I moved slowly toward it, step by step, desperately trying to remember which floorboards creaked and which were silent. When I was close enough, I stood to one side of the doorway and peered through the steam into the bathroom. I couldn't see Danny anywhere. I entered the room. Water was starting to run down the sides of the tub. The bath was full to the brim. I turned off the taps and walked out onto the landing.

Searching methodically, I opened each door on the first floor. None of them contained Danny. That only left our bedroom at the top of the house. I walked up the remaining flight and found him lying on our bed, fully clothed and snoring softly. His lips were parted as if he were about to make an "Ah" sound. His arms were spreadeagled, and the fingers of his right hand were still entwined around the Kimber.

I inched closer to the bed, expecting Danny to jerk awake and point my own handgun at me. But his eyes remained closed, his mouth gaped, and his chest rose and fell gently until I was close enough to stab him. I looked down at him, trying to work out where to inflict the wound. Would cutting his throat work best? Perhaps, but I didn't have the stomach for that. The thought of sawing through his windpipe made me feel ill.

If I plunged the knife into the left side of his chest, through his shirt, it would pierce his heart but might only feel like poking him. So that was what I decided to do. I held the blade high, left hand clasped over my right, and prepared to deliver the fatal blow.

While I took aim, I thought about what I was doing. This was Danny, whom I didn't hate and had once really liked. Yes, he'd stolen my girlfriend from me, but I couldn't condemn him for that. In the end, Caro had dumped him, a ruinous blow from which he had clearly never recovered. All right, Danny had called me lots of names. He had burned down my shop. But unhappiness makes men reckless. Did he deserve to die for being in pain?

No. But I still needed to get rid of him. He was a deranged person who knew that Caro and I had committed murder. With my eyes averted, I slammed the knife down into Danny's chest. There was a crack, and half the blade broke off and flew across the bed. The knife had broken on Danny's bones.

Danny drew in breath sharply, opened his eyes, and sat up. He looked at the broken knife in my hands, opened his shirt, and found a fresh scratch on his sternum that was beaded with blood.

"It's not how it looks," I protested.

"You stab me, then tell me it's not how it looks? Okay, pansy boy. If it's not how it looks, how is it? Eh? How the fuck is it?"

Danny scowled in contempt as he leveled the gun at my belly.

"It's funny," I said, "how you keep using words like 'pansy' as an insult. Because when we were at school, you were one of the few teachers with liberal views. You always taught us that names like queer and nigger and paki were invented to dehumanize minorities and make it easier to hate them."

"Did I?"

"Yeah," I said. "You were a pretty inspirational guy. Danny. What the fuck happened to you?"

"I was struck by lightning, man. The same fucking bolt that hit you." Abruptly, Danny's expression changed. The dark loathing in his face gave way to a look of dejection. "You didn't actually *want* to kill me, did you?"

"No," I admitted.

"Caroline forced you to do it, didn't she? Come on. Be honest with me."

I tried not to respond, but Danny must have read the answer in my eyes, for he nodded and said, "Oh, I don't blame you. She can be very persuasive. She once asked me to do the same thing to you. When I'd started seeing her and you wouldn't stop following her around, she begged me to kill you."

"I don't believe you."

"Oh, yes. I came very close. I once spent a whole day following you around in the car, just hoping for a chance to run you over." I could think of absolutely nothing to say. Seeing me sweating, Danny pursued his advantage. "See this?" He held out his hand to indicate his wedding ring.

"What about it?" I said.

"I notice you're not wearing one."

"Caro and I don't bother much with social conventions."

"Maybe she thinks wearing your ring would be a lie too far," said Danny, grinning unpleasantly.

"What are you talking about?"

"Caro isn't married to you. How could she be? She's still

married to me. I got a quickie divorce from my first wife in the spring of '96. Then I married your wife. Or should I say, my wife."

"That's shit and you know it."

"Ask her," said Danny.

"She took out a court order against you," I said. "The marriage was over."

"It was never formally annulled," said Danny. "Technically, she's a bigamist. As well as a murderer, a fraudster, and a first rate bitch."

I swallowed noisily. Danny gazed down at the gun in his hands. "But what am I telling you for? You know what she's like as well as I do. It doesn't stop us from wanting her." He flicked off the safety catches and aimed at my head. "But Mark, we can't both have her. One of us has gotta go."

"Don't shoot," I said.

"I have no choice," said Danny.

Then he pushed the muzzle of the weapon into his own mouth and squeezed the trigger. There was a short, ludicrously loud *BLAM*. The back of Danny's head burst open, bucketing oily red blood all over the wall behind him. Death was not instantaneous. Danny lived long enough to blink twice and murmur one last word. It was muffled by the gun in his mouth, but I'm pretty sure he said, *"Ow."*

I didn't like seeing him there, sucking on a gun barrel, so I took the Kimber from him. Then Caro rushed in, to see Danny's blood everywhere and me holding the gun with its gory red barrel. Naturally, Caro automatically assumed I'd shot him myself. "God," she said. There was real awe in her voice. "You don't fuck around, do you?"

"Get away from me," I said.

"What?"

"You heard. Fuck off, bloodsucker."

She backed away in fear. "I understand," she said. "You're all psyched up. That's all it is. I'll talk to you later. Okay?"

* * *

I COULDN'T stay angry with Caro for long. I had barely digested what Danny had told me before I started making excuses for her. Maybe she did tell Danny to kill me. So what? She didn't mean it. She was seventeen, little more than a child.

She must have said something rash in the heat of the moment that Danny had taken seriously. He was obviously sick in the head, even then. He had to be. What kind of forty-year-old man would be insane enough to embark on a sexual relationship with a seventeen-year-old girl?

What kind of forty-year-old man would be insane enough not to?

I found her lying on a bed in one of the empty rooms. You could really tell that paying guests used to sleep here. The bed was covered in a pink candlewick counterpane. On the wall hung a bad watercolor that some idiot had painted in his sleep. Probably while he was having a nightmare. The room had its own washbasin that gurgled when you turned on the tap.

We lay in each other's arms, dozing without really sleeping. I noticed that she was shaking and wondered whether she was scared of me or the fact that there were two corpses in the house. I was vaguely aware of the light arriving and birds singing. I closed my eyes and drifted for a while, then heard someone shouting my name. "Mark! Mark?"

The room faced onto the square. I went to the window and peered out through the curtains. To my absolute horror, my mum and dad were standing down in the square, beside their well-polished Citroën. They were staring straight up at me. I ducked back into the room, but it was too late. I knew they'd seen me. Mainly because my mother had waved.

"Fuck, fuck, fuck!" I said.

"Is it the police?" said Caro, sitting up in bed.

"No, worse," I said. "It's my fucking parents."

During this exchange, my dad continued to whistle and shout.

"You'll have to talk to them," said Caro.

"How? There's a dead body in the back room!"

"Use the window," advised Caro.

I opened the window and leaned out.

"Hi," I said.

My dad smiled up at me. "Are you still in bed, you idle bugger? It's half past eleven in the bloody morning!"

"We had a late night."

"Pardon?"

I repeated myself, this time shouting so he could hear me.

"Are you going to let us in or not?"

"I can't."

"Don't be so soft," said my dad. "Open the bloody door."

"It's not a good time."

"We wanted to surprise you," said Dad.

"You have done."

My mother's face darkened. "Is that all you've got to say? We've driven a hundred and odd miles to see you."

"Caro's really ill," I explained. "She's got chicken pox. We've been told not to come into contact with anyone."

"We've both had chicken pox," said my mum.

"But you can still get it again," I countered.

My mother looked skeptical. "Stop making excuses and let us in."

"I'll tell you what," I improvised. "There's a pub round the corner. I'll meet you there in about ten minutes. We could have lunch."

"All right. But you're bloody paying," shouted Dad.

They held an emergency conference. I saw my dad trying to be reasonable, my mum waving her arms about and shaking her head. I felt like crying as I watched them walk away. Mum and Dad. Dad and Mum. They had only ever wanted the best for me, and here I was, two corpses in the house and Christ knows how many more on the way.

* * *

"I suppose Tom told you where to find us?" I said.

Dad nodded.

"You look terrible," said my mum.

"What's going on?" asked my father. "Hasn't Caro been feeding you properly?"

"Dad, we're a modern couple. The woman isn't expected to do all the cooking these days."

"Oh, I see," he said. "And just what exactly is she expected to do? Sit on her backside all day, I suppose?"

We were sitting at a table in the pub's dining room, each holding a crap menu. My mother still hadn't recovered from being turned away from the house. "You could at least have offered us a cup of tea," she said.

"We can have tea here," I said brightly. "Should I order a pot now?"

"I think you know what your mother means," said my dad, warning me with his eyes.

"I don't know whether you've heard of it," I said, "but there's this wonderful new invention called a tel-e-phone. That's what people do nowadays. They phone to arrange a visit."

"We shouldn't have to arrange anything," said Mum. "We're family. When I was little, my mum's sister and brothers were always dropping in unannounced."

"It was a bit of a bloody nuisance, though," said Dad, laughing.

"No!" said mum. "People liked to see each other. We saw each other because we all got on. We didn't try to get rid of each other by making up cock-and-bull stories about chicken pox."

I suddenly felt a massive gush of love for her. I got out of my chair, walked over to her seat, and kissed her. "Mum, I'm sorry."

Tears came to her eyes, and I knew I was forgiven.

A waitress arrived to take our order. We asked her to come back in five minutes.

"It's just that things between the two of us haven't been working out," I said. "That's why I made up the chicken pox lie. The atmosphere in that house is poisonous. We're at each other's throats twenty-four hours a day."

"I know," said Mum.

"How do you know? What do you mean?"

My dad smiled indulgently. "You know your mother's dreams. She's been dreaming about you a lot lately."

"What kind of dreams?" I said.

Mum took a tissue from her bag and blew her nose. "Oh, terrible, mixed-up things. I just knew something wasn't right."

Dad nodded. "That's why we came to see you, son. She couldn't stop worrying about you."

"Caroline was never right for you," said my mum. "You should never have married her."

"We're stuck with each other now," I said. "She's pregnant."

They were both so stunned they could barely speak. I was

aware of their reservations about Caro, but until that moment I had no idea how much they actively disliked her. "Didn't you know it's customary for parents to be happy when they find there's a grandchild on the way?"

"Well, she'd make a terrible mother," said my father. "She's only interested in herself."

"You think she's a bad person?"

"Not exactly. We just want to see you settled, and we don't think you could ever be settled with a girl like that. It's like when I was younger and bluffed my way backstage after that Wings concert."

"Oh, no," I said. "Not the dreaded Paul McCartney ancedote."

"Hang on," said my dad. "I've never told you the full story. Yes, I met Paul McCartney. Yes, I talked to him in his dressing room, and yes, it's my only claim to bloody fame. What I didn't tell you was that while we were chatting, McCartney's eyes kept darting round the room, looking for someone more important to talk to."

"What's this got to do with Caro?"

"Well, if you ask me, that's what she's like," said Dad. "Always on the lookout for a better offer. She'll never be happy with someone ordinary."

My mother was nodding in agreement.

"Who are you calling ordinary?" I said. "I'm not ordinary."

"Ordinary isn't the right word," said my mother. "Normal. You're normal."

"That's even worse."

My dad cleared his throat. "I drove by Caro's old flat the other day," he said. "All the windows were boarded up. The porch had caved in. I never realized what a bloody slum the place was. Looks like it's been hit by a bomb."

"That's landlords for you," I said.

"Oh, and someone was asking after you," said Mum. "Nice chap. Came round to the house. Tall with long hair and a beard. What was his name? Victor something. Said he wished to be remembered to you and did I have your address?"

"You didn't give it to him?"

"I thought I'd better check with you first," she said.

"Don't tell him where I am," I said.

My parents exchanged worried glances. "He's just someone I met in a pub," I added quickly. "He's a Jehovah's Witness. You know how persistent they can be."

"What was he doing in a pub?" said Dad. "I thought Jehovah's Witnesses didn't drink."

"Who said he was drinking?" I said.

My dad gave me a look to show he wasn't fooled.

"What about this baby?" said my mother. "Was it planned?"

"Not exactly."

She tutted. My dad sighed.

"Things have been bad," I conceded. "But listen, I want you both to know something. Nothing that's happened or may happen is your fault. I couldn't have wished for better parents. You're not to blame for the way I've turned out."

"Son," said my dad. "What are you talking about? We love you. We couldn't be happier with the way you turned out."

*   *   *

AFTER LUNCH we took a stroll by the seafront. It was a dry, windy day. The clouds rolled like gunsmoke. The waves were tall, their white crests rising far out to sea. "You know, it's a shame," commented my father. "This wouldn't be such a bad place to live if you and Caro were getting on better."

I walked my parents back to their car, waiting until they had driven away before entering the house, quickly slamming the front door behind me in case the smell of death leaked out.

The lino in the hall was damp, and there was a reassuring smell of disinfectant. Caro, wearing a headscarf and rubber gloves, came down the stairs to greet me, a wan smile on her face. I could see that I had redeemed myself and was back in her good books. Once again, I was her indispensable personal assassin.

"I've been cleaning up the bedroom. The blood has come off the walls, but we'll have to dump the bedding. Luckily, nothing seeped through to the mattress. But I'm never sleeping in that bed again. Or that room."

I nodded darkly.

"What's the matter?" she said.

"Before he died, Danny told me something. He says you asked him to kill me."

"That's crap," said Caro.

"Are you sure? I did almost get run over outside my house."

"Well? You always were a clumsy fucker."

"And another thing," I said. "What's this about us not being legally married?"

Now Caro looked affronted. "What about it?"

"Is it true?"

"Well, if you're going to be really pedantic . . ."

"So it *is* true?"

"Legally, maybe," she said. "But not spiritually."

"Of course it's true! If you and Danny never got a divorce, it's true."

"I decided we were divorced," she said. "I didn't want to see him or hear him or be near him or be touched by him ever again.

That's about as divorced as you can get. As far as I'm concerned, it was official."

"It's up to a judge to make that decision. Not you."

"Why? Why should some dirty ex–public school prick who's into child pornography have the authority to say whether I'm married or not?"

I sighed. "If no one but you has the right to say whether you're divorced, no one has the right to say you're married. So why did we get married? You should have married us yourself."

"You're right," said Caro. "I should."

"And Wallace. You even screwed Wallace? For fuck's sake!"

Caro didn't seem to think this warranted a response.

I followed her upstairs, to be shocked anew by the sight of Danny lying dead on the bed. Caro's optimism about the walls was slightly misplaced. Although she had indeed sponged most of the gore away, the once-white walls were now tinted pink. The whole room seemed to be screaming murder.

"I'll tell you about me and Danny, shall I?" she said. "When I married him, I thought he was a romantic figure. Then I found out he never washed properly. He always had dirty fingernails. He ate with his mouth open. What's worse, he taught art but he didn't have the remotest spark of talent. His paintings were like smears of shit. He was always scratching himself and farting. I might as well have married a chimpanzee."

We tried to put trash bags over the chimpanzee, only to discover he was as stiff as a board. "How long does rigor mortis last?" Caro asked me.

"A few hours, I think. It might not make any difference. We can't move the bodies before midnight, anyway."

"And just exactly where are we going to move them?"

"The same grave as before. We might as well."

"What if someone's noticed it's been tampered with? What if Danny didn't bother to fill it in?"

"Then we're fucked."

*   *   *

WHEN IT was dark I took a flashlight and went next door to see if Danny had left anything incriminating behind. The back door was unlocked, so I went inside, my footsteps echoing through the empty rooms. In one of the bedrooms, I found a greasy sleeping bag. Underneath the pillow was an ancient, crumpled Polaroid. It was a picture of Caro at seventeen, sitting in a field. She was smiling at the camera, a piece of straw dangling from the corner of her mouth. On the back, in smudged ink, someone had written "free and in love."

That was all. It was just an empty, unfurnished house, sad and neglected. Unlike the house next door, which we'd brightened up considerably by splattering blood over the walls.

When I stood in the kitchen, I could hear a radio booming through the wall. Ricky Cragg was listening to the World Service. The old man seemed so cheerfully self-contained, so willfully indifferent to the world around him. I wondered if he ever got lonely. Then I bolted the back door and returned to the house next door.

Caro was in the kitchen, playing a Durango album at antisocial volume. I went up to the bathroom, took the gun out of my trouser belt, and sat on the toilet seat, trying to analyze our situation. This is what I came up with. Most of the trouble we were in had been caused by Caro. Some of it was God's fault. None of it was my fault. I was blameless. In fact, I admired myself tremendously.

So what was I worrying about?

Feeling better, I left the bathroom and began to descend the stairs. Then I stopped. I saw there was a man standing in the hall below, looking solemnly up at me. A cold wind blew through me as I recognized the Jazzman. Bad Jesus had found us. And there was no doubt in my mind that Bromley and Flett had led him to our door.

The Jazzman was holding a shotgun. I glanced back toward the bathroom, where I'd left my gun, resting on the linen basket. I couldn't decide whether to go back for it or not. The Jazzman helped me make up my mind. In a rapid flowing motion, he pumped the shotgun and aimed it at my head.

"Down," he ordered, as if I were a very bad dog.

Caro and Jesus were seated at the kitchen table. Caro had tears in her eyes and a red handprint on her left cheek. Jesus was holding her hand, more out of sadistic ownership than affection. There was broken glass on the floor where the Jazzman had smashed the window in the door to get in. Cancer Boy, chewing gum noisily, was smiling as he counted our money.

Bad Jesus wasn't smiling. He looked stern and cold, as if he were about to rebuke the Pharisees or cast the moneylenders out of the temple. "You're the dirty rat who killed my brother," he said.

"No," I said. "I liked your brother. I wouldn't have done anything to hurt him. I know exactly who planted the bomb."

I tried to sit down. The Jazzman yanked the chair away, and I fell over. Cancer Boy thought this was hilarious. I picked up the chair and sat in it.

"Now," said Bad Jesus. "Have you anything to say before we turn you inside out?"

"You know those e-mails you've been getting? The guy who's been sending them turned up."

"I know the very guy," said Jesus. "Green hair, long nose, wears a jester's hat."

"He's a real person," I insisted. "You'll find him in the room at the top of the house."

"Is this true?" said Jesus to the Jazzman.

"How the fuck should I know?"

"Go and look."

The Jazzman hesitated as if he wanted to refuse but didn't quite have the nerve. Then he did what he was told. A minute later, he called down to Jesus.

"Boss? You'd better see this."

"Watch them," said Jesus to Cancer Boy. Then he joined the Jazzman in the attic. They almost ran down the stairs. The Jazzman looked bewildered. Jesus had a wild look in his eyes. "Tell me it again, from the beginning."

I told him all about Danny, which meant that I also had to fill him in on Mrs. Mather.

"Woah," said Jesus, stopping me. "You saying you killed somebody else?"

Caro started to confess, but Jesus snarled at her like a rabid dog. "You speak when you're spoken to, bitch." He turned to me. I pointed to the hall. "First door on your right."

This time they all went to see. I heard Cancer Boy gagging when the smell hit him. Jesus reentered the kitchen and banged his fist down on the table. Cancer Boy and the Jazzman now surveyed me with a kind of sickened respect. Jesus' face had turned dark, and a vein was throbbing on his forehead.

Cancer Boy whistled softly. "Seems you were right, boss. This guy *really* is a killer."

Jesus didn't look happy at all. "So let me get this straight," he said. "These crazy e-mails this guy sent out, they were all because he was driven mad with jealousy. Because Lizzie Borden here was still his wife?"

"That's right," I said.

"So when I decided to leave her alone out of respect for her marriage to you, she wasn't married to you at all?"

"No."

"In that case," said Jesus, "I've got as much right to fuck her as you have."

"You've never fucked anyone," said Caro scornfully. "You wouldn't know how to. All creeps like you ever do is masturbate inside women's bodies."

Without the slightest alteration in his breathing or his facial expression, Jesus belted Caro across the face with the back of his hand. She fell off her chair.

"Look," I said, "why don't we just write you a check for whatever you think we owe you? I'm genuinely sorry about Rock, I mean it. So we'll even slap an extra hundred grand on top. Call it compensation. Then we'll be quits."

"Oh, no," said Jesus, pointing at me. "This isn't about money anymore. Even if you're telling the truth, I'm still holding you responsible. It was your car, man. It was you who offered it to my brother. It was up to you to check there wasn't a fucking bomb underneath it. Cancer Boy? Bring me the implements of torture."

"Fuck *off!*" said Caro from the floor.

Jesus kicked her in the ribs.

Cancer Boy went out and returned with a large leather doctor's bag. He emptied the contents on the table. There were pliers, a small blowtorch, a nail gun, a small bottle of acid, a set of kitchen knives. A drill, a pair of handcuffs, a blindfold, a collection of fishhooks, a club, a syringe, a length of rope, a leather whip, a cutthroat razor, a hammer, some very large nails. Everything, in fact, except a cuddly toy. "Tie him to the chair," ordered Jesus.

Cancer Boy picked up the rope, but Caro stepped between us. "What do you need to tie him for?" she said. "Are you afraid of what he might do to you?"

"Oh, yeah," said Jesus. "Look at me. I'm shaking all over."

"It doesn't take any courage to tie someone up and torture them," said Caro. "It's what the *fucking* police do."

"Shut up!" yelled Jesus.

I could see where Caro was going with this. "How about it?" I said to Jesus. "A fair fight. Just me and you, man to man."

Jesus looked like he was considering it.

"I don't know, boss," said the Jazzman, looking me up and down. "The guy don't look much, but he made a right fucking mess of Kev and Phil."

"So?" said Jesus, approaching the Jazzman threateningly.

Cancer Boy stepped between them. "Might be tricky, that's all he's saying."

"This guy likes *books*," said Jesus. "See those muscles of his? He got them in a gym. They're not real. Real muscles are like this." He flexed an enormous bicep. "I was born with these. I didn't have to fucking *grow* them."

Neither Cancer Boy nor the Jazzman reacted.

"What? You honestly think this little prat could take me?" said Jesus.

"You got to be careful with those karate types," said Cancer Boy. "They know all the deadliest points of the body. Like the Adam's apple. Hit someone hard enough on the Adam's apple, you'll kill them."

"That's right," agreed the Jazzman. "And if you hit someone

hard enough on the nose with the heel of the palm, you can knock the nose bone right into their brain."

"I asked you a question," said Bad Jesus. "Do you think he could take me?"

There was a long silence.

"Right, that's it," said Jesus, shoving me. "Outside, now. We'll soon see how hard you are."

Cancer Boy waved his hands in protest. "No, no, no. That's just wild, boss. You'll bring the cops down on us. Probably even try and blame us for the two dead bastards. If you're going to fight, do it here. Not in a public place, man."

"There's no public out there. This place is a ghost town by the sea. Come on."

Now I was so scared I could hardly feel my legs. "I'll fight you on one condition," I said. "It's just you and me. When you start losing, I don't want your friends to join in."

"Getting scared, are we?" Jesus shoved me forward. "Outside."

I started walking, and the others trooped after us. There was a black Cayenne Estate parked outside the house. It was the kind of car an American dentist would use for family vacations. I vaulted over the gate and clambered onto the hood of the car. As Jesus came through the gate, I launched my entire body at his head. It wasn't karate, it was street-fighting on a prepubescent level.

Jesus fell, crashing like a true heavyweight, and for a few moments I had the unlikely experience of sitting on the Son of God's chest and pounding his face. Because I was scared and desperate, everything Lenny had taught me seemed completely irrelevant. I couldn't even *remember* what he'd taught me.

Jesus grabbed one of my wrists and turned sideways, taking me with him. Not wanting a sixteen-stone psycho on top of me, I yanked my wrist free, rolled clear, and got up. My divine opponent, showing an agility I had not anticipated, was already on his feet and facing me.

I backed away, and Bad Jesus followed me, until we were standing on the gravel of the village hall parking lot. Cancer Boy and the Jazzman, with Caro between them, walked alongside us to monitor the fight's progress. "Hit him, Jesus," said the Jazzman, like some kid in the playground. "Fucking leather him."

Jesus might have considered himself an expert in violence, but he charged me like any out-of-condition football thug, brutal arms swinging frenziedly. There was no art or accuracy in the attack. He took the pragmatic approach, believing that if he launched twenty undisciplined blows in the approximate direction of my head, at least two of them would connect. He was right.

I've heard fighters claim that in the heat of battle, you don't feel the pain of your wounds. But when Bad Jesus caught my right eyebrow with his left fist, it was like being at the center of an explosion. The impact jarred my teeth, cowed and diminished me, threw me off balance.

My response was an ungainly kick that would have made my karate instructor despair, yet it slammed into Jesus' crotch with a satisfying thud. Even in the dark, I could see his astonishment and indignation. But my boot must have missed his balls, because a few seconds later he retaliated.

Taking one punch from an angry man who is larger and stronger than yourself can never be pleasant. Being hit a second time is, to say the least, discouraging. Jesus retaliated with another school-bully onslaught, and one of his punches caught me in the chin. He probably thought he had floored me. I still contend that I slipped. Either way, the end result was the same.

I fell over.

I was hurt and demoralized, but not beaten. Had I been able to rise swiftly enough, the outcome of the fight might have been different. But as I was pulling myself up, Jesus took a run at me, and I knew what was coming. His boot whacked into my left temple, sending two hundred volts of pain through my skull. Then he kicked me again.

After that second kick, the pain retreated. Time seemed to falter in its course. Shadowy figures danced slowly around me like Apaches circling the wagon train in an old cowboy movie.

My life didn't flash before my eyes. Instead, I saw a fancy parade of all the things that had ever made my life bearable: the sea, DC Comics, Marlon Brando, Modigliani, "Ode to a Skylark," Sinéad O'Connor, Dirk Bogarde, Bertie Wooster, Johnny Depp, Laurel and Hardy, J. M. Barrie, Kurt Vonnegut; a wonderful, shamefully obscure novel called *Fata Morgana* by William Kotzwinkle; Selma Hayek, with or without clothes; Billy Wilder films; "Everything Is Cool" by the Serenes, old American sitcoms of the fifties and sixties; Oliver Reed; guitars; the Beatles; Boris Karloff as an old man; my family; the stars; the smell of fireworks; the *nyow nyow* sound that passing cars make when you're parked in a lay-by; snow; Christmas morning when I was a kid; Easter eggs for breakfast; that wonderful first album by Jim Nightshade; and Caro. Caro. Caro.

There I was, about to die and still making fucking lists.

Then the world came back into focus and Bad Jesus was standing over me. I heard Caro shouting, "No, no!" and sobbing. Jesus' arm was fully outstretched, and I knew he was aiming a gun at me.

"Not here, you pill," complained Cancer Boy. "Shoot him and you're leaving forensic evidence behind. Ballistics, man."

The voices seemed intrusively, mindlessly loud, like voices from the TV when you're falling asleep on the sofa.

"Well, what, then?" said Jesus. "I know. The car's got a towbar. We could tie him to it and drag him behind."

"Down a public road?" said the Jazzman. "Don't you think someone might notice?"

Jesus sighed as if his men were being deliberately obstructive. "All right, who's got a blade? Someone give me a blade."

The Jazzman withdrew a short knife from his belt and passed it to Jesus, then yanked me to my knees and held me there. Jesus held the knife close to my shirt and, with a series of deft little cuts, ripped it open. "Don't worry," said Jesus, "I'm a doctor. I trained at the Harold Shipman School of Medicine."

Caro threw herself in between us. "No!"

"Out of the way."

"Please. I'll do anything you ask. Just leave him alone."

Her hair was so fair, her skin so pale, that she appeared to be glowing in the dark. Jesus looked at her, and I knew he was thinking what I'd always thought, that loveliness so extreme excused any amount of scheming and lies.

"Okay," said Jesus. "Be my bitch. No one else's."

"Yes."

"Yes, what?"

"I will be your bitch. Whatever you ask for, I'll give to you."

"And I still want the money you owe me, with interest. I think you should pay for the wonderful privilege of being fucked and abused by me."

For a whole two seconds, Caro hesitated. "Deal," she said finally.

"Okay." Jesus nodded to Cancer Boy. "Put her in the car."

Cancer Boy escorted Caro to the Cayenne Estate. I tried to

move, but the Jazzman tightened his grip, forcing me back down onto my knees. "Well, Killer," said Bad Jesus. "You're a very lucky boy. It turns out the whore cares about you after all."

Then he drew back his foot and kicked me full in the mouth. The impact almost snapped my neck. My mouth and nose filled up with blood.

The Jazzman hurled me forward onto my face. I coughed out blood and lumps of teeth. Then I felt hot breath on my face and heard Jesus say, "When you're lying awake in your lonely bed, remember this. *I'm the only man who ever made her come.*"

Car doors slammed, and a bright light washed over me, followed by the sound of an engine thrumming into life. I started crawling, knowing they were going to drive over me. The gravel cracked and spluttered as the heavy-duty tires rolled forward. Then a second engine roared, and out of the darkness came a second pair of headlights, set at full beam and aimed directly at the Cayenne. It was a large van, and its driver could evidently see what was about to take place, because he began to sound his horn in protest. The Cayenne swerved past me and skidded out of the square.

As defeats go, mine had been fairly comprehensive. I'd lost the fight. I'd lost the woman. I'd lost my teeth and my good looks, or what passed for them. Despite all these setbacks, I was possessed by a strange euphoria. Caro had saved me. She had traded her body in exchange for my life. That could only mean one thing. She loved me.

She really loved me.

CHAPTER 13

HOW TO BE BAD

WHEN I opened my eyes there was a strong smell of antiseptic and I was lying on the sofa. Dad was kneeling beside me. At first, I thought I was hallucinating. Then I remembered the blazing headlights and the angry horn and realized Maurice Madden, purveyor of quality meats, had come to my rescue.

Dad was swabbing my face with a ball of cotton wool. In his other hand, he held a bowl of warm water. The water was the color of cherryade.

"Why are you here?" I asked him.

"Your mother made me come. A bloody good job she did."

Then I remembered that there were dead bodies in the house and sat upright so abruptly that the room went out of focus. "I've just got to do something."

"There's no bloody need," said my dad. His voice sounded thick, as if he'd just woken up. "I've seen them. What the bloody hell have you been doing?"

Dad went out of the room and returned with two large brandies in balloon-shaped glasses. He crouched down by the fire, holding the glasses as close as possible to the flames to warm them. Then he lit a cigarette, something he only did when agitated.

My father downed his brandy in one gulp and held the other to my inflated lips. "You should see a doctor, really," he said grimly. "And a bloody good dentist. And a fucking psychiatrist by the looks of things."

I started to speak, and the pain of the cold air on my broken teeth made me wince. Dad passed me some tablets. "Codeine," he said. "I take it for my back. Might help."

I sat upright and swallowed the pills down with the brandy. When I'd finished, my dad sank back into his armchair by the fire. "Okay. Now you can tell me what's been going on. I don't want any excuses, any made-up silly bloody stories. The truth. *Now.*"

I hadn't seen Dad so angry since the school parents' evening when I was fifteen, when all my teachers had assured him, with astonishing unanimity, that I was a charming boy with great potential who just happened to be bone idle.

Weeping with shame, I told him about Caro's debt to Bad Jesus, the car bomb, the accidental death of Janet Mather, and Danny's arrival and suicide. I didn't bother mentioning Warren or Gordon. I didn't want my father to see me in a bad light.

Dad stared at me for a long time. "And the police really said that, did they? That they'd leave you alone if Caroline let 'em, you know . . ." He squirmed in embarrassment.

"That's exactly what they said."

He got up and paced the room. "Well, then. That's blackmail. Even if you'd wanted to call the police, tell 'em about your accidents, you couldn't trust the buggers, could you? So it's not as if we want to break the law, is it? We've got no choice."

"That's exactly the way I see it."

Dad stopped pacing to glare at me. "You realise all this'd break your mother's heart if she knew about it? You know that. Don't you?"

"Yeah."

"She isn't to know. Understand? Not ever. If you ever breathe a word of any this, I'll break your bloody neck."

"Okay, okay."

He blew out cigarette smoke in a despairing cloud.

"I'm sorry, Dad."

"I told you Caroline was bad news, didn't I? I bloody warned you. What the fucking hell did you have to marry her for?"

I told him we weren't married, that the marriage between her and Danny had never been annulled. "Oh, charming," remarked my father, unconsciously echoing Danny. "So now she's a bigamist, too, is she? As well as being a thief, a prostitute, a drug addict, a murderer, and *a stupid bloody cow!*"

With this, my dad stormed out to his van, returning with some old sheets and a bag of tools, cigarette dangling from the corner of his mouth. "Okay," he said. "I'm going to help you. On one condition."

"What?"

"That you don't go after Caroline, you don't try to contact her, that you end it now. While you're almost in one piece."

"Okay," I said.

He nodded and sorted through his tool bag.

"What're you going to do?" I asked him.

"I've got some clearing up to do."

"I'll help," I said.

"No, you won't," he said. "You'll wait here in this room until I've finished. I don't want you peering over my shoulder. I wouldn't want anyone to see what I'm about to do." He looked at me again. "You're a bloody pillock. What are you?"

"A bloody pillock."

I went to the bathroom. While I was pissing, I spotted the Kimber handgun, still resting on the linen basket. I opened the lid and hid the weapon under a pile of dirty laundry.

Dad was upstairs with his bag and the sheets. I could hear the sound of chopping and sawing as he dismembered Danny. Then he brought down four bloody bundles and dumped them in the hall. When I'd provided more sheets, he went to work on Mrs. Mather. Every so often, he stopped to swear and curse. Finally, all the body parts were tied up in neat little bags.

"What are you going to do with them?" I said.

"I'm a butcher, aren't I? I've spent my life cutting up bodies and getting rid of the waste. Don't ask stupid questions."

After checking there was no one about, Dad took the bundles out to his refrigerated van. He went upstairs again, returning with a bloody mattress and a roll of carpet. This also went in the van.

"Okay," he said. "Get your stuff together. We're leaving."

"I can't leave yet," I said. "I've got things to sort out."

"What things?" For a moment, Dad seemed to be considering clipping me round the ear. "You're not going after Caroline? Tell me you're not."

"No."

"You swear?"

"I swear by almighty God that I am not going after her. But I need to clean the house, sort things out with the estate agent, re-place the mattress and carpet. If I leave in a hurry, it's going to look too suspicious. Plus, my face needs to heal a bit before mum sees me. Don't you think?"

After a long pause, he nodded. Then he stared at me. "You've been a fool. A real bloody idiot. You know that?" he said. Then my father's bottom lip trembled and he started crying. He reached for me and hugged me to him, squeezing me so hard that I could scarcely breathe.

I started snivelling. I just couldn't help it. I'd always wanted to bond with Dad but never known how to. He didn't understand my love of books, just as his enthusiasm for football left me cold.

Now, at last, we were father and son. United at last by horror, darkness, and death.

*   *   *

Without Caro, Prospect House seemed dark and full of menace. I took a leisurely bath. After dressing, I went to see an emergency dentist in Cromer, a ham-fisted lout who charged me a fortune to place ill-fitting temporary caps over my broken teeth, then had the audacity to say I didn't floss carefully enough.

I went home, ate some lukewarm soup and returned to bed.

In the early hours of Easter morning, the mobile phone beside my bed bleeped to tell me I had a text message, which I sat up in bed to retrieve. The sender was JESU. The message was SW1 HTL. I felt sure that the text was from Caro, who must somehow have got hold of Jesus's phone to send me a hurried cry for help. She seemed to be saying that she had been taken to a hotel in South West 1. This wasn't much help. There were probably hundreds of hotels in that part of London. Anyway, what if I was wrong?

It then struck me that I could use my strategy for finding lost books to solve the problem. Rather than surrendering to panic, I wandered about the house aimlessly, watched a little television, made myself a cup of tea, allowing my unconscious time to throw up an answer.

I went upstairs for a piss. When I came down, I passed the table in the hall and noticed *Things to Do in Suffolk and Norfolk*. I picked it up to see if it said anything about hitting people with spades. The book fell open at an ad for a hotel. The hotel was in Southwold. It was called The Swan. SW1 HTL.

And I knew I'd found her.

Remembering what Caro had taught me, I took the gun into the kitchen and dismantled it. Bad Jesus's torture implements were still heaped on the kitchen table. With great care, I oiled the Kimber and cleaned it. Then I reassembled the gun and loaded it. There were just six shots remaining.

So far, I had failed every test of manhood. I had failed in business, failed to keep my woman, failed to defend myself against attack, and most seriously, failed to live with honor. If I failed again today, I would almost certainly die.

Caro's coat was hanging on the back of a chair. When I picked it up to sniff it and press it against my face, something fell out of one of its pockets. It was the card that Caro had bought from the fortune telling machine on the seafront. I must have misread it the first time, because now it seemed to say:

Someone close to you may murder a neighbour later this week. Social events are highlighted and an old teacher will blow out his brains in your bedroom. You will get your head kicked in by a psychotic gangster, who will then abduct your girlfriend. Never mind.

* * *

As I traveled south across the border, the glowering dinginess of Norfolk gave way to lush fields, bright windmills and rows of smart, well-kept cottages bedecked with plants and flowers. It was England as it must have looked fifty years ago.

Like Holeness, Southwold is a seaside town on the East Coast of England, but all similaritities between the two resorts end there. Southwold, with its whitewashed lighthouse and its newly-renovated pier, resembles a middle-class Caucasian child's painting of the seaside in which there are boats, shells, and sand castles but absolutely no suspicious foreigners or poor people. The promenade is free of litter and the only bad smell emanates from the gents lavatories above the beach.

I had read about Southwold but never been here. I knew that George Orwell spent time here, writing against the class system in a nest of genteel comfort. Various lovers of Englishness had praised the town for being unspoiled, meaning that there weren't enough working-class people there to spoil it. I found Southwold charming, its aura of prewar gentility marred only by the view of the Sizewell B nuclear power station further down the coast.

I parked the Audi on the road above the sea and walked slowly into the town. In the market place stood the Swan Hotel, a white mock-Georgian building with a dash of Victoriana. In the center of the square stood an old cast iron pump. There was a butcher's shop with a clock commemorating the Queen's 1977 Jubilee. To-day, the shop's blinds were down. It was Easter Sunday.

Most of the other shops were open. There were window displays of miniature lighthouses and toy boats. A bookshop full of browsers. A real-estate agent advertising properties so expensive that the conspicuous absence of paupers ceased to be a mystery. Families straight off the back of cornflake packets and old people from pension ads walked by me, the smiles on their clean pink faces evaporating when they drew close enough to see my smashed-in mouth.

I am one bad motherfucker.

I'd only been walking for about a minute when the shops began to peter out, so I crossed the road and walked back on the other side. Outside the Swan Hotel, I pretended to read the restaurant menu. Next, I slipped down a narrow passage that led to the hotel car park and found the Cayenne Estate. I was thrilled. They hadn't checked out. And they had no idea what was coming.

I walked into the hotel through the back entrance. The women on reception were chatting and didn't pay me any attention. No one in hotels, least of all the staff, can ever tell the difference between a guest and a well-behaved gunman. Unchallenged, I crossed the lobby and turned left into the lounge, where I sank into an old armchair with a view of the lobby and waited.

Two old ladies sitting by the window were discussing British celebrities who had stayed at the hotel. "Michael Palin has stayed here. And that nice Maureen Lipman brings her mother. Do you know Maureen Lipman?"

"No. But I know the woman who presents *The Weakest Link.*"

"Anne Robinson? Has she stayed here?"

"I shouldn't think so. But I know who she is."

I picked up a copy of the *Mail on Sunday* and leafed through it. Food smells drifted through from the hotel kitchen, reminding me that lunch approached and I hadn't had any breakfast. After forty minutes, I got very bored—although on this occasion, the *Mail on Sunday* wasn't entirely to blame. What was I waiting in the hotel for? It was a fine morning. Caro and Jesus were more likely to be walking by the sea or on the pier. If they saw my car, they would be forewarned. Whereas if I went out to meet them, me and my gun might still come as a surprise.

I left the hotel via the front door and headed down to the water's edge. Even the beach huts were more up-market here, almost good enough to live in, although a stern notice warned that sleeping in the huts was a capital offence. It wasn't warm enough to sunbathe but there were people walking dogs and a family playing ball on the sand.

Despite my recent head injuries, I was thinking clearly. I was thinking, *I used to play ball like that family. Today I am carrying a loaded gun, with intent to commit mayhem.*

HOW TO BE BAD

The Kimber was thrust into my waist band, its metal cold against my hip. There was no sign of the cropped blond head that I knew and worshipped, so I walked to the pier, which may have been renovated but was as windy, pointless, and dull as any pier in Britain. Walking back to the hotel, a hideous thought occurred to me. What if Caro was already dead? What if they'd fucked her so hard that she'd died?

Then they would die too.

I passed a busy little pub and a photographer's shop, its window filled with framed retouched photographs of lopsided brides and gargoyle babies. Then I stopped walking and slipped into the shop doorway, because I had just seen Jesus, Caro, and Cancer Boy walking out of the Swan Hotel. Fortunately, they turned right. Had they turned left, they would certainly have seen me. I reached into my coat pocket, extracted a woollen Kangol hat and put it on, pulling it low so that it covered my eyebrows. Then I followed them.

Caro looked comfortable and relaxed. She was wearing a short blue dress that I had never seen before. No one would have believed she was a hostage, and at that moment, I was finding it hard to believe, too. She walked and chatted, waving her right hand as she made some typically searing point.

Jesus, walking beside her, nodded every now and then as if he was genuinely interested in what she had to say. Cancer Boy dawdled behind, not listening, glancing to left and right as he smoothed his sideburns straight. At one point, he turned and glanced behind him, saw me but immediately looked away, betraying no hint of recognition.

They entered a café, a twee little English teashop where you could buy cream teas with clotted cream, jam, and scones freshly baked on the premises. It was the kind of place where old people

231

met to discuss their operations. As I passed the window, I saw Jesus looking around for an empty table. Cancer Boy tapped an old man on the shoulder. The old man leapt up in alarm, preferring to leave his tea unfinished than risk provoking a marauder.

I passed the café and kept walking until I came to a chip shop with a CLOSED sign in its window. Now I was really shaking. I had a weapon but was I really going to use it? Then I realized I didn't have to. Waving the gun around ought to be enough.

What was it they said in action movies? *Spread your hands on the table and keep them there.* Either that or: *Put your hands in the air where I can see them.* Yes, that was better. That would be my first line. The next would be: "Caro, we're leaving." When we had made it to the door, I would back away, aiming the gun at Jesus and Cancer Boy. Easy.

I walked back to the café, the Kimber already in my hand. When I reached the door, a couple were just leaving. Not noticing the gun, they held the door open for me and smiled. I smiled back. *It's nice to be nice.* I moved past the chattering tables and crossed the room to where Caro was sitting. Caro and Jesus were staring at a menu. Cancer Boy was slumped in his chair, looking bored and petulant as he shunted a salt shaker around the table with his forefinger.

I didn't anticipate any trouble. This wasn't London or Chicago. It was a tea shop in deepest Suffolk. The Kimber was just my insurance. Bad Jesus was rash, but surely not rash enough to start a gunfight in a public place, surrounded by witnesses? So why was I so scared? My legs were so unsteady that I could barely walk. Sweat dripped off my chin onto the tiled floor.

Maybe it was like this for my grandfather, when he fought in World War II. Maybe all those brave old boys once shook as I was shaking now.

I stood in the middle of the café, seriously considering walking out before anyone noticed me. Instead, I raised my weapon and approached Caro's table. It was Cancer Boy who saw me first. Even before he noticed the gun, something about my demeanour made him sit up sharply in his seat. When he saw the weapon, his mouth formed a sickly, desperate smile. The table shook noisily as he began to rise, already reaching for the gun in his belt. His reflexes were much faster than mine, because I was still wondering what to do when he raised his revolver and fired at me.

But in his near-panic, Cancer Boy forgot to aim and the bullet brushed my left arm and penetrated an old lady in a green hat who was sitting at an opposite table. With a sigh of infinite weariness, the old lady slumped forward, her face coming to rest in a plate of toasted tea cakes.

There was a scream to my right. Before Cancer Boy could fire again, I raised the Kimber and shot him. A red carnation magically appeared on the lapel of his jacket. He grunted and spun sideways off his chair, involuntarily pulling the trigger a second time. The bullet ricocheted off the gilt frame of a seventeenth century map of *Suffolke* and hit a waitress in the back. As she fell, she overturned a table and the tray she had been carrying hurtled down, scattering its contents all over the floor.

Now the café was in uproar. People were hiding under their tables, a baby was wailing and a middle-aged man in a flat cap was having a fit on the floor, threshing about in a pool of Earl Grey tea.

I turned to Bad Jesus and saw he'd been too fast for me. He was already holding a dainty little low-calibre pistol and its muzzle was pressed against Caro's head. Caro was staring at me in wide-eyed terror but Jesus didn't seem interested in me or the gun I was holding. All his outrage and malice was directed at the woman who had betrayed him.

"You stupid, stupid slut," he said. "You told him where we were, didn't you? *Didn't you?*"

Caro jabbered something about not meaning it. I blurted out my next line but in my terror, got my words confused. "Spread your hands in the table where I can see them."

Jesus didn't seem to hear me. "Give me one good reason," he said to Caro, "why I shouldn't kill you here and now."

"I'm having your baby," said Caro.

Her words sounded so surreal among the gunsmoke and the screams.

Jesus stared at her. "Say that again?"

"I'm pregnant." She kept her eyes fixed on his. The tears were rolling down her face. "If you kill me, you'll kill your own child."

"You're such a whore it could be anyone's," countered Jesus.

"You could get a DNA test," said Caro. "Shoot me afterwards if I'm lying. But I'm not."

She was very convincing. I could see that Bad Jesus was beginning to wonder. For one fraction of a second he forgot what he was supposed to be doing and lowered the gun. I saw my window of opportunity and seized it.

I shot him twice, once near the heart and once through the left hand when he raised it to protect himself. Jesus dropped the gun and rocked in his chair, his chin sagging forward onto his bloody chest. With a strange animal whimper, Caro kicked the table aside and ran for the door. I followed her. As we were leaving, an old lady in a Margaret Thatcher suit unleashed a truly shocking volley of expletives.

A young couple who had been standing on the street, gaping at the carnage through the café window, jumped clear as we rushed out. They backed straight into the path of a car. The driver braked just in time but was hit by the car behind and shunted forward, knocking the couple over anyway.

We ran down the street, barging into startled tourists. It was not over yet. Turning left into the passage that led to the Swan's parking lot, we met the Jazzman coming the other way. His hair was wet and slicked-back, as if he had just stepped out of the shower. At the sight of us, he stopped dead and reached into his jacket. But I had the advantage.

In my witless confusion, I was still holding the Kimber. I fired my weapon before his was drawn, aiming for the Jazzman's chest but missing and blowing a hole through his neck. He reeled horribly, spraying blood all over the shiny parked cars before collapsing on the cobbles. The noises he was making made me sweat with shame. I shot him again. This time, the Jazzman lay still.

At the far end of the car park lay a narrow road that bypassed the local brewery. There was no one about. I thrust my hat into my pocket and gripped Caro's hand. "Walk," I told her. "If we walk, it'll be less obvious."

It seemed to work. The strollers on the sea front, dressed in their Easter Sunday best, paid us no attention as we made our way to the Audi. It was only when we were inside the car that I realized that Caro's face was spattered with the blood of her captors.

I turned the car round and drove sedately back toward the harbor end of town. Three police cars, lights flashing, tore past us on their way to the high street. I thanked God that we were escaping in a dull, insignificant car. The police didn't spare us a glance as they raced by. Why would they? We knew nothing about violence and crime. We were just two sweet-natured lovers out for an Easter Sunday drive.

* * *

CARO INSISTED that we take a slight detour. Feeling, not without reason, that our hands were contaminated by the blood of many, she asked to visit the holy shrine at Little Walsingham. She wanted to pray for our immortal souls. I didn't argue. Just because I don't go in for praying myself doesn't mean I'm not flattered when other people think I'm worth praying for.

Before leaving the car, I moistened a tissue with some bottled water from Caro's bag and used it to clean her face. As I wiped the blood away, her eyes took in my own battered features. "Poor baby. I'm so sorry. I've really fucked up your life."

"Not necessarily," I said.

Walsingham was even more genteel than Southwold, its timbered medieval houses breathing out an air of piety and foreboding. Today, the streets were flooded with pilgrims, all intent on paying homage at the Anglican shrine. When I saw the crowds, I tried to persuade Caro to turn back. She refused.

I arranged to wait for her outside the pub in the marketplace while she walked down Holt Lane to pay her respects to Our Lady of Walsingham. The pub was closed, so I couldn't get a drink, although I badly needed one. Instead I sat at one of the wooden tables outside, watching the priests, pilgrims, and backpackers happily milling about. There was a strong smell of dog shit, for which I charitably assumed the pilgrims were not responsible.

I took no pride or pleasure in the events of the morning. I had gunned down three men, probably killed them. Indirectly, I was also responsible for the shooting of a waitress and an old lady. Five casualties, eight if you counted the car-crash couple and the epileptic.

I had saved Caro. But I had also defiled England. The thought gave me a strange satisfaction.

Ten minutes passed. By now, I was bored with waiting. I heard an ominous marching sound, accompanied by the clamor of many voices. Two coachloads of nuns swarmed into the little square, all laughing and talking at once. The noise was tremendous. Most of the nuns were under the age of forty, yet as far as I could see, there was not a single sex bomb among them. They clamored around a small dark-suited guide who was striving in vain to maintain order.

"The historic village of Little Walsingham . . ." the guide kept saying, but the unruly women never let him complete the sentence.

I walked to the end of Holt Road to see if I could spot Caro returning from the Anglican shrine. After a few moments of peering through the milling hordes, I saw her unmistakable cropped blonde head approaching. Then I saw something else. Coming up behind her, a full eight inches above the rest of the crowd, was a man with long auburn hair, a neatly trimmed beard, and a face so pale that it was startling.

Bad Jesus.

Caro was now less than fifty yards away. I pointed frantically and shouted out a warning, but she thought I was waving and waved back. I saw something glitter in Jesus' hand. When the knife came down, Caro faltered. She put a hand to her shoulder, saw blood, and lurched forward. Then Jesus stepped forward to stab her again. With all the force available to me, I opened my mouth and roared.

"Jesus!" I called.

Something extraordinary happened. The river of bodies passing up and down Holt Road parted, clearing the way for Caro to run into my arms. A large patch of blood was spreading over her left shoulder blade. The nuns, all silenced by my shout, looked where I was pointing and saw a huge, pale man swaying in the street, his clothes stained with blood, his face shining with an unearthly waxen glow. Here was the man from Nazareth, returned to earth.

There was a collective sigh, and as one the nuns surged forward. I hugged Caro to me as they rushed by, leaving a cloud of Bible dust in their wake. Jesus held up a hand to halt the holy sisters, but the sight of the gory hole through his left palm only served to increase their fervor. Bad Jesus spread his arms wide in one last desperate appeal for calm. Then he was lost to view as the black-clad bodies swept over him.

*   *   *

In the car, I examined the injury to Caro's shoulder. It was an ugly slash, about five inches long, but it wasn't deep, and it wasn't going to kill her. I tore a sleeve from my shirt and pressed it against the wound to stanch the flow of blood.

"Today in the café," I said quietly, "when you told Jesus the baby was his. That was just a trick, right?"

Her silence confirmed my worst fears.

"How do you know it's his?" I asked her.

"Because I can count," said Caro.

CHAPTER 14

IRON MARK

I PHONED Detective Sergeant Bromley at work. He wasn't there. Then I discovered that he was listed in the Richmond-Upon-Thames phone book. I phoned the number and his wife answered. She sounded friendly and bubbly. I guessed he was a jolly family man, when he wasn't trying to bribe attractive female suspects to suck his knarled old cock. "Who is it?" she said.

"Geoff Sadler," I said. "We went to school together. Is he there?"

"No, dear. Where do you think he is? I'll give you one guess."

"In the pub?"

"No. He's playing golf, ain't he? Right here in Richmond."

I knew I could get onto the golf course by cutting across the western boundary of Kew Gardens. It was a sunny afternoon in early spring. The green was so lush that it was almost a shame to walk on it. When I found them, Bromley and Flett were just about to tee off on the ninth. I didn't know what I was going to do. I had no gun, and there were two of them.

I was prepared for anything, but the police officers still managed to surprise me. Seeing me approaching, Flett dropped his club and started running. His flight was flabby and comical, punctuated by stops and starts and frequent glances over his shoulder.

Bromley, too proud to bolt, plucked an iron from his trolley and brandished it like a weapon. A purple nerve rash showed under his chin and around his sagging jowls. "I'm warning you, don't come any closer."

"Why? What'll you do?"

"Nothing." His voice was trembling. "Just don't come any closer."

My reputation had evidently preceded me.

"We want our passports back," I told him.

"Yeah?" said Bromley. "I can do that. Yeah. Fine." He was so relieved he almost wept. "No hard feelings, then?"

"All I want is the passports," I said.

"Great. No problem. I'll get 'em to you tomorrow."

"Today," I said.

Bromley hesitated, then nodded with excessive enthusiasm. "I could drop 'em off at your mum and dad's. Sometime early this evening? That okay?"

"Fine."

Bromley bared his teeth like a chimpanzee. "And that's it? That's the end of it?"

* * *

NOT QUITE the end.

There was one more thing I had to do. Armed with a brickbat and a can of fly spray. I returned to the Wheatsheaf. I was ready to reclaim one of my favourite pubs. I invited Wallace but he turned me down, claiming he was staying in to wash his hair. I knew this was a lie. Wallace didn't have any hair.

It was just after seven. There were only about a dozen drinkers in the bar. Wuffer was already slouched at his usual table by the window, wearing the Hawaiian shirt he'd worn at our last meeting. Tonight he was alone, staring morosely down at his empty beer glass. I walked up to the bar and Phil the landlord raised his eyebrows in that slightly unfriendly manner he reserved for irregular customers. His carpet slippers were looking a little threadbare.

"A pint of Guinness extra cold," I said. "And don't have one for yourself."

The landlord tutted and grumbled. I heard a shuffling sound behind me. Wuffer appeared at the bar beside me and placed his empty glass on the counter. Then he looked at me and nodded.

"Do I know you?" I said.

"Gah?"

"Your face is familiar. Have we met before?"

He shook his head humbly. "Ah gan nose yers, maid."

Wuffer wasn't faking it. He didn't know who the fuck I was. And suddenly my revenge mission seemed futile and vaguely shameful, like subjecting an old man in the advanced stages of Alzheimer's to a war crimes tribunal.

The fly spray had been intended for Wuffer's face. While he was choking and rubbing his eyes, I had planned to whack him with the brick. I felt it was the very least I could do. This malignant little bastard had attacked me twice and cost me a friendship.

I had come here believing that a man has to do what a man has to do. I now saw that a man needn't do what a man needn't do. I didn't have to fight to prove myself. Being unafraid was enough.

"Ah, bin stinking whacker late, yeah?" Then Wuffer smiled. I looked at him in amazement. Unless I was much mistaken, Wuffer was making conversation about the weather.

"Can I buy you a drink?"

"Gah?"

I pointed at his empty glass. "What are you drinking?"

Wuffer blinked and stared as if he was now trying to determine which language *I* was speaking. Then, in a perfectly clear, well modulated voice, he said, "Well, thanks very much. I'll have a pint of best bitter, please."

CHAPTER 15

THIRTY-ONE SENTENCES

CARO AND I went to Switzerland, the traditional refuge for rich scoundrels with ugly secrets. That summer, we hired a house near Geneva while we assessed our situation. Our assessment was that we should quit murdering people while we were ahead. One lunchtime, we were walking by the banks of Lac Leman when I finally told Caro the truth, that until that afternoon in Southwold I had never intentionally killed anyone.

It took a while to convince her. I thought she'd be angry or even disappointed. When she saw I was telling the truth she put her hand over her eyes and laughed. "You and Jesus had more in common than I thought."

"What do you mean?"

"He was no killer, either," explained Caro. "That was why he was so upset when he walked into our house and found two dead people. He'd maimed and scarred a lot of poor bastards but for some reason had never actually gone the whole hog and killed anybody. He had a bit of a complex about it. So when he saw that he'd been outslaughtered by a book collector, he felt he'd been made to look weak in front of his men."

Instinctively, she placed her hand over the small bulge beneath her dress, and I knew what she was thinking. "It's just a baby, Caro," I said. "It may not really belong to me, but nor do you. You never have done. It hasn't stopped me loving you."

Lately, my interest in owning Caro or anything else had greatly diminished. You don't chase possessions when you're self-possessed. Now that I could finally afford a signed, mint first edition of *The Catcher in the Rye*, I no longer wanted one. I had

243

stopped falling over things, and the only lists I made were shopping lists.

"You realize someone will come after us?" said Caro. "You know that, don't you? We'll never be truly safe."

"Who is?" I said.

A nice old couple walked by. He had a gray mustache like Carl Jung; she had bright, intelligent eyes and a steady smile. They were linking arms, proud of each other and wishing harm to no one. "Do you think we could ever be as happy as that?" said Caro, staring wistfully after them.

"Not a fucking chance," I told her.